Elgar Somerville

CAPTAIN ORTUGA AND THE ELOHIM THRONE

D1641118

AUSTIN MACAULEY PUBLISHERS™

LONDON · CAMBRIDGE · NEW YORK · SHARJAH

A CIP catalogue record for this title is available from the British Library.

ISBN 9781788236881 (Paperback)
ISBN 9781788236911 (Hardback)
ISBN 9781528953757 (ePub e-book)

www.austinmacauley.com

First Published (2020)
Austin Macauley Publishers Ltd
25 Canada Square
Canary Wharf
London
E14 5LQ

Table of Contents

Author's Note

Work on this first book of the Ortuga Jukebox Trilogy began in the early spring days of 2015, in the Blue Mountains in New South Wales, Australia. The writings of the first GAIA literary book took place next to the beaches, in the Bushland hillsides and tropical rainforests throughout New South Wales, ending in the autumn of 2017.

The titles of the Ortuga Jukebox Trilogy are:
Book One – Captain Ortuga and the Elohim Throne
Book Two – Captain Ortuga and the Art of Noise
Book Three – Captain Ortuga and the Aquarian Dawn

Conceived, researched and developed in the Blue Mountains, the new family board game, Ortuga, was released onto the market in 2012 and is set to forge a new vanguard and galvanise the board games market. Subsequently, the global, not-for-profit service – GAIA – Global Altruistic Industry Accreditation, was founded in 2013 from humanitarian insights and knowledge. Highlighting the creative pathway, Ortuga became the World's First GAIA Product, with a percentage of profits from sales being donated to homeless communities and disadvantaged families. Supporting the Ortuga brand is the first book of a Trilogy – *Captain Ortuga and the Elohim Throne* – written by the author under the pen name Elgar Somerville.

Chapter One
As Time Goes By

After the boundless journey of 5000 miles across three principal waters of the seven seas, the Indian, South and North Atlantic Oceans transporting Indian oils, spices and dried fruits, the merchant trading ship of Ganji-i-Sawai was drawing closer to its destination of the British seaport of Bristol. The freight vessel was heavily armed and each and every crew member carried weapons to fend off attacks by pirates or other plundering, aquatic fleets. The notoriously known vessel of frequent combat slowly entered the mouth of the Bristol channel that led to the cargo port where the goods would be unloaded and inspected by the HM Revenue & Customs Office in the district of Temple Back; then the goods would be transported further to the depot warehouse and re-distributed to retail outlets and shopping centres around the united kingdoms of England, Wales, Scotland, Ireland, France, Germany and Spain.

On its way along the reefed channel, an English pirate, Henry Avery, tagged along behind the merchant trading ship in a single mast sloop vessel. When the pirate sailing craft reached the rear of the cargo vessel, Avery threw a grappling rope up to hook onto the timber railings. Most of the crew of the cargo vessel were based at the front of the ship preparing to dock at the port as Henry Avery climbed up the stern and walked towards the bridge to see if the Indian Captain, Fateh Muhammed, was in there.

Opening the door to the bridge, Avery stood quietly behind the Captain; reaching inside his coat, he took out a cloth soaked with a natural anaesthetic liquid. The Captain pressed an inquiry into the atmosphere.

"Who is there, what is that smell?"

Before he could turn around, Avery shoved the cloth onto his face covering his mouth and nose causing the Captain to fall unconscious. He collapsed onto the bridge decking and Henry Avery then bent down to remove the hat and uniform jacket from the Captain. At the very same time, the crew lowered the anchor and docked the vessel at the port of Bristol, then they walked down to the ship's berth to settle into their hammocks to sleep for the night to regain strength for the future working tasks of unloading the goods the following morning.

Of a Celtic, northern Irish heritage, the Chief Customs Officer, Joseph Tullman, was mildly chauvinistic but overly fanatical to the importation and accurate inspection of goods from other countries. Usually, he would not allow full cargo to be removed from any ship before he opened and inspected the sample goods in several of the shipping containers.

The night was the planetary timing of the full moon and feeling physically empowered but mentally absent, Joseph Tullman allowed the cargo to be unloaded by his colleagues. When the pottery oil jars, spice baskets, crates and barrels – each filled with various goods – arrived at the warehouse in Temple Back port, they were stockpiled next to his office for him to obsessively inspect each container to ensure that they were not packed with any illegal spices or recreational substances that would devastate his employment seniority. After his inspection, he would order his forklift operator to carry the shipment onto the main storage flooring area within the warehouse for distribution. That night, the rare moonlighting was the second full moon in the month of February 1959; the power of the Blue Moon made him restrain his time to sleep, and he carried on working through the night. By midnight, he had inspected all the handmade pottery jars, woven storage baskets and wooden containers. He unwittingly seized hold of kilogrammes of each of his favourite aromatic powdered Patchouli, Sandalwood, Frankincense and Nag Champa. As the fragrances deeply absorbed into his clothing, he sat down at his desk to fill out the allocation paperwork. Joseph felt so peaceful and stress free that he turned on his cassette player to listen to a magnificent song titled *Something in the Air* by a band called Thunderclap Newman.

The musical rhythm was so penetrating that a newly employed, young Security Guard charged down from outside of the building into the warehouse where he hid behind the storage baskets to observe what was going on. Joseph emptied out every one of his pockets and placed the powdered fragrances into his briefcase. As the outro of the song faded away, Joseph fell into a stunted power nap and began snoring.

Believing that Joseph was a criminal burglar, the Security Guard walked out from behind his camouflaged hiding into the office; he pulled out his gun and shoved it against Joseph's temple. Shaking his body to energise himself, Joseph nervously stared into the Guard's eyes, that were filled with aggression. The guardsman blurted out his conviction insight:

"I have witnessed your criminal act of stealing goods from this warehouse, who are you? I will have to use that phone to contact the local police to arrest you before the night moves on."

Forcefully, Joseph swung his right arm upwards, barging the steel gun barrel away from his head, then plunged his fist into the Security Guard's stomach which made the young man collapse onto the concrete flooring; falling down heavily, he banged his head on the slate and fell unconscious. Joseph Tullman dragged the dishevelled body of the Security Guard, Stuart Hirst, back into the warehouse and flopped it close to the warehouse entry door, thinking that when the staff arrived in the morning, they could assist the Guard to regain his health. Then Joseph returned back to his office; silence and stillness of the full moon re-emerged in the office atmosphere whilst he emptied the fragrant powders out of his briefcase into large recycled envelopes; putting pen to paper, he scribed his signature for full authority on documents of the cargo to be dispatched in the morning. Sitting at his desk, he then heard chaotic, jangling sounds coming from the back of the canvas partition where the straw baskets filled with spices were stacked. He assumed that the noise was of the young Security Guard or possibly that of rats eating some of the dried fruits or contaminating the expensive spices. Opening the bottom draw of a filing cabinet, he pulled out a torch and a hefty wooden mallet with a view to slaughter the creatures before they destroyed the natural healing effects of the herbal seasonings. He acted quickly, for if the creatures contaminated the goods, the infection would erode his reputation and senior position of the Customs Office. Jumping up from his seat in silence, he moved toward the rustling sounds that were coming from inside one of the large calendula straw basket containers. Lifting his presence up into the night air and expanding his chest, he felt empowered and commanding enough to kill any other life forms without any revenge or mental disturbance. Silently moving nearer to the basket where the tinkling noise was coming from, he lifted the mallet high above his head and used his left hand to remove the basket lid. Bending down, he bellowed a constricted command into the darkness of the basket:

"Come out of there right now, you destructive idiots. I am the Chief of this customs warehouse and your beings will be terminated!"

Unbalanced, the basket stirred around on the ceramic-tiled flooring making Joseph peer deeper into the shadows. Covering the objects or creatures inside was a layer of orange linen; reaching into the basket, he snatched the material away and raised the mallet again in preparation to bring it down onto the rats before they could leap out of the basket and scamper to another hideaway. He then saw two large brown eyes, looking up at him, pleading him not to kill. A highly attractive, olive-skinned female form rose up from out of the basket, dressed in a colourful wedding sari and wearing golden jewellery with her long raven hair draped over her shoulders.

Smiling, the beautiful Indian woman fluttered her eyelids and flourished her lips with carefree admiration. Joseph whispered:

"Hello, Beautiful One! Sorry for being so nasty. What are you doing in my life?"

"Namaste, Hello Sir! My name is Parvihn Kadisha."

Speaking in pidgin English:

"I am only sixteen years old. I was born on 19th of November, 1943, in the historic southern Indian village of Pondicherry. Please allow me to migrate to the United Kingdom for the British military invaded our country in the 1400s and we never received any appreciation or thankfulness for their aggressive colonisation, but I do admire the traditional British history of witchcraft, paganism, druidry and spirituality; the associated ancient megaliths and legendary stone circles like Stonehenge."

"Please – Please let me live?"

Sensing her adorable vibration of passionate energy, Joseph Tullman opened his arms to embrace the Indian Goddess of mesmerising beauty, replying kindly to her:

"Major oceans never refuse any river inlets. Come into my life, apologies for my anger to you."

Rolling the basket sideways down onto the floor, Parvihn Kadisha shifted her weight and crawled out. She then stood up, fronting Joseph's handsome, square-jawed glowing façade. He then said:

"Parvihn, let's go outside to view the stars and planets, for the planetary energy of the Capricorn blue moon is very strong and it will assist us both to make the best decisions of which future pathways and destinations we should follow. Take my hand."

Joseph grabbed hold of Parvihn's hand, and they walked up the grass hillside adjacent to the customs warehouse, sitting down they began to talk about their current lives and past existences.

In the moonlight, they both noticed the pirate man, – Henry Avery, walking across the top of the rolling hillside carrying the body of the Merchant Ship Captain Fateh Muhammed, over his shoulders. Parvihn thought that the two men were migrating from their native lands to seek a new home in England. She said:

"I possess a very compassionate and humanitarian attitude. I like to help and counsel refugees and people from all cultures. I have been working for the global charitable community – Save the Children. But I decided to leave my hometown of Pondicherry, for my parents arranged a marriage for me to become the wife of the devious and greedy gangster businessman – Ali Ganatra. He is an extremely wealthy forty-year-old bachelor who fights with all business opponents to take their lives and also embezzling competitors that seek to solicit his clients and business products only to increase the size of their own financial empires. He slays their motivation by poisoning their drinks."

Parvihn expressed her element of deep sadness to Joseph, leaving her parents and departing from her sister and two brothers, but she was enthused and happy to become a companion of the authoritative British principal she was sitting with, as he possessed the knowledge and had created a network that would gain consent for her stay in England and efficiently obtain British citizenship. With her power of love, she wished Joseph Tullman would become her Good Samaritan:

"I did not want to be the wife of Ali Ganatra so I left my parents' home on the day of my wedding ceremony and travelled down to the port of Netaji Nega, clambered up the rope ladder to the cargo hold in the ship and emptied the powdered Calendula out of a basket and then I hid inside for the journey across the ocean."

Gazing into the striking blue eyes of Joseph Tullman, Parvihn expressed her contemplation:

"I feel wonderful tonight; I like to walk amongst the stars at night because they help me find love in my life. I love the thought of being with you; we will always be together for love never ends – Always and Forever, I will love you."

As Joseph moved his face closer to her lips, a column of soft, yielding blue light shone down from the moon blanketing over their bodies. The sparkling column of blue light was projected from the Universal Pleiadian Photon Beam, engendering a consciousness of love, romance, understanding and acceptance across the planet Earth which filled Joseph's soul. He spoke lovingly:

"After I was born in the Irish town of Dublin, my parents moved to the south western English, pirate seaport of Bristol. I have much appreciated my profession as a bureaucratic Customs Officer, because the career made me a respected political representative for the local conservative party. Your humanitarian, Hindu friendship and compassion has inspired me to be brave."

As a political businessman – workaholic, Joseph Tullman, was highly successful, structuring his own world for he socialised and drank alcohol with a lot of friends, neighbours and business colleagues. He then went onto to speak of his family:

"7 years ago, my mother passed away from consumptive tuberculosis, she was free like the wind, and, unfortunately, 2 weeks ago, my father toppled over a cliffside adjacent to his guest house, The Charter Inn, falling 100 metres down to his death onto craggy rocks on the ancient pirate beach front in

Cornwall. His inheritance left me his public house, his financial estate and vinyl record and book collections, which will pleasurably help us continually move forward together to greater happiness. Parvihn, would you like to move down to the southern region of England to become my wife, give birth to my children and work as my Landlady in The Charter Inn in the Cornish village of Cam Mellyn?" A broad smile came onto Parvihn's face as Joseph cuddled her warmly under the night sky.

When they moved from Bristol down south to the Cornish county of Penzance, Joseph Tullman became the local political candidate for the Liberal Party and married his divine female Indian companion who soon became pregnant, giving birth to their first child – Davy Tullman in March 1961, and then a few years later, a baby girl – Jasmine Layla was born.

After the two children reached the ages of 8 and 5 years, Parvihn decided to find employment. Because of her happy disposition, she became a part time Assistant for a marvellous eurythmic teacher at the local Steiner Primary School, which focused on the individual talents and inspirations of every child; to create their optimistic futures, leading to the most appropriate career path for each personality.

Both Davy and Jasmine went to the school for their primary education. Davy had such great talents to help his friends with any of their personal troubles and, as he was quite artistic, he also painted superb portraits of his mates and gave them to their parents. After school, he would meet up with friends down by the river in the local recreational park and watch small-crested newts and stickleback fish moving around in the shallow ponds. Davy and his mates would excitedly observe the growth of frogspawn turning into tadpoles followed by the next stage of tiny frogs, initially with only 2 legs and then 4 legs. The enjoyable motivation of feeling good and making the most of every moment, created confidence and happiness in Davy. He explained that all living creatures and human life forms living together spiritually, evolved forward with motivation to become kind-hearted, to openly accept other beings and their characteristics and religious insights without any aggression or battles.

Parvihn had told Jasmine how she fell in love with her father, Joseph, just 10 minutes after meeting with him. Jasmine wondered how her mother and father fell in love so quickly. Respecting her brother Davy's admiration for boys and girlfriends, Jasmine spent early morning time with her brother, talking about how she could create friendships with his companions, to build up her balanced network of male and female energy to gain more confidence, to create a global consciousness for the future. Her naturally gained insight of the powerful resonance of the energy of every individual also demonstrated why her parents were attracted to each other so promptly.

Her adorable mother, Parvihn, worked at the Steiner School in the mornings only from 8.00 to 11.00am, then returned to The Charter Inn to serve lunches and talk with the neighbours that frequently visited the guest house to gain her empathetic counselling and advice, but not from her heavy drinking intoxicated husband, who bureaucratically presented overbearing regulatory directives and political incentive gossip.

The widespread grass hillside leading down from the village of Cam Mellyn had a spectacular vista overlooking the panoramic span of the beaches, stone pathways and the rocky seafront, which was once the docklands of ancient pirate crews returning from voyages around the seven seas. The Charter Inn was built on the corrupted foundations of the original Customs House from the Tudor days of the 1600s, where all seafarers and nautical rovers had to declare the importation of goods and merchandise shipped in from overseas.

As with all custom book-keeping, before unloading the ship's hold they would have the cargo inspected to obtain legal authorisation from the officers. The regulations seemed pointless to pirates, because all pirate ships secretly sailed into the bay and smuggled their goods into the local townships, then travelled with the cargo into more populated regions and capital cities to illegally sell off the booty and stolen products. When senior members of pirate crews smuggled in any gold or treasures, they would hide the riches in the caves that lined the beach fronts.

Constructed on the clifftop at Lamorna Point, The Charter Inn opened only four days a week from Thursday night to Sunday. The three-storey sandstone building had an antique reception desk, a public drinking house and restaurant on the ground floor. Next to the timber reception desk were stairs that led up to the second and third floors, each with 10 rooms for registered guests. Fixed above the entry archway leading into the building was a large bronze casting of the face of Sir Francis Drake from the Elizabethan era of sea mariners.

Although very worn, most of the heavy timber doors, brass hinges and locks were still strong, and so they were restored and used again when the building was refurbished by Joseph's father, Adam Tullman, in the early 1920s. The original cellar and veranda that overlooked the beach front were restored to be part of the new building. The veranda watchtower was redesigned to project the appearance of the bow of an old Square Rigger vessel, and to protect patrons, the veranda was edged with metal railings to stop people, especially children from falling down the cliffside. Behind the antique timber reception desk was a spatial sized room, which was the original custom headquarters where Joseph's mother and father had rented when they moved from Belfast to Cornwall. When Joseph and Parvihn moved down from Bristol, they set up their belongings in this room. At the back of the room was a dog kennel, homing a burly black Labrador Alsatian cross and placed in front of the kennel was a large hand knotted Persian rug. One morning, whilst walking over the rug, Joseph nearly sprained his right ankle, for his weight broke one of the old floorboards positioned underneath the rug. Hidden under the rug, Joseph discovered a trap door leading down a slippery stone stairway into a cave below the building. Upon Parvihn's humble request, Joseph became a low profile people smuggler, trafficking only a few refugees from around the world each year to live in harmony in the southwestern counties of Britain.

From legends taken from historical books in his father's library, the friendly political publican, Joseph, chronicled many tales about renowned pirates of the 1700s and 1800s that didn't declare their freight. Additionally, he explained the daily news and reasonings of current local and global conflicts. Favoured by the local community at weekends, The Charter Inn overflowed with locals who brought their children with them, allowing them to play on the theatrical ship decking veranda, the rear entry passageway, grassy hills and cliff walks flanking the left and right sides of the Inn.

A lot of the younger children played on the timber veranda overlooking the seafront, for it had a crow's nest platform, and they were protected from falling down the cliff faces by the metal railings and ropes erected around the edge of the decking.

As the ancient building was recognised as the famous venue for pirates of Penzance, many adults and children would dress up in pirate costumes. The three children, Molly Swanson, Tim Yates and the homeless boy Quinton Morris that were schooled together with Davy at the local Steiner School, became very chummy and visited The Charter House Inn with their parents every weekend.

After Davy and his young sister, Jasmine, left Steiner to advance to their high school, Parvihn also moved on to seek a new role to help locally abandoned families. Davy and Quinton resonated so well with Parvihn's kindness that they helped her after schooling hours and at the weekends.

Thirteen years of age, Molly Swanson was born in Wales, in the capital city of Cardiff. The girl was pleasant as well as pretty – no one had ever seen her frown or speak badly to others. Her caring political parents moved down to Penzance, for they were offered full time positions in the council chambers to market the tourism campaigns, historical pirate features and landmarks throughout the entire county of Cornwall.

Always possessing a sparkling smile, Molly was super entertaining, and unlike her mate Tim Yates, she open-heartedly spoke to each and every fellow human, without any hostility or commanding behaviour.

From Northern Ireland, the young, powerful empire builder, Tim Yates, was dedicated to his own victory – fifteen year-old Tim was greatly inspired by the knowledge of the global history of political victories and colonisation between conflicting countries and religious cultures. Consequently, he used these realms of knowledge to find the greatest route to reinforce his 'I am' monarchy and leadership.

Mentally and physically strong, he ordered people around with burly directives and rudeness. Being an authoritative idea's person, Tim always developed schemes and employed personal insights to impress people, especially men, with the view to gather their abilities as well as in order to gain more personal power, leadership and financial legacies.

Enjoying life, the happy, homeless boy, Quinton Morris, adored travelling and speaking with all communities, in both England and around the world. His military based father was so overly disciplined that his authority made the colourful character of Quinton very loose, understanding and accepting of poor families and the homeless, and all beings who wanted to change the world, helping each other to protect animals and the environment itself. With his laid back, larrikin attitude he liked to be identified as The Jolly Roger as he was always telling jokes and pirate stories to his friends and other people he met, for he was significantly admired by those folk.

The children's friendships and knowledge grew stronger as they moved onto secondary education. The three boys, Davy, Tim and Quinton, were labelled by the teacher's community as 'The History Boys', for they savoured all historical teachings and lessons in the form 3Q at their school; Penwright Grammar. Always mutually together with Molly, the three boys cleverly mimicked famous historical characters from the past when playing imaginary games. In the long grass-laden rolling hillside, dressed as pirates with stripy T-shirts, wooden swords and toy pistols, the group of schoolmates excitedly performed as pirates searching for buried treasure.

"Right," shouted Tim:

"Ahoy there, mateys! Show me the way to your hidden treasures, or I will take you as prisoners onto my ship and sail with you out into the ocean where I will strap a cannonball onto your body and drop you off the stern!"

Molly giggled at the play-statement and screeched back:

"You cannot take my treasures, for they are gifts for my sick grandmother."

Grabbing Davy by the collar of his school blazer, Molly pointed at him:

"But I do know that him over there knows the whereabouts of a secret stairwell leading into a treasure cave down on the beach. Let's all fight with him until he says that he will lead us to his treasure."

Davy turned around and pulled his sword out of the scabbard:

"I am the Captain of The Charter House crew! It's My Life! I have the genetics of a spiritual yoga guru from India, so don't try to force me to show you my hidden treasures."

Thirteen years of age, typically of privileged birth, a boy of Hindu ancestry, self-governing silent achiever, Davy Tullman was of a unique birthright. His mother, Parvihn was from the Indian state of Tamil Nadu where she cared for many homeless people, but she was violently discriminated against in her own town of Pondicherry, for she belonged to the lowest Hindu caste – the Dalits. Davy inherited her genetic compassion, for they both worked together in Cornwall helping many people.

Being chased by his three friends, Davy ran quickly along the pathway at the top of the cliff passing by the point where his grandfather fell to his death. Tim roared at Davy:

"Why run when you have nothing to hide?"

Running from his three pirate mates, Davy moved carefully along a pathway in the long grass on the cliff side, heading down towards the beach front to search for the cave that led up to the trap door inside the guest house. Before moving on, he dropped down into the grass, hiding for several minutes so his friends could not see him fooling around. His friends suppressed their encouragement to revenge and skipped back to the rear entry of The Charter Inn. Davy courageously stood up and headed down the path towards the ocean, arriving on the beach about 500 metres south of the cave below The Charter Inn. Contemplating with optimism and glee, Davy was deciding to explore inside the hidden cave to discover the doorway leading up to The Charter Inn. As he boldly walked towards a concealed cave entrance, where at its entry, he noticed a glimmer of gold shimmering from the base of a small, but deep rockpool. He then glanced back up the hillside to make sure that no one was following or watching him. Upon realising that he was by himself, he excitedly kneeled down onto the sand at the edge of the rockpool and stared into the water to make a close scrutiny of the object that was partly hidden under a clump of seaweed.

What Davy did not notice was Tim, who was observing him through a rusty telescope from the crow's nest platform on the veranda at The Charter Inn. There was a slight current running around at the bottom of the pool, waving the villi of anemones in harmony with the motion of the slow water current that was shrouding the golden object embedded in the sand. Davy thought that the shimmering was reflected from mother of pearl inside an oyster shell or possibly a piece of pirate treasure; he reached into the water to brush away the seaweed and exposed the object – a golden spiral Mollusc shell. When Davy touched the shell, suddenly a mental picture of a sea Captain flashed into his mind:

"Woaargh!"

Davy identified the image as Sir Francis Drake, as his historical school knowledge merged with the character of the ancient slave trader. Born in Devon around 1540, Francis Drake was the first Englishman to circumnavigate the earth and was secretly commissioned by Queen Elizabeth to demolish the Spanish colonies set up on the Pacific regional coast of South America. During his voyages, Drake attacked numerous pirated and foreign vessels, stealing masses of gold, silver and other booty to bring back to Britain.

Progressing the vision, it expanded to show Drake walking unaccompanied along the Cornish beach front of Penzance where Davy was crouching. Holding a leather bag of treasured antiques and a timber chest, Sir Francis Drake was singing a melodic tune of ancient sea mariners'.

In the vision, Davy saw the Captain striding towards the cave, when a golden Mollusc shell fell out of the pocket of Sir Francis Drake, into the rockpool that Davy was presently sitting by. Not noticing the object falling into the water, Sir Francis strolled into the cave to hide the bag and chest of treasures behind a large rock at the very back end of the cave, he then opened the bag to reveal numerous golden Mollusc shells, which he placed on a ledge above the rock concealed by seaweed; then the vision faded away.

With the cold water reaching up to his armpit, Davy moved his head downwards to focus on the shell. From behind the seaweed, appeared a large aggressive Blue Fiddler crab, which moved harshly towards his hand and snapped its claw into the bulbous part of the palm of Davy's right hand, producing a deep incision:

"Arrghh!" screamed Davy.

In agony, with blood flowing from the cut, he quickly reached deeper into the water to try and seize hold of the golden shell, but when he grabbed the shell, he was rapidly catapulted onto his back on the sandy beach and a soft melody spiralled around him, similar to the tune Drake was singing. Unbeknown to Davy, the melody was the Elohim Mantra, orchestrated by advanced Light Beings from the Pleiades used to open energy channels to teleport life forms back to the past or forward into the future depending on what vision or thoughts were released in the mind of the character that was transported. The rhythmic melody swirled in the atmosphere around Davy:

"T'Jen Yar Day, Yar Day Ta M'kas

Beautiful Day, Beautiful Life

You Need to Love Yourself to Love the World

Show Me the Way to Love – Cha Guru Day Lah."

Mystical images also came into his mind, presenting hieroglyphic carvings on the rock face of a hidden gateway and a stairway leading up to an ancient stone throne created by the Elohim. The imagery visualised by Davy demonstrated how the Elohim Throne transported people to past and future events, and how the golden spiral Mollusc shell is used as a Turnkey.

Placing the shell Turnkey into the right hand side of the throne opened access to visitations. When the shell is turned clockwise, the person is carried into the future, and anti-clockwise carried back to past historical events.

In order to return safely back to the Elohim Throne from the engendered visitation, the traveller must carry a Turnkey on the journey; when needing to return to the original point of entry, the shell should be held firmly and the memories contained in the shell would return the holder to the location where the teleportation journey began. Another alternative to gain travel to the past or future is to impart speech or inquiries into the inside of the shell.

The Mollusc Turnkey can activate transportation of an individual or groups of people and creatures, taken through cosmic gateways such as the Bermuda Triangle, Glastonbury, Avalon and Stonehenge in England, The Parthenon in Greece and Uluru in Australia. Located north of the Aztec citadel of Machu Picchu, the Bermuda Triangle, sometimes known as a wonderwall, is a mythical fragment of the Atlantic Ocean – situated north of the Caribbean Sea.

Wonderwalls are keys to the universe, having been created by the Pleiadian group as gateways for tribes and their means of transportation to travel through to the Photon Beam, to the Pleiadian Galaxy or other desirable destinations by using the power of the Mollusc Turnkey. Any groups travelling close to the Bermuda Triangle or other gateways that were not aware of the opening, would be swallowed into the invisible region and teleported somewhere into the past or future of the universe.

Back at The Charter Inn, whilst viewing the happenings on the Penzance beach front from the crow's nest, Tim shouted down to Quinton who was playing a board game with Molly and Jasmine on the hotel veranda, commanding him to track down to the beach where Davy was and help him get back to the Inn for lunch with his mum and dad.

"Hey, Quinny! Davy has hurt himself on the rocks down there. I can see that his hand is bleeding badly. Can you get the first aid kit from behind the bar and take it down to the beach to help him?"

Quinton got hold of a bottle of antiseptic and some dressings for the wound from the first aid box, then leapt over the veranda railings and rushed along the stone steps that led down to the Battery Rocks. Unfortunately, Quinton tripped over on a cluster of seaweed and collapsed onto his knees on the sand quite far from Davy. Glancing over towards Davy, who was still lying on his back with his eyes closed, holding the shell Turnkey, Quinton observed Davy was suddenly dragged out to sea by the king tide, which flowed up to the sand where he was lying.

The power of the tide picked him up and carried him down the beach onto the ocean waves. Quinton could not understand or accept the way the tide was stealing his friend away, with questions flashing in his mind:

Is he dead, and where is the ocean taking him?

Quinton turned his head to rub his left knee and then glimpsed back at the position where Davy was on the water front, but he was not there, he had disappeared:

"Oh no, Davy has drowned! He has been kidnapped by the power of the seven seas!"

The coastal dwellings in Cornwall where Quinton and many other homeless youth lived and arranged weekend rave parties were the large caves on the beach. The cave where Quinton slept was the one where the treasure of Francis Drake was hidden. After the loss of his friend Davy, Quinton wandered back into his home cave and talked caringly to his pet Golden Retriever dog – Monty. He dragged his skiff boat out of the cave to the waterfront and skipped around the aquatic waters with his watchdog – trying to find Davy and both listening for any sounds of life.

Chapter Two
The Liberty Bell

The energy of the golden Mollusc Turnkey compounded with the silent power of the ocean carried Davy Tullman rapidly back into the past, to the Argentinean port of Valparaiso. Davy did not realise that he was being teleported from the 1900s to 1700s – two hundred years back to the Golden Age of Piracy. He thought he was travelling south across the English Channel to northern France. Floating into the past, he noticed a green coloured glow surrounding him, radiating from below the wave he was carried on; wondering to himself what the light was indicating as it formed an atmosphere of optimism and excitement for him to move forward to his new destination with confidence and belief.

Securely holding the shell Turnkey, Davy sat upright on the wave, riding it like a magic carpet as he gazed closer at the iridescent light. He saw the shape of a sea creature, appearing like the silhouette of a Manta Ray.

"Where are we going Manta?" yelled Davy. "Please, Mr Fish, take me to a beach front in Cantabria in Spain, St Tropez in France, or to St Ives on the English beach front of Cornwall? I am having a really good ride, so anywhere you want to take me is alright for me too."

As the Turnkey was half-filled with salt water, his voice was slightly muffled, lost in translation any commands could not be conveyed inside the shell to instruct the energy to teleport him. Alternatively though, the memory retained in the Mollusc taken by Sir Francis Drake was rolling Davy away to the continent of South America.

Both European countries, Britain and France were constantly at war with Spain, seeking to destruct the Spanish territorial monopoly of trade and constant vision to expand the Spanish empire by overpowering foreign and indigenous cultures.

The historical events of the 1600s when Francis Drake broke the nautical rulings to engage in piracy, he was attacking the Spanish colonies on the western coastline of South America to destroy their communities. Additionally, the happenings that had occurred to promote the future building of the Spanish empire, were both recalled by the Turnkey memory. After Drake docked his buccaneering ship, the Golden Hinde at the port of Valparaiso, he travelled north with 20 of his crew members to the earliest Spanish fortress city of Espina, seeking to wipe out the community and its political councillors. After annihilating most of the township, Drake walked up into the mountainous hillside where the Pleiadian sanctuary of Machu Picchu was built.

By entering the safe haven at the top end through the higher woodlands, up on the Xanadu hillside, the guards did not halt him as they stood at the main gateway at the lower end of the hillside, at the opening to the stone corridor and stairway. That is when Sir Francis Drake first discovered the visitation energy of the Elohim Throne, visions entering his mind to feature events in the past or future, founded by the statement that was permanently set into his intellect.

"Only the brave or the foolish dare to enter the future."
Francis Drake sat on the throne and contemplated about what may happen in the future after the Spanish colonies were demolished. His thoughts teleported him to the future days in the 1700s, to glimpse how his hostile victories helped facilitate the Elizabethan empire, making the Queen of England so rich that the majestic lady named Drake as her personal pirate. Before Drake returned to England, he stole eight shell Turnkeys from under the Elohim Throne and took them back to the village of Penzance in Cornwall, which is why Davy perceived the Elohim Throne, hearing the Elohim mantra and seeing Sir Francis Drake strolling along the Cornish beach front; entering into several caves where he hid his stolen jewels and treasures for the glory of England. Drake's aggressive intent and revenge were so feared by Spanish fleets, they called him El Draque – The Dragon.

All of a sudden the green luminosity emanating from under the high wave carrying Davy faded away, looking behind himself out onto the ocean Davy saw the glow reappear, drifting out towards the horizon.

Davy turned back to face the beach where he felt thrilled at being in another time of history, as the wave settled and washed him up onto a sandy bay near to the Chilean port of Valparaiso under the bow of a square rigger ship.

The heavily armed Galleon was a length of 55 metres with a main mast and one other sail mast with a crow's nest platform fixed to the top. The ship's hull was covered with barnacles and sea-weed and the huge wooden vessel had a title written on its stern – Liberty Bell. The luxury Captain's cabin was located above the large rudder at the stern of the ship, 5 windows overlooked the ocean wake and any vessels that may chase the ship to attack and plunder its treasures. For the Captain to move swiftly to the bridge to implement commands to his crew, there was a stairway leading out from his cabin, up the stern to the top decking.

Next to the ship's hull, Davy stood up on the beach, pulled open his long pirate coat to conceal the Mollusc shell inside. Walking along the beach towards the long line of multicultural, community folk seeking seafaring work he passed by a young orphaned boy, sitting together with 2 Oriole birds on a dirty blanket against the stone sea wall of the port with a hand written message hanging around his neck. The writing was in Spanish:

"Sin hogar, solo tratando de pasar otro día Toda la ayuda sería muy apreciada, gracias."

Luckily, because Davy had been influenced by the power of the intellect and memory of the Mollusc shell, he found that he could interpret the wording:

"Homeless, just trying to get through another day

All help would be greatly appreciated – Thank You."

With the humane thought seeding in his mind, Davy turned around and walked back to the homeless urchin:

"Let me take you by the hand, and I will find somewhere for you to sleep tonight and get you some food from the market up there on the fisherman's wharf."

The two tropical birds bounced onto his shoulders. The boy removed the sign memo from his neck, rolled up his blanket and walked along with Davy to the group of men seeking work on the Liberty Bell:

"Gracias, Senor."

When they both came closer to the assemblage of local buccaneers and knowledgeable nautical men, several looked at him, smiled, bowed and waved at him with joy and interest, for they knew the young homeless rascal and were so pleased that Davy revealed his compassion and open hearted tolerance to help the homeless and needy. The gifted Captain, who stood in front of the group was talking with each person to recruit senior crew members and strong deckhands to assist him on his ship. Admiring Davy's kindness, the man who stood in front of the group reached out to shake hands with Davy.

"Are you the Captain of that ship over there – the Liberty Bell?"

"I am indeed! My name is Juan Ortuga, from Argentina, and I am seeking more crew members to sail with me around the oceans to help poverty-stricken families and uneducated and homeless communities. That's why I am so impressed with your insight to help that local, abandoned, young orphan boy – Leeron Ali."

Gripping Davy's hand, the master mariner squeezed it so hard that the jagged scratch from the fiddler crab bite opened and began to bleed again; the blood squirted out in between their hands. The Captain, Juan Ortuga, quickly pulled his hand away and questioned Davy:

"What's your name boy, how old are you? Would you like to be my Cabin Boy? You will face the same perils as the rest of my crew: battles, shipwrecks and storm damage."

"Captain, my name is Davy Tullman, from the English seaside county of Cornwall. I am 13 years of age, a young boy with blood on his hands – a Child of the Universe. My mother is of an Indian bloodline ancestry, my father is of Irish origin, and I have many refugee friends from countries all over the planet, whom my mother helps to migrate to England where they become residents."

The young wide-eyed boy from Cornwall accepted the Captain's request for him to be a Cabin Boy on the Liberty Bell. He stood next to the marine folk hero and listened to the other likely recruits talking about themselves, their marine skills and courageous talents that would help Juan Ortuga with his desire to make the world a better place.

He had engaged twelve deckhands to proceed with hard labourings, but wanted 6 skilled senior crew members to control navigation, maintenance and the most disciplined, winning ways of sailing to numerous destinations. Juan Ortuga then asked each chosen recruit to tell him about their lives. Moving together along the line of men and women, Davy and Ortuga stopped and spoke with a bald Chinese man.

"Ni Hao. When the senior crew have been enlisted, we will be sailing across the South Pacific Ocean to visit the communities of Easter Island, Tahiti and The Pitcairns, where we can help the homeless families. Can you just tell me why you would want to join my crew on such a journey and what your expert skills are?" said Ortuga.

The Asian fellow of a typically light build replied softly:

"Thanks, Captain, I am a Tibetan Monk and my name is Han Lipling. I lived in a Tibetan monastery for 20 years and left there last year when it was invaded by the ranks of Mongolian military. Before I arrived in South America, I travelled to the Jewish community in Israel where Jesus of Nazareth was visited by a Tibetan monk one thousand, six hundred years ago. I returned there to reaffirm the prophecies, and religious insights of Taoism. I offer courtesy, understanding and acceptance to all cultures."

"My solemn talents include a broad repertoire of acupuncture and the energy pathways of ancient Chinese health. Also, I have magical powers and expert knowledge of fireworks and explosives. Since I have lived in the town of Valparaiso, I have been working as a ship's Carpenter to maintain and repair any damage to the masts, hatches, yardarms and the hull; I also play a Pan Flute to keep the crew spellbound, happy and clear-thinking when we would sail to search for treasure or rally swashbuckling with other ships."

Captain Ortuga shook hands to verify the role for Han Lipling:

"Han, you are a genius! You've acquired the position of Carpenter and Tibetan Chaplain Counsellor on my ship, the Liberty Bell. Is that ok for you?"

"Thanks, Captain! Just one query though, can I please have one hour off each morning and late afternoon to meditate and pray?"

"Yes, my friend," replied Ortuga.

He moved along the recruitment line, passing three other men and then stopped in front of a heavily built, strong, red-headed Scotsman wearing a tartan kilt:

"Who are you, sir?"

"Och aye Sasanach – I am Richard Flintlock. I hold the rank of a Bosun from the Edinburgh fleet. Captain, who's that wee laddie crouching on the sand behind you with the 12 deckhands? As there is a highly poisonous box jellyfish washing up onto his leg that might cause his death!"

"That youth is my new Cabin Boy, Tuli." Flintlock pushed past Juan Ortuga and stomped on the jellyfish, squashing its dangerous venom out of its body. The highly potent Scottish braveheart drummer, Flintlock, had five children who lived in Scotland; he possessed a vast knowledge of sacred spaces like Templewood stone circles in the township of Loch Gilphead, east of Edinburgh.

Sailing from Penzance, Flintlock travelled across the Atlantic Ocean to South America in a Scottish Fleet. A Bosun or Boatswain holds the duties of supervising the maintenance of marine vessels and its stores. He is also responsible for a daily, morning inspection of the ship, its rigging and sails. Being in charge of all deck activities, he would select several junior Officers to assist him in overseeing the general morale and efficiency of the crew as well as the maintenance and repairing of the hull, riggings, sails and deckings. Ortuga grabbed Flintlock's hand and shook it:

"Richard Flintlock, you've now got the same role on the Liberty Bell. You are my right hand man, my second in command," alleged Ortuga in a very welcoming manner.

At the beginning of the recruitment alignment, the group of 38 people that had lined up on the beach front was made up of a majority of men and several women, who were waiting to talk with the Captain. After two hours, together with the deckhands and the homeless orphan Leeron, a number of the group walked off the beach front, up the stone stairway to the port market to find food.

The nautical opportunists that remained on the beach were a Mexican Quartermaster, Javir Sanchez; an Iranian Linguist, famous but insatiable Treasure Hunter, Bijan Bonapart; a Sail Master, Pablo Medellin; the ship's Cook, Aturo Deshah; and the ship's Physician, Amir Noorian, who had worked for the King of Persia.

The group of superiors stirred intention and moved nearer to each other for a group talk with Ortuga about how, where and when the Liberty Bell would sail to find treasure.

Striving to be a Captain of the sea, Javir Sanchez was a strong man with a pigtail, wearing ragged clothes. He was a highly charismatic, charming, womaniser. Although he adores women, he does not like them to be part of any ship's crew. When Ortuga was interviewing potential crew members, a female stepped forward from the line to ask if she could travel with him and cook food for the crew. Sanchez blurted out that the problem with females being on ships is that their beauty can cause aggression and quarrels between the men; women halt all conflicts and killings with other ships because females don't enjoy fighting and stealing wealth and riches from enemies. After the Captain's leadership, the Quartermaster is next in line in the chain of command over the crew and the day-to-day activities of the ship, and decision-making regarding navigation. His authority would take over when Captain Ortuga retires to his quarters or is out of action.

Whenever the ship is not in chase or battle, the Quartermaster makes most of the decisions. His responsibility included the distribution of rations, work and punishment. Serious crimes are usually tried by a jury of senior crew members, but a Quartermaster could personally punish minor offences. The selected Quartermaster, Sanchez, leads the boarding parties when attacking other ships. He also makes decisions on which booty to pilfer from opponents, taking the treasures back to the ship and those which should be left in place. Sanchez would also watch over the treasure until it was divided amongst his crew. Peruvian by birth, he had a lot in common with Juan Ortuga. Three years older and highly educated, he knew his place when dealing with the Captain. Although his sharp intellect sometimes did get the better of him when dealing with the crew, for he knew their trades sometimes better than themselves. The instrument that Sanchez enjoyed playing is the acoustic guitar.

The skilled Linguist, Bijan Bonapart, who could competently speak five foreign languages, angrily stared at Sanchez after Ortuga shook his hand and told him that he would become the most senior member of the Liberty Bell crew. Bijan realised that with Sanchez as the nautical director, he knew that he himself would not be able to steal any treasures from the ship's hold, or even when they filched gold from other vessels and discovered treasures without being roughly punished by the forceful Quartermaster.

Contemplating the scathing outcomes for several minutes, Bijan shook hands with Sanchez and Ortuga, snorted phlegm up into his throat and spat it on them, then ran off along the beach.

Captain Ortuga turned around and knelt down at the waterfront next to Davy, were he washed his hands to remove the gooey phlegm in between his fingers that the sun had solidified to a sticky substance. Jumping up, he cradled hold of Tuli, asking him to be with him to discuss role potentials with the last three men up on the beach, for the Liberty Bell needed a cook, a physician and a person to maintain and mend shredded canvases.

Davy and Ortuga then marched up to Pablo Medellin:

"Who are you, can you cook good, healthy foodstuffs, fix sails and flags on our ship or perform operations on male bodies to regain their health and strength?"

The young man spoke gruffly:

"I can do anything because the universal energy guides me along all pathways with brilliance and success. I will do whatever you believe I can do."

Accepting their understanding, Pablo bowed his head in respect and shook hands with Tuli and the Captain. Ortuga then went on to speak with Aturo. Because Pablo's voice was also soft and shrill, Tuli stayed and gave him a man hug, and being this close, Tuli felt that under Pablo's muscular male physical form, were two bulging breasts like that of a woman.

"Why are you pretending to be a man looking for work on our ship, are you a woman?"

Pablo Medellin sat down on the sand and pulled Tuli down next to him.

"Look! To confirm the speaking of Sanchez about women as crew members, women cannot be taken onto ships because their single energy does not resonate well with pirates or swashbuckling males that kill each other to steal treasure and gold. Men also want to be in love with women, and due to crews being of males only, just having one female on a ship causes abrasive flare-ups and conflicts between the males. That is why I am using a male disguise. My name is Evangeline Moreau, and perhaps when we can get together in a quiet space, I can tell you more about my character, but please don't tell anyone about my disguise."

"My male outfit and false bushy beard is worn so no one can recognise me as the royal daughter of King Philippe of Spain, for he is searching for me to take me back to his homeland. I want to stay in South America."

Evangeline Moreau inherited a Royal bloodline and mild petulant nature from her father's lineage, who descended from the Spanish House of Habsburg.

The Habsburg dynasty ruled a vast but fractured empire from 1581 through to 1640. Of French descent, she was a very beautiful, kind-hearted, humanitarian. Evangeline spoke fluent French and Spanish; refusing to forsake her mother's tongue, she spoke little English but when she did, she mixed the two languages, which she referred to as Frenglish. Dressed in her disguise as Pablo Medellin, she was recruited by Captain Juan Ortuga as a male Sailmaker in charge of all canvases on the ship – sails, flags, hammocks and other materialistic equipment and utensils.

Only two men were still there on the waterfront with Tuli and Ortuga, the others had grouped together and walked up to the fisherman's wharf. Aturo Deshah learnt Voodoo as a child on the Caribbean Island of Jamaica, but he wants to make some money to donate to his parents so they can retire. Aturo is always complaining about other people's approaches, their attitudes and opinions. More often than not, most nautical cooks are isolated from the crew, and are only allowed to remain on board to make food that doesn't hinder the crew. This, not so able seaman takes many herbs to help him slow his mind and allow him to relax and sleep.

Pretending to help others in order to gain a few friends, mainly in the hope of larger portions of high quality food that he smuggles past the Bosun to sell to other crew members, he would hide and listen to the inside whisperings and information he was privy to, gained from the nightly conversations that took part between the Officers in the Captain's quarters.

"What can you do for me on the Liberty Bell?" Ortuga asked Aturo.

"I have such a great knowledge of herbs and foods that strengthen mental and physical attributes, so with my expertise your crew would become supermen?"

The last character on the beach was Amir Noorian, the tall, mild-mannered Physician wearing a powdered wig. In the past, working as the surgeon for the King of Persia, he retained many relationships and family links to the Royal Family, for he had an affair with the King's wife. Although he smokes plenty of dried mangrove leaves, locally grown tobacco and other herbal substances in his clay pipe, he boasts grand knowledge about native teas and bush medicines, brewing concoctions and distillations that will naturally heal frailties.

While he stood next to Ortuga who was talking with Aturo, Amir repeatedly heard how beneficial herbs and natural foodstuffs were, which positively would lower his stress levels of daily diagnosis and demands to keep allocating pills, potions and operations relating to each person on the ship. Wearing glasses, Amir reads medical books in his times of relaxation and researches for the cure of all diseases and illnesses to further support his capability leading to stable employment. Captain Ortuga was so impressed with Amir's knowledge and personal talents that he realised how valuable his skills would be for both the trouble-free, hard labouring deckhands and his senior crew members.

He firmly shook Amir's hand and told Tuli to shake his hand as well, to strengthen their relationship.

"Gosh, you are my most credited senior crew member, can we please have a discussion about my illness and cures when we get to the ship?"

Davy Tullman went forward to shake Amir's hand, without sensing any visions of the Turnkey, he removed the golden shell from his long coat:

"What is that treasure, is it solid gold?"

Ortuga questioned:

"No troubles, Captain, I'm yours to command. I will tell when and where I found this golden shell in England, let's talk on the ship!"

Ortuga shouted up to his comrade crew on the fisherman's wharf, who all walked down to the waterfront, chatting, joking and laughing and marched along in harmony, singing together to the Liberty Bell.

Han was expressing his devotions to the whole group as they descended from the market:

"Life, it is the destiny of all of us received from the universe, all treasures will be ours. Life – Live it, Love it. May Love and Light shine to help the World.

"We are all Superheroes that will help each other to help the world, accept and understand each other with no discord or demanding conflicts. The Universal Soldier knows he will put an end to war and bring Peace to the World without weapons.

"No man is your enemy; everyone is your teacher. He is the Braveheart who devotes his Body and Soul to bring Peace to all Nations.

"Your Love is King, Crown your Power with Devotion and Surrender.

"Hey, hey, hey – Ooooohh. Yeah…"

Aturo was telling jokes to his mates. Yo ho ho…

"Where do shellfish go to borrow their money?

- The Prawn Broker!"

"Why don't oysters give money to charity?

- Because they're Shellfish!"

"What do you get when a parrot is cross bred with a shark?

- A bird that will talk your head off!"

"What does a mermaid wear in her maths class?

- An AlgaeBra!"

Even though all the recruited men, 12 deckhands and five senior crew members were greedy and taking on their roles to hunt for gold and steal treasure from other parties, they all laughed benevolently, and they smiled and patted each other on the back and slapped their hands together high in the sky:

"Yaarrrgh!"

Heading along the waterfront to the Liberty Bell, the band of men were feeling so super energised and excited about finding treasure to help the world; their high spirits all sung to Juan Ortuga, together in harmony and power.

They knew that they would have to be involved in conflicts and plundering with other ships and people in order to gain wealth and treasure, but it would have to happen to move forward with the Captain's faith:

"We are The Champions, my Friend, and we'll
keep on fighting – No time for losers, cause we are
The Champions of the World.
We've all taken our bows, and the Wonderwalls are
Calling. The Universe has brought us fame and
fortune that goes with it –
We give thanks to you all
There's going to be no bed of roses, no pleasure
cruise – we consider it a challenge for the whole
human race, and we're not going to lose 'cause we
are The Champions, my Friend!"

Chapter Three
Bad Moon Rising

The rolling tide was high and the sun was fading as the nautical squadron arrived at the starboard side of the Liberty Bell. Gathering together under the bow of the vessel, the men all looked around at the magnificent workmanship of its classic construction and at each other; smiling and shaking hands.

Captain Ortuga leapt up onto a small rock ledge on the beach front to cast his welcoming speech into the twilight atmosphere, presenting his five senior crew members to the 12 deckhand sea-dogs:

"Ahoy there, mateys, welcome to my ship, the Liberty Bell, which was originally captained by the mean slave trader, Francis Drake. His ship was named the Golden Hinde, but I removed the lettering and got a sign writer to repaint the new title on the stern escutcheon, the starboard and portside. When we set sail, our first port of calls will be the South Pacific islands of Tahiti and Easter Island."

Stretching his hand out, Ortuga introduced each of his senior associates to the recruited deck labourers:

"Avast, ye landlubbers, I run a tight ship discipline! You swashbuckling pioneers are very welcome to the seven seas. Right, here they all are, your high-ranking seniors; each one of them has much knowledge of their own skills, meaning that you must always follow their commands."

"This Scottish fellow here, Richard Flintlock is the ship's Bosun. Here is my Mexican Quartermaster, Javir Sanchez. This man, Pablo Medellin, will repair and maintain the sailcloths and riggings. These two men, the ship's Cook, Aturo Deshah; and Amir Noorian, the ship's Physician, will take care of you all."

Suddenly, the weight and unstable movements of Juan Ortuga with his enthusiastic public speaking made him lose his foothold. His left foot slid into a crack in the rock, which scraped off the skin around his ankle; losing his balance, he fell down heavily onto the sand and twisted his ankle.

"Wooarrghh!"

The deckhands cheered loudly and clapped as the kind-hearted Physician, Amir Noorian, rushed over to help Ortuga. The crew were so distracted by the accident of their Captain that they did not notice the Iranian Linguist, Bijan Bonapart clambering up the hefty anchor rope onto the main deck, on the portside of the ship. Reaching the top of the gunwale, the upper edge of the side of the ship, he grabbed hold of the balustrade and hurled his body over the railings, and landed on the decking. Then he sneaked inside the ship to hide in the bridge wheelhouse, the shelter where the ship's steering wheel is placed. Using his sword as a walking stick to support his leg, Ortuga stood up and asked the deckhands to ascend up the ladders, walk along the gangway down into the ship's hold to become aware of their sleeping hammocks slung from the ceilings. The men quickly began climbing upwards, and stampeding down into the hold to find the best sleeping spaces. As twilight was settling over the port, most of the crew were snoozing loudly in their hammocks. Their collective snoring bellowed around the hull, which scared all the creatures aboard the ship, rats, chickens, the dogs and the newborn lamb, from out of their hiding places and nests onto the timber planks under the hammocks to glance up at the noisy deckhands.

The Captain allocated admirable sleeping quarters to his superior crew members with washing basins, mattresses, pillows, quilts, and portholes over-looking the ocean. Ortuga had his own luxurious cabin at the rear of the ship above the huge rudder with five lead-glazed windows facing out onto the wake of the ocean waters. Inside the Captain's cabin, a door opened to a set of wooden steps leading up to the stern decking which led to the bridge for secret observations. The three senior men, Amir, Han and Sanchez, shared a communal cabin. The Bosun, Flintlock, shared his quarters with Pablo the SailMaker, and the Cabin Boy, Davy Tullman – Tuli. The ship's Cook, Aturo, slept in the food storage space in the galley using a bag of flour as his pillow and five empty hessian sacks as blankets. Loaded into the galley were barrels of drinking water that weighed roughly one ton each, serving as ballast to keep the ship stable until the casks were emptied; refilling the barrels was to be carried out by the deckhands when the ship docked at its destination. But in the case that the ship would be unbalanced and unable to confidently repel dangers, the ship would dock at an island to fill the casks with sea water.

The planetary timing of that night in April was a full moon night – a bad moon. The harmful power of a bad moon rising has influence on the earth and its inhabitants, creating a low tide and generating ferociousness in the animals, who were racing around the ship, squealing, howling and yelping at each other and any other life forms that they banged into.

As the night became mildly darker, there appeared a small golden glow from within the ocean on the starboard side of the ship. The only senior staffer who remained on the decking was the commanding Scottish Bosun. Whilst observing the glow, Flintlock leaned over the railings and spotted an ancient-looking glass bottle bobbing around in the waters, encircled by a subtle glow of illumination emanating from within the bottle. The Liberty Bell had been docked in the port of Valparaiso for roughly ten days, and no one had noticed the object until the day of the full moon, which activated the coloured liquid inside the bottle.

Using his telescope, Flintlock took a close inspection of the bottle, and noticed there was a misty liquid vapour swirling inside the bottle, flowing around in an almost molten gold-like manner. Looking over his shoulder to make sure nobody was watching his actions, he climbed down the anchor rope to collect the bottle. Thinking that it contained a priceless treasure, Flintlock shoved it under his jacket, concealing the strength of the glowing illumination to securely smuggle it back onto the ship, and into his quarters without any brazen crew members confronting him.

Due to the twilight darkness of the sky above his head, he did not notice that there were two deckhands watching him. However, when the red-bearded, booming Scottish-born hulk began to scramble back up the chain to the ship's bow, he looked upwards and saw two deckhands; a close companion of his,

Johan Gallagher, and one other deckhand, both gazing down at him:

"Hey, Bosun, what's in that bottle? It looks like liquid gold. Do you think it's from the city of Eldorado?" hollered Johan.

Speaking back in a deceitfully planned reply, Flintlock made up a story to relieve himself of the responsibility of the smuggled gold:

"Arrr! Oh no, lads, after I picked the bottle up from the water, it slipped out of my hand and smashed on the rocks. The golden liquid flowed down onto the seabed to dilute into the water and lost its golden glow."

"Why don't you both get back into your hammocks, for Captain Ortuga implied that tomorrow we are sailing over to the South Pacific islands. Make sure you sleep well tonight in order to gain some strength; for tomorrow, your tasks will be massive; you will have to scrape the barnacles off the ship's hull and scrub all the timber deckings before we set sail."

"What is that glow coming from inside your jacket?" enquired Johan.

Flintlock expressed his intention to the deckhands:

"Oh, it must be the phosphorescent sand from the beach in my pockets reflecting the moonlight. I took off my jacket when I was talking to the Captain when I was trying to gain the role of Bosun and I placed my coat on the sand for more than a few hours. Go on both of you, get back to your hammocks or I will dismiss you from your roles on the Liberty Bell for not carrying out my orders."

Under fearful disillusionment, Johan Gallagher strode back down to the sleeping berth quarters in the sail locker room. Rolling quietly into his hammock, he landed on top of a rat, which slithered down into the back of his shirt. He became so irritated and afraid that the rat might bite into his backbone that he pulled himself upwards to the timber ceiling and dropped back into the hammock, trying to kill the creature by flattening it without waking any of his shipmates. Terrified, the rat forcefully sunk its teeth into the flesh of Johan's lower back and squeaked to its death.

The other deckhand buddy of Johan Gallagher, Calvin Thurman, remained in his position behind the railings on the decking of the ship's bow where Flintlock was climbing higher to meet him. Stretching up his right hand, asking Calvin to help pull him up over the railings:

"Yes, you! Grab my hand and pull my body up to the decking."

Calvin spoke out into the night sky:

"Only if you will offer me some of the golden treasure you have hidden in your jacket. I have been watching you climb down to that ancient bottle and saw that the bottle did not break on the rocks, as you told Johan and myself."

"Go on then, I will only give something to you if you help me!" bawled Flintlock.

Flintlock moved upwards to the railings, Calvin gripped his hand and heaved him upwards. Flintlock violently yanked the man over the railings. Calvin tumbled down onto the rocks below the ship that were revealed by the low tide produced by the full moon, breaking his left hip; Calvin rolled into the water and drowned.

Flintlock dragged himself up over the railings, stood on the decking and glanced around to see whether anyone else had witnessed him smuggling the bottle of gold and his killing of the deckhand. Flintlock didn't notice the young Cabin Boy, Tuli, who was hidden by the faint darkness up in the crow's nest, way above his head.

The emergent light of the moon began to reveal the hideaways of many creatures stowing away on the vessel as Flintlock rushed along the capstan corridor to the ship's stern, arriving at the door to the sleeping quarters that he shared with the disguised male SailMaker, Pablo, and the Cabin Boy, Tuli.

Outside the door was a black Labrador puppy that snarled and started to bark at him. Flintlock kicked the dog in the ribs, booting it away from the door as he turned the key to open and enter the quarters. The dog padded up to the top deck and yelped for someone to hold him. Davy climbed down from the crow's nest podium and cuddled the animal to heal its rage and bruising.

Inside the quarters, Pablo was sitting by a porthole gazing out at the bad moon rising, which was channelling negative energy down to the ocean causing massive waves to heavily roll in, washing over the sand and rocks, carrying the body of the dead deckhand Calvin Thurman, out from the shallow sea front to bottomless waters, hundreds of metres from the Liberty Bell.

To ensure her femininity would not be exposed, Evangeline Moreau gifted more power to her male identity of Pablo, stroking his bushy beard, she howled masculinely:

"Ahoy there, Bosun Flintlock! Quickly, look out this porthole, there is a bad moon rising. Someone's body that was lying on the beach has been carried out by the waves to a deep burial chamber in the depth of the ocean. It is still floating on the ocean, you might be familiar with the clothing on the corpse and therefore identify who the dead person is!"

Flintlock angrily claimed:

"Pablo, be aware of your aggressive behaviour to me and my response, for I am the ship's Bosun. If you do not show me courtesy or any respect for my power of seniority, then I will arrange some way of dismissing you from our crew."

The only light glowing within the cabin was a wax candle that Evangeline had lit when she took her belongings to the room, about five minutes before Flintlock returned to the shared quarters.

The golden light from the bottle hidden inside Flintlock's jacket glowed so intensely, it penetrated into the thick cloth material to illuminate the entire woollen sheathing and further spread around the cabin. Evangeline's eyes widened with anticipation at the golden glow shafting from under Flintlock's jacket, she thought that she knew what the light was:

"That glow looks like a light I have seen before about three years ago when I was searching for treasure in the valley leading to the city of Eldorado."

"Pablo, I told you not to interfere with my activities tonight, just go to sleep and let me relax or I will throw you off the ship," blurted Flintlock.

There was a knock on the door to the cabin. Ignoring the slight sound of entry, Flintlock walked away from the door to his bed at the back of the cabin behind a timber wall, as he was thinking that the person knocking on the door could be a buddy of Calvin Thurman trying to discover who killed him. Removing the ancient bottle from under his jacket, the glow faded gradually as he slid the bottle under the thick mattress. Lying down, he began to snore, pretending he was sleeping, but he stayed awake to listen to any conversations.

Evangeline stood up from the porthole, walked over to the heavy timber door and pulled it open. Leaping past Evangeline was the labrador dog chasing a rat and barking at the full moon. Following behind the dog, Davy walked in and shook hands with Evangeline:

"I have just watched the cold blooded murder of one of the deckhands, the killer was our house mate, Richard Flintlock!"

Knowing that Flintlock was awake in his bed at the rear of the cabin, Evangeline placed her index finger to her lips to indicate that Tuli should be quiet, not to say any words or express statements that would offend his or her being. Tuli sat down with Evangeline, who he knew possessed wonderful wisdom about the moon and energy emanating from planets that influenced all planetary life forces such as plant and animal life plus all creatures including humans and the power of the oceans.

Davy wanted to befriend her so he could learn some of her spiritual knowledge and compassion to help him benefit poverty stricken islanders to greatly improve their lives. He whispered softly:

"Pablo, what's happening, where is Flintlock? Is he down there at the back of the cabin?"

"Tuli, let's go back up to the top deck, okay? Take my hand and we will walk together and I will tell you about the happenings produced by the energy of a bad moon rising."

When they reached the outside, under the moon, they strolled along to the stern wheelhouse and sat on the helm decking. The light of the moon had become so strong that it sheened across the ocean and highlighted the ship's form, canvases and mechanical structures, casting eerie shadows on the decking.

"The phase of the robust Scorpio moon tonight contains a life-threatening influence that demands domination and control of individuals who do not resonate with its energy. The moon's gravitational pull upon the ocean and all life forms has been so strong that it produced anger and loathing of other individuals. That is why the animals in this ship have escaped out of their nests and kennels and also why Flintlock killed the deckhand, but you and I are very harmonious. We must have similar energies that contain compassion and surrender. Mutually, we can cultivate the desired spiritual vision that Captain Ortuga inspires.

"Help Each Other to Help the World."

Pointing out to the horizon, Evangeline muttered: "Right, Tuli, please tell me about the killing of the floating corpse of that man out there."

Davy moved closer towards Evangeline and began to whisper, he thought that he should keep his voice down while he was re-telling the story of the ship's Bosun because he wanted to keep his role on the Liberty Bell

"The killing happened due to the greed and aggression of two men recruited by Captain Ortuga: the Scottish Bosun, and a deckhand, Calvin Thurman. They both had a strong desire to open the bottle that Flintlock found and keep the treasure for themselves. I suppose, it was the rising of the bad moon that enthused their gluttony…"

Downstairs in his sleeping quarters, Flintlock was getting more intrigued about the contents of the smuggled bottle hidden under his mattress. Rolling over, he slid his hand under the mattress and grabbed the mysterious object. The glow was more powerful than before, so strong that he had to squint his eyes to reduce the extreme flow of harmful light into his eye sockets. Even so, his eye pupils had received a minor burning effect that fogged his vision; irritably, he thrust the bottle back under the mattress and stomped over to the brass porthole, squinting through the round glass to observe the current activity of the effect of the moon on the ocean.

Flintlock reflected his thoughts and imaginations back into himself:

"Even though I am driven by my insatiable energy to build my own empires and demonstrate tough orderings to higher-ranking colleagues and inferior deckhand buddies to elevate my lifestyle, the rising of the bad moon tonight has caused major issues and excessive disturbances in my mind, producing conflicting aggressions towards my fellow cabin mates and brutal yearnings to the deckhands. I must be careful tomorrow before we sail off to the South Pacific and I will make an effort to befriend my fellow senior crew."

Chapter Four
Threshold of a Dream

The following morning, the Aztec sun rose at 6.30am. As the light of the sun surged down into their sleeping quarters, the 12 deckhands aroused from their deep sleeping patterns. They all rolled out of the hammocks and strolled up to the food galley to find some breakfast. The stowed away animals – rats, chickens and dogs – that had wildly circled the ship through the night time had returned to their concealed nests and kennels but also woke up to search for food and any leftovers to maintain their vigour.

Only a few of the senior crew members had woken up with stalwart scrutiny to appropriately prepare the ship for its long, distant journey across the South Pacific. The seniors who had woken were Flintlock, Sanchez and the ship's Cook, Aturo Deshah. The other seniors remained in their quarters, in sound sleeps administered by the effect of the intense energy from the bad moon. Also that morning, Captain Ortuga found that he still could not walk correctly, so he too decided to hang about in his own private cabin quarters, for his sprained, tender right ankle was still aching when he stood up to load his weight onto the body part. By chance, he found a walking stick in the wardrobe next to his bed, which might have belonged to Francis Drake; Ortuga used the stick to help him walk around his cabin.

The ship's galley was packed with the men yawning and enjoyably eating the breakfast that Aturo had prepared since 5.00am. The incredibly powerful foodstuffs and potent fodders consisted of smoked mackerel fish with kale leaves and brown rice laced with fried garlic, coriander and fresh red chilli.

When the deckhands and the two senior comrades, Sanchez and Flintlock arrived in the food galley, Aturo knew that the super foods he cooked would bestow them with balanced strength to encourage them to maintain the ship with basic duties and endow the minds of all crew members with optimism in order to set sail on the ten-day journey across the ocean.

The disturbed deckhand, Johan Gallagher, spoke to Flintlock:

"Bosun, what happened to my good friend Calvin Thurman, he hasn't returned to his sleeping berth?"

"Your friend slipped and toppled over the railings at the starboard side of the ship and fell onto the reef under the ship's bow. He damaged his hip and drifted out to sea where he was taken down to a sea graveyard by a strong current."

"Oh no! He was my best friend – I have known him for 15 years, since we schooled together in Buenos Aires. My life will have to change now that he is dead, but I can now tell you of our tales of trials and tribulations when he searched for the City of Gold. We were planning to travel there to acquire some gold, which is why he was so interested in the gold that you hid under your coat."

Whilst the crew were hastily scoffing their breakfasts, Aturo ordered one of the deckhands to go with him up to the Valparaiso market place to purchase more food supplies for the journey to Easter Island. As they walked out of the galley, the remaining men clapped hands, giving thanks to Aturo for the magnificent breakfast. Walking to the upper deck, Aturo and the deckhand met up with Tuli, and Evangeline dressed in her male disguise.

"Morning, young lad, what's your name? Can you please help me and this deckhand here to carry some food supplies from the portside markets back into the galley?"

Tuli replied:

"Yes, sir, my name is Davy Tullman from the Cornish pirate port of Penzance in southern England, but the Captain has nicknamed me Tuli. I am the ship's Cabin Boy, and, yes, I will help you with any tasks that will be of benefit to the Liberty Bell."

Back in the galley, a number of the restless animals had sneaked through the door and passed under the tables into the kitchen area to gobble the food left on the preparation benches and any scraps on the floor. Out in the canteen arena where the hungry crew were eating, a vigorous chicken pounced up onto a table and pecked away at some brown rice on a plate. The person whose plate the chicken pecked at was annoyed; he grabbed hold of his fork and thrust it into the chicken's chest. Blood from the chicken sprayed all over his breakfast.

The injured creature squawked so loudly, it made all the other senior crew members, Amir, Han and Pablo, make their way to the galley to find out what the rowdy noise was all about. The Chinese Reiki Master, Han, glanced over at the table where the chicken was wobbling about on. He walked over and picked up the chicken, clinched it in his arms and swiftly healed the bird with his magical power. The chicken became active, widely opened its eyes, stretched its neck upwards and squawked again, in poultry communication, to imply:

"Thanks for saving my life, Chinaman."

Still cradling the chicken, Han jumped up on top of the table and stated to the men in the galley:

"Can you all please stop eating animals?"

Han moved the chicken on to his left forearm, sitting like a bird of prey, then began to speak mystically to the men:

"Animals have the same life force that we humans have, and all humans possess astrological characteristics of certain animals which define our personalities. When you don't believe in things that you understand, you will then suffer. I was born in 1696 – I am a Chinese Wood Rabbit."

When the chicken heard Han's comments, it began to violently peck at his wrist. He shook the bird off his arm, and it scuttled off into the kitchen to be with the two dogs that were eating the leftover food. Han's protest was perceived by the deckhand grouping as a threat to their mentality; they all laughed and yelled back at him:

"You Chinese people eat dogs, cats and rats!"

Furthermore, they demanded a response of what foods could replace meat in their diets. Before Han had replied, Aturo returned to the galley wheeling a trolley of fresh vegetables, melons, coconuts, pomegranates, sacks of rice, cereals, kebabs and two meat shanks of beef and pork. Back at the market, Davy carried a barrel of rum and after several minutes, the weight became overwhelming, so he began to roll the cask on the street. Bumping along, one of the metal rings sprung off from the barrel, and rum leaked out onto the stone paving attracting a friendly baby lamb from a butchery trader stall where its mother had been slaughtered and prepared into kebab sticks.

The deckhand, wheeling the trolley stopped and helped Davy lift the barrel back up onto the barrow, a tad of rum still dripping invited the young lamb to lick the rum off from the stones.

Following behind the trolley the lamb padded across the plank onto the ship's top deck and skipped down to the galley.

Aturo then blurted out his belief:

"Han, I am a Jamaican Voodoo child. I heard what you said about eating animals. Meats taste really good though, and are eaten to increase energy and mindful grounding. But eating meat is like any food stuffs; only eat in moderation to balance your addictions. Then you can remove animal products from your diet; replacing them with super foods like artichokes, brown rice, green vegetables, oats, berries, nuts, seeds and herbs. Much like these food types that I have just bought from the farmers' market on the wharf that I will be cooking as provisions to feed the crew on our future journeys, searching for gold. When we find the gold, I will roast this lamb to serve a luscious, congratulatory meal for the deckhands."

The men stood up, and all went up to the main deck to begin preparing the ship for the first journey. Standing on the helm, Captain Ortuga asked his Quartermaster, Sanchez, if he could temporarily take over his captaincy rank to command the crew, as his ankle was aching badly, defecting his mind power and methods of instruction. Sanchez smirked, as he told the Captain about Han's healing powers. Ortuga muted:

"Hey ho, that sounds so good, I will get him to channel some energy to heal me as well and also heal any of my crew when they injure themselves. So let's both work together to get the ship ready to sail off into the Pacific Ocean, then you can take over my commanding responsibilities for several days so I may rest my ankle, until we reach Easter Island." A stage manager, striving to be a Captain, the charismatic Sanchez, blurted out an expressive statement to impress his audience:

"I have such a great knowledge of the most efficient techniques to sail well on the ocean that I can sail the Liberty Bell to any destination Captain Juan Ortuga would ask me. I will take on the role as Master and Commander of this ship."

Gesturing Han, Ortuga waved his sword, beckoning him over to heal his ankle. In front of the crew audience, gently placing his right hand on the Captain's hair-laden leg, Han massaged the injury to infuse positive energy over the swollen skin. The audience all raved loudly with respect and amazement at his incredible magical powers after which Han strolled up to the bow of the ship to look at the carved wooden figurehead mounted on the bow.

Because women were not to be recruited on many nautical vessels, the figureheads termed as Neptune Angels depicted female forms, highlighting their beauty and compassionate characteristics. Being a creative Carpenter, Han pictured himself carving a new figurine in the shape of a commanding creature such as a buffalo, elk or a rhinoceros.

Although the primary tasks of the Bosun are supervising the maintenance of the vessel and its stores, Flintlock also had the daily responsibility each morning to inspect the ship and its sails. Being in charge of all deck activities, he would select another officer to assist him in overseeing the general morale and efficiency of the crew as well as the maintenance and repair of the hull, lines, cables, sails and anchors. Flintlock did not want Sanchez to be his master. He, himself wanted the role of Captain, and, therefore, highly aggressive anger entered the eyes of Flintlock when Ortuga requested Sanchez to take on the temporary position of Captain.

Expressing his rage, Flintlock turned around and stared loathingly at Sanchez:

"Look, even though you were boasting of your supposed skills to the Captain, I have much greater knowledge than you do, especially concerning galleon vessels like the Liberty Bell. I have spotted leaky seams in the hull of this ship, which, if not fixed, would sink us into the depths of the sea, drowning all the crew on our journey to the islands. You must be my co-worker, so we can discuss things together, but I will make the decisions."

Preparations and maintenance work began. The deckhands were cleaning the timber decking and sails to remove seaweed and slippery substances that would cause the crew to lose their balance, fall over and roughly harm themselves. Han reached into his pocket, took out his Pan flute and began to play a tune that motivated the crew. Flintlock yelled from the helm to the bow:

"Han, stop playing that flute. We need you to fix up the ship's leaky seams with wooden plugs and oaken fibre, and then we can set sail."

Dressed in her disguised male outfit, Evangeline laboured along with Tuli to raise the main sails and tauten the riggings to secure the battens and canvases. After they had fastened the main sail to the mast, Tuli climbed up the rigging to the crow's nest, looking over the horizon to observe any dangers such as hidden reefs, sunken vessels and enemy ships of pirates and bandits that would cause damage to the Liberty Bell.

Half way up the rigging, Tuli misplaced his footing on the yardarm and he spun upside down, the golden shell Turnkey fell out of his trouser pocket, toppled down and thrust into the dampened timber decking.

Luckily, not one of the governing commanders or labouring deckhands saw the marvellous, teleporting object. The higher-ranking trio of Evangeline, Aturo and the Chinese Taoist monk, Han, saw the shell falling down though. Evangeline bent down; in harmony with the military rhythm, she pulled the shell out of the timber and threw it up to Tuli. He caught it and put it back in his pocket. Han then came dancing along the deck playing his flute and glancing up to the crow's nest, he said:

"Rock Stopper, what was that golden shell? I have never seen anything like that before, it looked amazing as if it is out of this world, from another planet."

He clambered up the mast and stood with Tuli in the crow's nest, looking down at the crew who were turning the capstan to heave up the anchor, but Tuli did not want to talk with Han about the shell Turnkey. Evangeline returned back down to her cabin to have a brief power nap, to regain some strength after the bad moon had drained her energy. Whilst laying down, she had a dream of the future gateway to help the world; it was in the grassland hillside of a South American, Incan citadel called Machu Picchu, which she knew as the threshold to another galaxy.

After waking up, she thought that she could talk with Ortuga about her spiritual insights, as she knew it would empower his vision for people to change themselves to change the world.

Evangeline decided that the right time to meet up with the Captain would be before they arrived at Easter Island.

The only senior members remaining on the ship's deck were Sanchez, Han and Flintlock. Captain Ortuga was sitting on the helm talking with Johan about the death of his best friend Calvin Thurman. When the anchor was raised up, the ship drifted away from the port, out to the ocean. Everyone's focus was on the anchor and looking over the side of the ship to ease its way through the rocks. Tuli glimpsed down to the stern and noticed Bijan Bonapart creeping out from the wheelhouse and getting into one of the rescue boats to stow away from the malicious seafarers, the strong Quartermaster, Sanchez and the Scottish conservative empire builder, Flintlock.

Sanchez joined Ortuga at the helm and steered the ship out from the port of Valparaiso towards the coastal heads leading out into the ocean. Sanchez was holding a frayed cloth which was the navigation map showing Ortuga the location of Easter Island as well as the distance and the estimated time before arriving at the destination.

Ortuga expressed his gratitude to Sanchez and told him that he was going to his cabin to rest for a few hours and then prepare the space for a party gathering of his senior crew before they reached their destination. On his way down the steps to the ship's berth, he walked past the quarters of Pablo, Flintlock and Tuli. He knocked on the door and waited for it to be opened. Dressed as the bearded Pablo, Evangeline opened the timber door and welcomed Ortuga into the cabin:

"Hello, Captain, would you like to have a glass of ginger beer with me? I would like to tell you about the life of a very close friend of mine, Evangeline Moreau. I met Evangeline when I was a Senior Commander with the Spanish armada on her father's – King Phillipe's – sailing ship, the Santa Rosa, whilst working in the King's chain of command to successfully operate the ship when they fought with pirate vessels and attacked communities in South America. His daughter, Evangeline Moreau, lived on the ship, and we had a relationship together. She was my girlfriend for eight months."

"She knows such great stories about South America and the City of Gold, and would let you know about the threshold gateway that the world will go through in the future. I am really impressed by your consciousness to heal the world. Let's talk together about the many ways of searching for and acquiring treasures and gold to be donated to poor communities."

Ortuga moved his face closer as Pablo spoke in a lovingly deep male voice about the life of his female friend:

"My girlfriend is living in Valparaiso. She told me that she inherited a royal bloodline and petulant nature from her father, who descended from the Spanish House of Habsburg. Of French descent, her mother, Eyvette Dupont, was extremely beautiful, but of common birth from the French fishing village of Marseilles. She met the prince whilst working in one of the local shipyards. The clandestine relationship was doomed from the start and could never be spoken of in open conversation."

After falling pregnant, to avoid persecution and possible death, Evangeline's mother fled from France, stowing away on a merchant ship sailing to the unknown seas of South America. Taking final refuge on the Caribbean island of Barbados, her mother gave birth to Evangeline in 1709 in a galactic period when the earth and the moon aligned with the central planet of the Pleiadian galaxy, Alcyone. This era of ingenious enlightenment occurs only once every three hundred years, and those earthbound human beings born during the seven-day period are sheathed with a cosmic mantle and are termed as Starseeds.

These extraordinary human individuals possess an innate, inner spiritual wisdom bestowed upon them from the universal intelligence which the Elohim beings desire to channel back to their Pleiadian planet to seed their society to further advance their race with greater transcendence, compassion, understanding, altruistic insights and prophecies. Wisdom and compassion are channelled out of the Starseeds on the nights of a rare planetary alignment, opening galactic pathways to interconnect the Pleiadian system with the earth.

The intuitive wisdom of Evangeline Moreau enlightens her to open her mind to allow peace and loving energy to flow to and from the Pleiades. Her youth was embroiled in the early days of piracy in the seas that separated the two Americas. Growing up, surrounded by shipwrecks and drunken buccaneers, she possessed more knowledge about ships and their workings than most of her male peers. She also took on the larrikin charm of her seafaring comrades and was able to embellish and re-tell the many tales she overheard in the local port of Bridgetown. Although the island of Barbados was colonised by the British, she retained her French accent and strong sense of pride of the homeland of her mother.

Ascending the throne to become King Philippe V of Spain, history does not, unfortunately record Evangeline's birth or any association with the House of Habsburg. Because of his love for Evangeline's mother, the king eventually accepted and honoured their relationship. As a consequence, a search party was dispatched to find his daughter, Evangeline Moreau, and bring her back to Spain to fulfil a promise of succession. Hiding from her father and his armada made King Philippe irritated; he started to attack many vessels, kill the crews and destroy migrated communities.

Juan Ortuga was so impressed by the story from Pablo about his girlfriend, that he thought that if they returned to Valparaiso, he could meet up with her, and she could show him the way to the City of Gold, Eldorado. He posed a question to Pablo:

"Hey, buddy! Can we get together with Evangeline Moreau when we sail back to South America? I believe she can help our crew to open their hearts, and find gold and treasures that can be given to needy communities."

Chapter Five
Pacific Eardrum

At midday, the two deputy captain rankings, Richard Flintlock and Javir Sanchez, were standing together on the bridge behind the helm watching the deckhand, Helmsman, Johan Gallagher steering the wheel on the passageway between the two peninsula heads. Arriving to the open ocean, the ship was caught up in a strong wind. The wind bellowed into the main sail and powered the ship forward onto its course to Easter Island. The movement of the vessel's speed was so rapid that Sanchez thought that instead of ten days to reach their destination, it could reduce to just about seven days.

Whilst managing command of the deckhands, Sanchez, would not allow Flintlock to interrupt his words, relay orders or adjusting any commands hollered out to the deckhands. Feeling so unwanted and uninspired, Flintlock left the company of Sanchez and stomped away from the bridge down to his quarters where Ortuga remained sitting together with Pablo. Dressed in her male disguise outfit – Evangeline was still perceived by the crew as a muscular, strong, well-built, male seaman.

Walking towards the ship's bow, Sanchez punched his hand up into the air; he wanted to speak with three men who were trying to hide from the view of their commanding senior authorities. As Sanchez passed under the crow's nest, Tuli glanced down and focused on him following his way to the three deckhands when he met up with the men he barged the group apart and began shouting:

"Listen, you scoundrel seadogs! I am the quartermaster of the Liberty Bell and you must always follow my commands or else I will get rid of you from the ship's legion, and you will have to walk along the gangplank – off the end to a new ocean life!"

As Flintlock was not on the upper deck, Davy decided to climb down and speak openly with the welcoming Helmsman, Johan.

Tuli was just about to vocalise his witnessed observation when Flintlock appeared at the top of the stairway leading up from the hull. Carrying a large military tenor drum, when he reached the mid-ship point where the crew deckhands were gathered, he began to play a Scottish marching theme. The thunderous rhythm empowered the men, making them advance to the bow to look out over the horizon. Below the gunwale, the upper edge of the ship, there was a school of dolphins and a soft, green glow shimmering upon the hull. The pod of lively dolphins appeared above the water after the drumming; they swam in and out of the waves, up and down in harmony with the military rhythm.

The creatures swam in front of the bow, weaving across their tracks and gliding back to the sides of the ship where they seemed to be rapidly carried along by the immense power of the waves driven by the glowing green light. Tuli also noticed a slight glimmer of the green illumination emanating from the rear of the ship.

Because the piercing noise of the drum was so loud, he could not talk with Johan about the killing of his best friend, so Tuli ran to the bow and leaned over the railings to peer downwards into the water; he was amazed at the movement of the dolphins, and the green glimmer caught his eye. It was now just two days after he had been teleported from Cornwall to Valparaiso in South America.

He thought back to the time he was carried over the ocean by the same influence of the glowing green light to the port of Valparaiso for recruitment by Juan Ortuga. Another thought entered his mind about his parents and how they were feeling without him being there. Reaching into his trousers' pocket, he touched the golden shell; a vision flashed into his mind of his parents, Joseph and Parvihn, and his three close school friends in his British hometown of Penzance, Molly, Tim and the homeless boy Quinton.

Davy sat down on the deck, closed his eyes and gave an long solo focus to the visualisation. The images that passed into his mind began with his parents down on the waterfront standing at the spot where he had found the golden shell Turnkey. His mother was shattered by the grief of her son's unseen and indefinite death; weeping harshly, she was shrieking comments into the horizon conceived from her emotional misery:

"Where on the seven seas has the body of my son been transported? Is there a spirit out there that could notify me about my son – has he died or is he still alive? Davy is one of the major loves in my life, he has a little sister called Jasmine, who misses his sympathetic energy, his personality and kindness to her and all of her young, juvenile friends."

Davy's father, Joseph Tullman, wrapped his arms around his wife and whispered softly into her ear, saying:

"My darling, our young son may still be alive, for there has been no notification of his death. I spoke with Robert Scanlon of the Coastal Rescue squad and he told me that no dead bodies had been washed up on the Cornish shoreline which indicates that no one had drowned in the last three to five days."

Parvihn paused her sobbing heartache, she turned around and walked towards the rock pool where Davy found the Turnkey shell; glancing down into the water, she saw the intensely coloured sea anemones. Moving further on past from the rock pool, she walked into the entry point of the big cave calling out to her husband Joseph:

"This is the location that Quinton told me about where Davy was taken out to sea; perhaps, Davy's body was washed back to the shore and entered this cave. I am going to search inside."

Parvihn walked into the darkness and tried to look around on the sand and behind the rocks, but the shadowed obscurity made her eyes sightless. She started to weep again and returned to Joseph – sitting with him on the sand – they looked up to the hillside and noticed Davy's three friends strolling down to the beach. Molly waved at them and ran to the spot where Davy's parents sat, then the boys, Tim and Quinton, rushed down into the water and started to splash at each other...

"Let's all get into the caves and search for the stairs leading up to your house," said Molly.

Shivering, the two boys exited out of the cold water, Tim grabbed his towel and flicked it at Quinton's chest. Quinton then grabbed hold of the end of the towel and jerked Tim down onto the sand. He splashed into the rock pool where Davy had collected the golden Turnkey from. Assuming that Tim was a predator seeking to kill, the fiddler crab that bit Davy scurried out from behind the aquatic flower anemones and sunk its claws into Tim's thigh:

"Whoaargh! What's that in the water that has bitten into one of my veins? I can't move now. Quinton, please help me quickly get out of this torturous position."

Regrettably, Quinton had moved on into the enormous cave, to pacify the dreary howling of Parvihn. On the sand next to the rock pool, Joseph stretched his arm over, Tim clasped his hand and stood up, the fiddler crab was attached to his left buttock. Seeing the creature, Joseph took hold of a towel from the sand and flicked the crab off him. They both wrapped towels around themselves and walked into the cave passing Parvihn exiting out of the cave, crying as she still could not see into the darkness of the cave or find anything that would help her find her son.

Molly sat on the beach with Parvihn talking about Davy and how kind he was helping homeless communities in the townships of Cornwall. She told Parvihn that Quinton was homeless too, and that he slept in one of the caves along the beach front. Inside the cave, Joseph followed Tim, and close to the entrance, he saw a sleeping bag with a retrieving watchdog laying on it. Next to the sleeping bag was a paraffin lantern, a pair of reading glasses with several books, a torch and a fish bowl housing some crested newts and sea anemones.

"Which homeless being lives here?" asked Joseph.

"Mr Tullman, this is my home. I have lived here for nearly four years after my parents fell down from those massive cliffs across the ocean, over there." replied Quinton, pointing up from the beach front.

Joseph picked up the lantern and lit it with a Swan Vesta match that he had in his pocket; the Swan Vesta matches can be stroked on any object or material to explode the match head flame. He strolled cautiously way back into the depth of the cave, glancing back he saw the two boys walking out of the cave to sit on the beach with Molly and Parvihn. He noticed a bold tattoo on Tim's right arm; the design was that of the pirate symbol of a skull and cross bones. Leading his way, Joseph held the lantern high in front of him to illuminate the rock walls and back of the cave. The sandy floor changed to slippery rocks covered with seaweed and algae near the rear of the cave so he walked very carefully until he reached the back wall where a large rock was mounted vertically, and several rock ledges protruded to make shelves. Behind the base of the rock was a saltwater moat containing barnacles and other shell fish. Turning around again, Joseph saw his wife and the three playing chums walking into the cave, moving towards the light of the lantern, down to where he was standing.

Tim spoke out in the darkness:

"Hey, bossman, let's all get into these caves and search for the stairs leading up to your guest house."

Joseph swung the lantern around to light up the pathway so the group wouldn't trip over or lose their footing on the rocks covered with seaweed. Arriving at the back of the cave, they all stood quietly looking at the massive vertical rock, Joseph squeezed around the side of the rock with the lantern, creating slight shadows at the front position. Before the folk were out of sight in the darkness they followed Joseph. Because of the darkness, they couldn't see clearly as they walked behind the rock; deplorably, Tim bumped into Joseph and knocked the lantern out of his hand. Falling onto the rock floor, it smashed and the murky darkness obscured the whole cavern space.

Joseph reached into his pocket and pulled out the matches, striking one on the rock it produced only a flare of mild light, so he used the match to light the whole box of matches which flashed brightly into the air. He then raced back to the entry point where the battery torch was, and as he picked it up, the watchdog, Monty, snarled at him. Meandering back to the rear of the cave the retriever dog tagged along with him.

Sliding behind the rock, he shone the torch up onto the roof and scattered a colony of bats that fluttered down to the light of the torch, knocking it out of his hand the flock of bats soared madly out of Quinton's home and into a neighbouring cave. Silence veiled the darkness, Joseph stood in the shadows by himself for the other folk had walked back out to the beach. Glimpsing along the wall, he noticed a thin beam of light penetrating from the rock wall, putting his hand on the rock he slid it to the left revealing a stone stairway covered with dirt, moss and water dripping from the roof.

Back on the Liberty Bell, the stimulating green light emanating from below the ocean caused the visions passing through Davy's brain to fade away; he opened his eyes and stood up on the top decking. Next to him was Han, with a sheepdog that belonged to Captain Ortuga:

"Hey, brother," said Davy, "I have seen this type of green light before! Can you explain what makes this light illuminate under the water?"

Han's explanation was mind-blowing. He told Davy that the light below the bow was the power of an ancient sea-dwelling creature known as a Sledge Ray. The Sledge Ray was a magical predator that ruled the waves created by the planetary influence of the full moon using its light to frequently attract other sea animals from whom it extracted their energy, transferring it into its own body to furnish more strength and super power into itself. The radiant power lifts up vessels to carry them rapidly to their destinations. Although the beast drains energy from fellow sea creatures, it has great respect for terrestrial life forces, especially human beings. It would help oceanic voyagers to travel to their destinations on their selected sea routes. The mythical creature can also fly high in the sky, taking people on journeys to the past. The Sledge Ray emanates a coloured radiance to indicate the journey's predictions. The green light indicates that the moment in time is easily accessible and securely safe for travelling. When a red light illuminates around the vessel, it signifies a warning of danger, indicating that there could be hidden rocks or a reef in front of the vessel that would damage the hull and sink the craft. Furthermore, a stronger radiance of the red light indicates that there would be rivalry danger heading towards them or close by to take over the vessel; a warning of enemies, pirates, buccaneers who would attack the ship, launch personal conflicts and killings to steal treasures and booty being transported.

The Sledge Ray is a combination breed of a Hammerhead Shark and the related wide, flat-bodied Manta Ray creature. Indigenous communities of the islands named the creature Sea Goat because the creatures were often seen in the mountains.

The structure of the Sledge Ray's head is flattened, extended into the shape of a hammer and joined to the wide, five-metre body of the Manta Ray which has triangular shape fins and feeds on zooplankton krill. It swims with its mouth open to let the small crustaceans sail into its oral cavity and be digested in its stomach. The source of the light flows out from its horn shaped fins, and radiates from within its body. Most of the time, the amphibian swims in the oceans, but on a prevailing good full moon, it walks up onto the beach to find somewhere to stretch out and absorb the energy from the moon then it lurches up to the mountains or hillside to soar into the sky. Davy leant over the gunwale side of the ship, the light was still glowing green, but he could not see the dolphins, so he thought that morphed sea creature destroyed them all by draining their energy which stole their lives. He then climbed back up the mast head to the crow's nest and picked up his telescope to look behind the ship. In the distant wake of the ship's course the school of dolphins were motionless, they were dead, floating on the crest of the waves away from the illumination of the Sea Goat. Moving away from the school of dolphins, the Liberty Bell gradually rose above the sea level, carried aloft by the Sea Goat roughly one metre above the waves with its speed limit increasing from the average of sixteen knots to a powerful, skyrocketing rate of 30 knots bouncing over the waves.

Ortuga, Flintlock, Amir, Pablo and Aturo lingered in the ship's berth. Sanchez, Han and the deckhands were on the topside, the speed was so brutal it rushed the ship uncomfortably ahead across the ocean. Smashing through high waves, the crew secured themselves with ropes strapping to the main mast and handrails, because the random movement was like an earthquake. One of the men did not manage to secure himself, so he grabbed hold of the main mast but was shoved away by the shuddering motion and rapidly skimmed down the oily timber decking and crashed into the bridge platform where Sanchez was sitting.

Sailing over the ocean, the Liberty Bell passed two other vessels. The first was a galleon from the Spanish Armada, Gallo Conquistador, sailing away from the City of Gold, Eldorado, back to its homeland. The ship was laden with gold, silver, precious stones and jewels. The Captain of the Spanish vessel thought that the Liberty Bell would be crammed with treasure hunters and his crew should attack them to plunder their treasures; so he ordered his crew to fire cannons. Because the Liberty Bell was surging so rapidly across the ocean, the cannon balls shot past it, missing the target. Up in the crow's nest, one of the cannon balls zoomed past Davy, luckily he ducked down onto the podium as he saw it soaring up towards the upper mast head.

The second aquatic vessel that confronted them was a small, single mast, pirate sloop. Of course, they were sailing so fast that the pirates could not chase them, but they did try by commanding their crew to row into the strong wake behind the Liberty Bell.

The powerful, controlling wake of a vessel carried by a Sledge Ray is a deep rut of turbulence that draws objects and other vessels into it. The pirate sloop was so very light, it was violently sucked into the wake. Trying to shift the Liberty Bell onto another direction away from the pirates, Johan Gallagher swiftly spun the wheel around. The pirate sloop rolled out of the wake and blasted along the starboard side of the Liberty to the bow. The mast of the pirate sloop vessel collided into the Liberty figurehead, smashing it off the front of the ship. The Liberty Bell pushed on, even though the ship was sitting one metre above the waves, the green light travelled under the vessel as it transferred so hurriedly across the South Pacific; after six days, three islands appeared on the horizon. The time was 4.20am – a meditation time – sitting cross-legged on the decking, Han noticed that the glow beneath the bow had faded away and the ship had fallen back down to the sea level. Looking out over the horizon, in the distance he noticed an island with five large stone heads mounted on the grassland adjoined to the coastline; the heads faced out to the ocean, the island was Easter Island.

The dramatic speed of the Liberty Bell had slowed down, extending the distance and increasing time of arrival to its destination longer, taking two to three hours. The crew freed their bodies from the railings and strolled down to their hammocks to have a brief power nap before reaching the island. They would soon be turning the capstan to lower the anchor and setting up the timber walkways and ladders from the boat to the island.

The sun was rising as Evangeline woke up and put her false, bushy beard back on her face and went up to the top deck. Davy awoke in the crow's nest podium, then climbed down to be with

Han and Pablo, they all gazed out on the horizon to view the magnificent statues on the outskirts of the island.

Davy spoke:

"Good morning to you both, what a marvellous day this is going to be. Pablo, what is your date of birth?"

Pablo replied in her gruff male voice:

"The 18th of October, 1709, I am 23 years old."

Han expressed his layered knowledge of Astrological animal characteristics:

"Pablo, you are a Libran Water Snake. What about you Tuli?"

"My birthday is on the 5th of March, I am only 13 years old."

"You are a Piscean Earth Rooster! As a meditative group of early morning beings, we each have the insights to converse with the energy of the universe."

Seeing that the existing year was in the early 1700s, Davy did not state his year of birth which was 1960 as he thought that if he did, then no one would accept it as a true reasoning yarn, and he would be cruelly challenged by the senior crew members, Flintlock and Sanchez, about his role as the Cabin Boy being part of the Ortuga crew in 1732. Steering the ship, Johan asked Davy to return back up onto the crow's nest to look out into the distance for any rocks that might damage the hull; the best way of avoiding the dangers would mean to change the route of the vessel. Davy said the he would stand on the bow of the ship and use his telescope, which was more defining and had better clarity than standing above the deck. Johan agreed; so Han, Davy and Pablo stood together looking for the safest route for the ship to sail on in order to reach the island. A noise appeared behind them. Turning around, Han saw the sniffer sheepdog, Arlee, that belonged to the Captain; he sat down with them at the bow and talked with the animal.

"Good boy, where is your master? Is he still asleep in his quarters?"

The dog barked once, which Han interpreted as 'Yes!'

The other animals crawled up from the ship's hold – five chickens, the young lamb that escaped from the butchery stall in the market of Valparaiso and the tetchy labrador puppy with a damaged ribcage. The animal group sat down in the warmth of the early morning sunshine next to the Captain's sheepdog. The chickens hopped up onto the railings fixed onto the bow and were joined by three Tahitian Petrel birds and a large Albatross that was perching on the broken figurehead, flapping its wings and squawking with the flock of chickens. Han knew that it was his kindness to tend animals that drew the varied species of creatures together in a group. He mentioned to Davy that animals, insects and even human beings sense the energy of predators – hence they snarl and bite. But those humans and other life forms that do not kill or eat animals become close friends of those creatures.

Sitting together in harmony on the front of the ship, the three humans and the group of mixed animals spoke with each other – twittering, chirping, woofing and baa-ing with no conflict or aggression. Davy strolled back towards the helm to talk with Johan.

Davy warned Johan about what had happened with Flintlock, and how Calvin's body was carried out to sea by the massive waves powered by the moon. Davy mentioned that, unfortunately, the power of the bad moon was what inserted the aggression into Flintlock's brain:

"Johan, I have not seen any rocks or dangerous reefs on the course you are steering, but the route we could take is marginally veered to the east – over there near those coconut trees, only about two degrees from this present route. It will let us easily dock the ship with no troubles in a lagoon close to the stone heads near the waterfront. That looks like a meeting place where the indigenous, sun worshipping Mayan communities would gather after eating their breakfasts," said Davy.

The Liberty Bell was now only three minutes away from lowering its anchor in the lagoon. The stone heads on the tree-less hillside were colossal; two of them were covered with green moss, which sealed the pores of the rock and didn't allow the air to circulate into the stone to freshen its mineral appearance. The other heads exhumed the presence of dominance and authority. The sculptured heads were spiritual repositories charged with the one universal dialogue that seeded global, human cerebral evangelism to build the core foundation of all religious beliefs. Han and Davy slid down a rope into the shallow lagoon. Davy's feet were nibbled by a cluster of little crabs snapping manically at his toes. Splashing in the water, he jumped up and down to try and scare them away from hurting him and then he waded off onto the sandy beach and ambled up the stumpy hillside to the five stone heads which were expressing such vast spirituality.

In her male disguise, Evangeline climbed down after Han and Davy and wandered towards them as they stood in awe in front of one of the stone heads; speaking in her male voice tone, she expressed her insight received from her birth as a Pleiadian Starseed.

"Let me tell you about these massive statues. Three thousand years ago, well before any religious faiths were founded throughout global communities, these giant heads were created by alien beings who dropped them down from the sky, facing the eastern mountainous region of Machu Picchu in South America. After several hundred years, the heads welded onto the rock formation below the hillside to form complete, gigantic figurines which are hidden under the earth."

Each one of the heads is charged with the same thinking patterns but in different languages. Speaking in tongues, they convey knowledge to structure the central format of many religions, Christianity, Shinto, Islam, Hinduism and Buddhism. For prayer and worship, Islamists and Taoist monks face the same direction, as the heads 'East', and as you may already know, many monasteries are set up in mountainous districts that are abundant regions of spiritual rock.

The insight about the Easter Island heads that did not enter Evangeline's mind was that the power of a bad moon, which only occurred about two or three times a year, raised the giants from their concealment. One of the religious rock figurine bodies, held below the surface of the earth would rise from its holding, walk around and swim over the oceans to attack communities that did not accept their philosophies. However, when the rock giants were held for longevity under the earth on the hillside of the island with only their heads emerging, their beliefs softened to gain acceptance of all indigenous cultures and religious faiths. Standing below the sculptured head of Arabic faith, Han and Davy gazed up to its eyes. An invisible fragment of words seemed to flow out of the eye sockets, channelling into the minds of Davy and Han:

"Hallelujah."

Their minds filled with the Arabic language, explaining about the holy prophet Muhammad and his preaching to commence the Islamist faith, neither of them could interpret what the language stated. Davy ran back down to the water and climbed back up the rope, he tapped on the rescue boat where he had seen the phlegm baited linguist, Bijan, stow away. The canvas cloth stretched over the rowing boat slid open and Bijan looked out:

"Tuli, what's going on?"

"Hi, Mr Bonapart! There are no problems, for most of the crew are still asleep in their hammocks. The men have not slept for three days because the ship was carried viciously across the ocean by a magical creature called a Sea Goat. Bijan, could you please partner with me onto Easter Island, and use your broad intellect to translate the words flowing out from the stone heads that have been sculptured by extraterrestrials?"

Bijan had been lying inside the rescue boat for four days. As he sat up, Bijan groaned and gripped the sides of the boat to help him stand. He pulled himself over the side and stood with Tuli, then walked with him along the top deck to a ladder that Johan had fitted onto the ship, taking him down to the beach front. Bijan's eyes widened with amazement at the sight of the five heads, he perceived all the different languages: Japanese, Hindu, English, Arabic and Chinese. Meeting with Han, he shook hands and told him that he would translate the speaking of tongues. The figurine head they stood in front of exhumed more speech vapour, which dropped down onto the four characters, Han, Bijan, Tuli and Pablo. Bijan was so impressed by the happening, he blurted out in the international language of Esperanto:

"Tiendu masee, Jen darbo Hienday!"

The words of Japanese language, expelling from the head above him fell into his mind:

"Kon'nichiwa Tamashi."

"Life is sometimes a mystery, everyone can stand alone. You can hear the universe calling your name to have a conversation with God…

The Power of God is Omnipotent, Omniscient and Omnipresent. Down on your knees to seek help from Heaven to gain power through Love, Devotion and Surrender – A Prayer Will Take You There…"

Davy was so thrilled:

"That is fantastic, Bijan, please let's move onto those other heads, to listen and learn what they have to say."

The group shuffled along to the next stone figure, where they calmly stood with hope and faith to aspire the words of wisdom out of the statue. The atmosphere filled with profundity and the words poured out of the stone figure's mouth. Bijan's mind took in the inspiration; he told the group the words were similar to what the first head had told them but in a different tongue, Indian:

"Marhbaan Sould."

"What does that mean?" Han asked.

"Both of those heads used the same welcoming phrase. Translating into English language, the words are, Hello Soul."

The third head of religious consciousness was covered with moss and grass, but because the moss covered the eyes, the wording could not be released. Standing in front, waiting for the expression to move into the surroundings, Evangeline understood why the spiritual communication would not enter the atmosphere. However, the tongue poked out and muffled words of the Buddhist pathway escaped from its mouth:

"Hailo Aatma."

The atmospheric words to serve the foundation of Buddhist religion did not appear.

High in the sky, the sun's position indicated that the time was 11.00am, unexpectedly the throbbing sound of the ships time bell rang behind them. Turning around, the group noticed that Aturo was surrounded by the deckhands ringing the bell as he called out that food was being served for breakfast. Hungrily, Davy and Han returned back to the ship, walked up the ladder and down into the galley where some of the other senior crew members were. Aturo welcomed Davy into the galley and offered him a breakfast of fresh grilled catfish with chips, greens and parsnips. Han said that he would like some rock melon with greens, walnuts and brown rice to bestow more sensitive energy to his physical fatigue, for he hadn't slept for five days since the Liberty Bell had left the port of Valparaiso. After eating, Han returned to his cabin to sleep for a few hours allowing the foods to be digested and processed into energy.

Remaining with the Iranian linguist, Evangeline moved along to the fifth head. She then heard the voice of Flintlock shouting at her:

"Hey, Pablo, get back here immediately, for we need your skills to repair the main sail which has ripped off the top of the mast on the forceful journey from Valparaiso!"

Evangeline mocked him, pretending that she didn't hear the demand of anger. She crept in front of Bijan, who was close to the fifth head, to hide from the Bosun's aggression. Akin to the third head projecting Buddhism, the fifth stone head was smothered with green moss that choked the voice of Chinese Taoism. Because no words were heard, Evangeline crawled back down to the fourth figurine, which depicted the religious beginnings of Christianity and Catholicism:

"Hello Souls."

Up in the blue sky, way above the stone heads, word soundings appeared in the atmosphere, swirling around the hills and settling on the sandy beach close to the waterfront 100 yards from the heads:

"Each Human Being is a Child of God. We all are Stardust. Every atom in our bodies comes from Exploding Stars. Life belongs to Every Soul. Help each other with Global Understanding and Acceptance to Help the World."

The head that expressed words of English, evoked a directive into the Pleiadian, Starseed mind of Evangeline Moreau:

"Lady of the Lake – Travel back towards the East, visit the tribal township of Machu Picchu where the sun rises to empower the indigenous communities of Mayan, Aztec, Olmec and Inca; all of whom worship the sun. Peace and nurturance are at the very heart of life on earth and the universe."

A group of eleven native tribesmen of Mayan ancestry suddenly appeared at the top of the hillside, they wandered past the stone figurines down to the waterfront to view the magical wording embedded into the wet sand. The communication was in English. Lost in translation, not one of the tribesmen could understand the meaning. Bijan decided to abandon the Liberty Bell and remain on Easter Island to join up with the Mayans, explain to them the inscriptions and live his future as part of their tribal community.

One of the Mayan tribesmen told Bijan what he knew about the statues:

"These statues are symbols of religious authority and power; they are actual repositories of the sacred universal spirit, charged by a magical spiritual essence called Mana."

United with global compassion, Pablo rushed back to the ship to repair the main sail and speak kindly with Ortuga, asking him if they could sail back to South America. Then, together with his senior crew and all the male deckhands he could search for Eldorado – the City of Gold, and collect masses of bullion for donation to needy islanders and poverty-stricken communities. Also, Captain Ortuga could, of course, uncover many treasures hidden by pirates to share with his crew members to lessen greed and enhance their kindness; the optimistic deed of constructive inspiration would progress the growth of altruism in his crew, thus helping the world. Ortuga still did not perceive the female form of Pablo but he resonated very closely with the incredible story of Evangeline's life as the girlfriend of his senior shipmate.

The Mayans greeted Bijan into their native community; they felt that he would have the ability to help protect them against the aggression of the Rock Giants who, in the past, had killed a percentage of their tribe. Knowing that Bijan could speak many languages, enabling him to discuss issues with each giant, the Mayans set up a congregational meeting to welcome him into their political council. Gathering around a wooden table, stories of the attacking Rock Giants began.

The premier Mayan Councillor stood up and began to tell a tale of the time when he watched the body of the Indian stone giant emerge out from below the hillside.

It happened one night whilst he was catching fish in a rowing boat with his son and two daughters. They were out in the bay, only 100 yards away from the beach front, when they heard a massive groan up in the rolling hillside. Relaxing down into the boat, the family turned it around to look towards the hillside, where the groaning sound floated into the night air and the moon shone down onto the ground. The group saw the eyes in the stone head open, glaring down to the beach; its head twisted around and rose up, causing the earth to break apart. The shoulders of the Rock Giant appeared above the ground, and gradually moved higher to reveal its arms. At this point, the empowered figurine placed its hands flat on the ground and surged its body out from the holding region embedded by soil and grass. When the massive figure had extracted its body from the entrenchment, it stood up. The Mayan family were amazed at its enormous presence and height of twenty-five metres as the enlivened statue shook its body to remove soil and insects that were embedded in its rock lesions.

After the shuddering quake, the Hindu giant stomped down to the waterfront, wadded into the deeper water, dived in and swam near the boat of the Mayans. Surging past the boat it noticed the four natives; it stood up and flicked its hand, springing the boat off the ocean into the sky, dropping it down onto the beach sand – KaahPow!

The Rock Giant then rushed forward across the ocean to the continent of India to suppress the Tibetan religious conversion of the Dalai Lama.

On arrival, it stormed into the mountainous monastery region where the monk was trying to convert the Hindu mountain folk to a Taoist faith using his sermon speech:

"There were no scripts or notes from the beginning. Words of enlightenment spring naturally from deep within yourselves to fill your bodies with courage and confidence. Taoism helps you to believe in the power to happily carry you through your lives."

Stomping its foot onto the floor of the temple – the religious leader was crushed under his foot. After squashing the sacred person, the Hindu giant inhaled deeply and shouted out at the audience of 400 people with the massive power of its exhaling breath pushing fifteen of the group off the side of the mountain: "Apologies for the death of your friends, it is the power of the Killing Moon that has intoxicated my brain, making me infuriated about other religious cultures, especially those that want to pressure all other races to convert to their beliefs. *The key to global multiculturalism is acceptance of all races, surrendering to their religions, cultures and devotions."*

The following morning, the glowing energy of the rising sun cleansed some of the toxic thought patterns from the Rock Giant as he swam back to Easter Island and slid back down into the hole where his body had been secured. Showing his own head on display above the ground next to the four other stone heads, the thoughts of his anxious killings created tears gushing from his eyes. Sensing his loathing deeds of cultural revulsion, the other stone heads swung around to face their fellow giant, as they channelled their philosophical foundation of religion into his brain to heal his being – through Peace, Love and Understanding.

Chapter Six
She Sells Sanctuary

All the swashbuckling crew members were huddled together on the main top decking of the Liberty Bell. With his well-trained, friendly sheepdog, Arlee, Captain Ortuga and Sanchez were standing on the quarterdeck bridge behind the helm. After Captain Ortuga's command, Johan Gallagher was preparing to steer the vessel to the new destination. Johan opened his hand to show Ortuga his compass lodestone. The lodestone was a magnetic rock that indicated navigational directions defined by energy of the universe. To find the direction of North East, which was the ship's new course, the port of Puerto Caballas. Johan rubbed the compass on a rock to magnetise it, it spun around on the top of the rock, and then stopped and pointed in the direction of the ship's new destination.

Twelve male deckhands were recruited at Valparaiso, but Calvin Thurman had been killed by Flintlock. Another lad, Alejandro, who slid down along the decking, had smashed into the iron bridge platform and damaged his hip causing multiple fractures in his spinal column. The ship's Physician, Amir Noorian, did try to treat the injury by fastening a poultice of Epsom Salts with menthol oil to Alejandro's backbone, but the mixture inflamed the broken nerves and flesh, causing insanity and suicidal impetus within his mind so much so that Alejandro lifted up a cannon ball and leapt over the stern down into the ocean depth.

Before he committed himself to the South Pacific's grave waters, he nodded goodbye to Pablo while he was rigging a sail up on the mizzenmast head at the stern of the ship. After Alejandro's death, only ten deckhands remained.

For most of the time, Amir and Aturo, relaxed in their cabins, taking insightful actions together, preparing potent foods and medical mixtures for the crew that would bequeath energy to empower their physicality. Davy, the welcoming young British Cabin Boy, spent a lot of his free time wandering continuously around the ship, asking the crew if he could assist them with any tasks they wanted help with or any equipment that they wanted him to find for them.

Han spent a lot of his time meditating with the animals, practising magic tricks and crafting fireworks from the ship's gunpowder and paints.

Impressed by Pablo's appeal to sail back to South America, Ortuga believed that when they discover the City of Gold, a vast bounty of donations could be given to poor and poverty stricken communities all over the planet. On finding the gold and treasures, he would load tons onto his ship and first sail back around to the Polynesian and Caribbean Islands to distribute the fundings to the Mayan and indigenous communities. He would then return to Eldorado with a combined fleet of other ships, reload more gold and sail to the continents of Europe, America and Asia.

The Peruvian port that Pablo had asked Ortuga to sail off to was below the Inca citadel of Machu Picchu, the port was named Puerto Caballas. From his position on the bridge platform, Captain Ortuga ordered a group of three deckhands to raise up the anchor, releasing the Liberty Bell ship from its holding, freeing the vessel to begin its return journey back to the western coastline of the continent of South America, where the brutal Spanish military was continually destroying the native communities. Weighing nearly 200 kgs, the heavy iron anchor normally had to be raised by turning the capstan numerous times. The three men commanded by Ortuga to raise the anchor, Delmar, Abdul and Febian, expanded their chests to confidently flex their muscle power and grabbed hold of the heavy rope cable attached to the anchor. Amir passed each one of them a glass of a super herbal, green energy beverage to ease fatigue that he had prepared with Aturo; a mixture consisting of Ginseng, Astragalus and Ashwagandha. Gulping down the super beverage, the men sprung their postures upward and bounced around the decking:

"Hey, medicine man! No wonder the wife of the king of Persia fell in love with you. When you offer this type of ecstatic drink to fuel anyone, it creates worshipping of your kindness and admiration of your handsomeness. I could love you."

Amir was very open-minded by this comment and he then said:

"Young man, you're right! Men can love each other, women can love women too. Friendship and devotion are the foundations of humanity and the credence of mankind."

Lined up, each man hauled the rope up onto the decking near the front of the ship; when the anchor appeared at the railings, Febian leaned over and exerted his muscles to yank the solid iron device onto the decking. As the weighing anchor was pulled out from its sand bed lock, the Liberty Bell drifted out of the lagoon. Johan turned the wheel to the direction indicated on the lodestone to steer the ship towards the ocean to capture the forceful wind into its main sail.

Surging off on its new journey of 2280 nautical miles, travelling with speed and nautical surprises, the Liberty Bell encouraged amiability to the men; engendering amazing willpower and skills to the crew. Sanchez, explained to Ortuga that the distance of the journey would take roughly seven days to complete:

"Ahoy, aye, Captain! Your ship is a magnificent vessel, for it catches the wind into its canvases and pitches strongly over the waves. Our Sailmaker, Pablo, has such valuable experience of the most excellent techniques that firm up the rigging to support the sails when they are bellowed with immense power from wind. We must not lose his talents or we will lose the power of the wind, so do not expire his recruitment. Ortuga, you must carry out all of my orders."

Feeling plagued by the dominance of Sanchez, Ortuga replied using his authority:

"Look, Sanchez! I am the Captain of this ship, you are the Quartermaster, so do not try to command me with your aggressive orderings or else you will have to leave my recruiting!"

After four days on the ocean, sailing with determination and courage, the Liberty Bell was slandered by a rival boatload mob of ten seafaring filibuster thugs. The offensive vessel was not pirate or buccaneer, it was a ship from the Spanish armada which had followed the Liberty Bell for two days and, eventually, closed onto the starboard side of the ship. When the vessel was parallel to the side of the ship, the Spanish freebooters tossed ropes with grappling hooks which clinched onto railings, the gunwale and the raised upper edge of the ship giving the attackers an ability to easily storm aboard and start a battle. Only three attackers climbed up onto the decking of the Liberty Bell.

Observing the incident, Tuli was up in the crow's nest together with Pablo. They both kneeled down onto the podium to hide themselves and peak through the gaps in between the rotted timber palings to observe what was happening on the top deck. Tuli noticed a line text on the bow of the armada ship, reading – Santa Ana. Whilst crouching on the podium, the Mollusc Turnkey in his trouser pocket ripped through and thrust into his thigh:

"Eaarghh!"

Uneasily standing up, Davy reached into his pocket and removed the pointed shell. Evangeline kindly looked at him with compassion and whispered in his ear:

"Jeepers, those golden Turnkeys are amazing objects. They are stored at the Pleiadian citadel of Machu Picchu, which is where we will travel to when we dock at the port of Puerto Caballas."

"Here Tuli, take this chain, you can wear it around your neck inside your shirt. When the shell is on a chain, it does not release any visions of the past or future because the energy is encapsulated by the chain connection, just like any chained force, animal, human or transporting vessels – captured and imprisoned."

Bowing his head with thanks, Tuli attached the chain through a small hole at the top of the Turnkey and placed it over his head and around his neck. Wildly raging, the three Spanish assailants who climbed onto the ship, fought with the Liberty deckhands, killing four of their opponents.

Johan Gallagher survived the deadly assault, the five other Liberty deckhands that were not slain, charged down into the ship's artillery shot locker to get hold of their muskets and prepared the cannons, ready to fire at the armada vessel.

Whilst the man-to-man skirmish was taking place, from the top deck of the Spanish vessel, the Commander sprung up onto the bridge of the Liberty Bell and went inside, Sanchez was there. The Spanish authority posed a question to the Liberty's Quartermaster:

"Do you have a beautiful woman called Evangeline Moreau travelling on this ship? She is the monarchy daughter of King Philippe – our prudent Majesty. He wants her to return to Spain to become the new princess and, where do you keep your treasure on this ship?"

"No way, boy! We have never had any women on our vessels, for they cause too many issues with the males, and we do not have any treasures on our ship either. These offensive questions you have asked me are none of our dealings." alleged Sanchez.

Barging past the Quartermaster, the Spanish Chief Officer walked out of the bridge. He stood close to the timber railings of the platform, watching his crew fighting with their mixture of cultural opponents. Sanchez sneaked up behind him and shoved him over the railings into the water; he then dropped a cannon ball down onto the hat of the Chief Spanish Officer.

The compounded weight of the arsenal object pushed the Spanish Captain lower into the water, demolished his brain capability, bounced off his head and smashed onto his elbow joint, therefore he could not swim back to gain protection in his galleon. He just clung onto the hull of the Liberty Bell and floated on the top of the ocean.

Rummaging around to find the Captain of the Liberty Bell, the three Spanish attackers that were on the top deck ran down into the hold to search the shot locker and the cabins. On his way past the front foremast, one of them seized hold of the sail, slashed his broad sabre sword through the canvas and ripped it off the yardarm. Stomping along the dark corridor to the rear of the vessel, one of the other attackers yanked open the door to Captain Ortuga's cabin who was lying on his bed sound asleep. The attacker threw his hands down onto Ortuga's abdomen, rumbling him to wake him up, and then posed a question:

"El Capitano, where do you hide your treasures? If you won't tell me, you will lose your life!"

Ortuga's sheepdog snarled vigorously, leaping up onto the invader's chest. The animal snapped at his chin, sinking its teeth deep into the side of his face, making a hollow reverberating echo that came from the cracking of the jawbone of the attacker.

The man yelled out for his two plundering comrades to enter the Captain's cabin to help him:

"Amigos, quick! Get down here and carry me back to the ship or else my flesh and organs will turn into food for this mad dog."

The defending hound unlocked its teeth from the enemy's jawbone and bolted underneath a table positioned in the midpoint of the cabin. Tumbling off the mattress, the Spanish foe fell onto the floor and banged his head into a state of unconsciousness. Lifting himself off the bed, Captain Ortuga glanced at the trail of blood leading underneath the table. He called his dog to him and together, they moved to the rear of his quarters onto the set of steps, leading up to the stern of his ship. The time estimated by the position of the sun was about 4.00pm in the afternoon. Outside, the weather condition was becoming extremely windy; with the bellowing of the sails moving the two ships to strongly surge together on the ocean.

Raising himself upwards from the podium, Tuli set his eyes down on the main decking, gazing from the ship frontage to the rear to observe if any of Ortuga's senior crew had been slaughtered. He saw Ortuga and the sheepdog exiting from the steps and walking onto the iron bridge platform.

Johan was sitting at the helm, Flintlock was walking out of the hold. Han was sitting on the bow, hiding under the sail that had been ripped off its mast by the Spanish attacker. Flintlock got hold of an axe to chop off the ropes that were hooked onto the ship with grappling irons. Tied tightly from the Spanish ship, the ropes sprung off the Liberty Bell and flopped down into the water. Firmly gripping onto the hull of the Liberty Bell, the wounded Spanish commander caught hold of one of the ropes and tried to climb up high to his vessel. His shouting floated upwards from the water, for he was being attacked by a massive, Great White shark dragging him under the keel of his ship and drowning the man of influence.

As the attached entry ropes had been removed, the Santa Ana vessel drifted away from the Liberty Bell to a distance of about 40 metres. The six crew members left behind on the Spanish ship began to roll out canons from their storage cabinets on the portside gun deck of their ship adjacent to the gunwale of the Liberty Bell. Because no Spanish attackers stayed on the topside,

Han shook the canvas off his body and walked to the bridge to be with Captain Ortuga, his sheepdog friend and Johan.

Sanchez, Aturo and Amir all remained in their quarters. The two agile enemy attackers that were still downstairs in the ship's hold searched for their injured comrade who had yelled out to them. Reaching the well-stocked quarters of Captain Ortuga, the two Spanish men cautiously opened the door to find their mate sprawled out on the floor with his head resting in a pool of blood. Bending down, they placed their arms under his rigid body, lifted him up and sat him into Captain Ortuga's wooden chair.

The Spanish ship, Santa Ana began firing cannon balls at the Liberty Bell, with one cannonball tearing through the wall of the bridge where Ortuga was talking with Han. Flintlock was commanding his crew to return cannon fire onto the Santa Ana ship, but they could not find any gunpowder because several days ago Han had used the bags of gunpowder to make his fireworks.

Han noticed that the Liberty crew were experiencing troubles with the artillery, and Flintlock was having an outburst of anger about the loss of the gunpowder he stored in the ship, that he had purchased from the military traders market at Valparaiso. In order to save the ship, Han used his magic influence to raise a curtain of energy from the ocean to create an invisible barrier facing the Spanish enemy vessel, along the starboard side of the Liberty Bell. The force field made up of energy particles offered such protection to the Liberty that all the men in the hull appeared on the main decking.

From up on the crow's nest podium, watching the shielding liabilities produced by the wall of energy, Evangeline noticed that the cannon balls fired from the Santa Ana bounced off the force field, mightily hurling back to damage the Spanish armada vessel and bestowing serious injuries to the men working their canons. The torrential power of the cannonballs thudding into the hull of the Spanish ship pushed it further away from the Liberty Bell, drifting out on the ocean towards the horizon.

Evangeline was very impressed by the density of Han's energetic influence and magical powers that protected everyone on Ortuga's ship. She scrambled down the rigging to meet up with Han and her cabin mate Tuli. The three kind natured souls together resonated words of compassion that hovered in the air around the ship:

"Everything in the universe, all life is formed from energy. By refining, caring for and by transforming the energy within ourselves we can transform and improve our lives for the better."

The loudness of the cannons blasting brought the two Spanish companions up the metal steps from the Captain's quarters to the ship's stern. Carrying their injured comrade up the steps to the rear of the ship was difficult; his gushing blood was flowing over their hands as they wobbled on the slippery decking at the rear of the vessel. Viewing across the horizon, they saw the Santa Ana ship roughly about 30 yards behind the Liberty. Above their heads was a cautionary sign, hand written and installed by Han –

ENTRAPMENT CAN RESULT IN SERIOUS INJURY OR DEATH DUE TO THE CONSUMPTION OF SEA CREATURES AND ANIMAL BEINGS – WHY CAN'T WE BE FRIENDS WITH ALL BEINGS?

The information sign stated the layered dangers of the slippery decking due to the space being used to haul up turtles, fish and other sea creatures for consumption by previous crews of the ship, as the skinned bodies of the filleted sea creatures caught at the stern left a deep residue of dangerous syrupy slime on the timber decking.

One of the Spaniards looked up at the sign, he accidentally dropped his injured mate onto the deck and his body slid off the stern into the ocean waters. Leaning over the railings, one of the last two comrades saw the Great White shark re-appear in the distance, hurtling to the stern to devour their bleeding companion. The other companion untied the small rescue boat that Bijan had used to stow away in before he began his new life with the Mayan tribesmen on Easter Island.

The two Spanish buddies stepped into the boat and quickly lowered it down into the waters. Arriving at the surface, they hauled their injured mate into the rescue boat and rowed towards the Santa Ana; the shark raced with them to their location and savagely barged up under the small row boat, throwing the blood covered man back into the water. The shark then opened its mouth as wide as possible, swallowed the body, then dived down to the seabed and vomited the carcass out of its stomach into a small storage cavern containing other marine foodstuffs, such as turtles and numerous large fish species. Out in the distance, a massive Blue Whale, 30 metres in length, saw the shark taking its burley human provision down to the ocean floor; it soared over the waves, bashed the two men out of the row boat, then opened its mouth and swallowed them both down into its cavernous stomach.

Once the men moved into the hollow organ, they sat against the wall and began to talk with each other about the tactical way of escaping out of the whale. They both crawled along the ridged gullet channel, where they tried to gorge open the massive creature's mouth, making the whale belch them out from its throat. They then swam to the Santa Ana and started to climb up one of the hanging ropes, with the Great White shark, snapping its jaws behind them as they climbed higher on the ropes.

At 7.00pm that night, as the two vessels had parted, the Liberty Bell was geared up to continue on its course to South America.

All the senior crew members were alive, but only six of the 12 deckhands recruited by Ortuga in Valparaiso remained alive. Out of the dark night air there flickered an arrow from the Santa Ana, breaking through the energy force field it thrust into the chest of the handsome helmsman, Johan Gallagher, reducing the number of deckhands to five.

That night, which was two days before arriving at Puerto Caballas, in order to capably sail the journey, the crew needed to re-energise their physicality. From the top of the hatch stairway leading to the food galley, Aturo appeared and said:

"Saluton Amikoj. Hello, friends – I have cooked some great food to boost your energy, for your health and immunity. The supper for tonight is turtle soup with brown rice dumplings and coca greens. I realise the selling of coca leaves may be illegal, but I purchased the greens from the law enforcement agency at the port of Valparaiso."

He continued:

"Tomorrow's breakfast is going to be a bone broth with pearl barley and kale. The Captain has told me he is going to have a party tomorrow night before we arrive in South America. For the special gathering, I am going to cook roast pork with apple sauce, potatoes, parsnips and broccoli plus homespun gravy. Let's celebrate the world vision of our Captain: to Help Each Other to Help the World."

As cheering rose into the night sky, Aturo was embraced by his fellow senior crew members. He then climbed up the rigging to the masthead to view the horizon where three planets – Venus, Mars and Saturn – were very closely grouped in the form of a noticeable triangle. Pablo sauntered lower down from the crow's nest platform to be part of the group gathering on the yard arm. Flintlock and Aturo sat on the right arm, with Sanchez, Amir and Han on the left. Positioned in the middle of the nautical seniors, Pablo explained the cause and effect of the planetary alignment. Evangeline spoke gruffly to intensify her male personality:

"In September, the brightest planet Venus settles lower in the twilight, it is surprisingly bright being so close to the horizon. It is normally higher in the sky but the energy of the solar system, consisting of the nine planets – Mercury, Earth, Mars, Jupiter, Saturn, Neptune, Uranus, Pluto and Venus – multiplies strongly in the beginning of the month of September, causing destructive earthquakes, hurricanes, tsunamis and heavy floodings.

"The compounding energy that draws the planets closer together becomes increasingly more powerful over the three month period ending in December. During this time, Starseeds or human beings that have open meridians can teleport their beings into the Milky Way and neighbouring galaxies."

Out of the five senior male companions sitting on the mast arms, Flintlock, Aturo and Sanchez listened intently to Pablo's explanation, thinking to themselves that the planetary energy would empower their ability to create their own empires.

"Right on, Pablo – you're a genius; can you tell me of the techniques about how to open my meridian channels to access the energy into my body?" asked Sanchez.

"Not tonight, as I have to repair the hammocks in the sail locker because the Spanish assailants pulled them all down from their fixings and ripped them into shreds.

"There are now only five of our deckhands remaining, who will have to work really hard sailing onto Peru, so they must have a good sleep. Let's talk tomorrow morning as the sun rises and I can demonstrate to you the methods to open your meridians."

The Santa Ana vessel disappeared over the horizon, its departure from the violent skirmish furnished the crew on the Liberty Bell with tranquillity and relaxation. Carefully climbing down from the mast, the seniors gathered on the bridge to discuss the fate of the lifeless body of Johan Gallagher. Two of the seniors lifted up his body and swung him off the bridge into the air without realising that the force field barrier was still active and much to their astonishment, the corpse bounced back onto the helm. The bewildered crew decided to leave the disposal of the body until the next day, then grouped together, the crew walked down to the galley for some fine energy foods to nourish their health; afterwards, they returned to their quarters to sleep well. Before Ortuga went down into the galley, he asked Tuli to stay by the helm and steer the vessel:

"Tuli, could you please remain here? Take the compass lodestone from Johan's pocket, wrap his dead body up in the torn hammock and slide it off the stern down into the ocean. Also, steer the ship towards the east and have a few power naps."

"Okay, Captain, I will carry out your commands. Good night, boss." Dany then looked at the cadaverous body of Johan. A number of rats were nibbling at his flesh and sucking blood from the hole in his chest where the arrow was inserted. Davy slowly pulled the arrow out of Johan's chest and lobbed the deathly projectile into the sea; blood gushed out from the incision like a water blowhole. Blood spurted over Davy's shirt; he removed the chained shell Turnkey from around his neck and placed it back in the pocket of his corduroy trousers along with the lodestone. As the Turnkey was covered with some blood, it could not discharge any visions into his mind. Davy then picked up one of the ragged, handwoven Mexican hammocks that Pablo had brought up to the helm. He rolled Johan's body into the flax material and securely tied it together with the strings at each end. After it was firmly assembled, he rolled the colourful cloth coffin to the rear of the boat but did not shove it over the stern. Noticing that the ship was drifting off in the wrong direction, he raced back to the helm and grasped hold of the steering wheel, opened the lodestone, rubbed the needle on his trousers and placed it on the flat side of the stone. The needle spun round and round, then stopped at the magnetic north point. Davy used some string from the hammock, tying it to the steering wheel to lock its easterly route in place, and then he fell asleep for several hours.

Rousing at 12.00 midnight. Davy felt the soulful, loving energy of Evangeline sitting close by him:

"Tuli, do you know its Juan's birthday tomorrow. He is having a party with the deckhands and his seniors. I think there will be some weird activities going on, for I have been talking with Flintlock tonight, and he said he wanted to take over the Captaincy. I still believe that Ortuga is the best commander; he will be helping the world if we can help him. What do you think?"

Davy was shocked by the aggressive actions of Flintlock:

"Evangeline, I think that Captain Ortuga is the best commander, he has been so good to me. Tomorrow, I will get together with Han and set up the fireworks to show the crew's recognition of Ortuga's diplomatic leadership. I am going back to sleep now, see you tomorrow."

"Sleep tight, my little one, I will be here in the morning when the sun rises, as I am meeting with Sanchez, to show him certain yoga practices to raise his levels of personal energy and breathing techniques to convey relaxation and calmness."

Thankfully, Davy replied:

"Fantastic, my mother is from India, so I am sure she would know much about yoga and meditative routines. I really adore your energy. When you turn up here tomorrow, can you please wake me up, and I will join you and Sanchez for the instruction session?"

When Evangeline delicately walked away, down into her sleeping quarters, she noticed that Flintlock was asleep but the golden glow from the bottle of treasure he had hidden under the mattress was emanating from behind the wooden partition near his bed. She quietly moved towards the space and peered around the wall, seeing that the glow was seeping from underneath the mattress; she wiggled her hand in to clutch the bottle, sliding her arm under, reaching up to her shoulder into the slight opening she took hold of the bottle. Drawing the bottle out from under the mattress slightly raised the bedding and Flintlock woke up. The golden light glowed around the space, highlighting his large hairy feet and presenting both their faces and attitudes. Although Flintlock awoke, his foggy mind was filled with annoyance at the disturbance of a person stealing his treasure. In her disguise, the false, bushy beard that Evangeline was wearing furnished her male appearance with the strength of a thief.

Flintlock drove his knuckles into Evangeline's cheek; she dropped the bottle onto the bed and yelled out:

"I am not a thief, I am your cabin mate, Pablo. Please, Flintlock, let me go to sleep, I was only searching under the mattress because I thought that the light was coming from a fire under your bed and burning you!"

Flintlock clasped hold of the bottle and moved it under his pillow:

"Okay, Pablo, sorry for hitting you. I am quite drained of my energy because I have not slept for the past four days on the ocean journey. And tonight, the attacking Spaniards made me so livid that my physical energy relapsed and I had a dreaded nightmare of somebody rolling me off a mountain top, as I was bumping over the rocks to my death; you woke me. I thought you were the man in the dream, which was why I punched you to stop the killing."

"Sorry Flintlock, I won't disturb you again, let's both get to sleep. Sweet dreams." said Pablo.

At 5.00am the next morning, the sun appeared on the horizon, its light flowed in through the portholes of the cabins waking Evangeline. The flickering, fiery sunlight stirred Flintlock, for he thought that the subtle golden glow was the light coming out of the treasure bottle.

Sitting up in his bed Flintlock noticed Evangeline in her male outfit walking to the door:

"Hey, Pablo, where are you going? The time is in the early hours and it is untimely to set the sails because all the deckhands would still be asleep down in the hull."

"Morning, Bosun, I am going up to the main deck to meet with Sanchez, for he wants to talk about the energy of the universe and how to channel it into his body to make him a superman." replied Evangeline.

She quietly moved on, tiptoeing out through the door of the cabin and up to the main deck. When she reached the top of the stairs the sunlight was becoming stronger with its light flowing across the ocean and the ship's timber decking. The ship's damaged wooden foremast figurehead was pointing towards the horizon where the sun was rising; looking in that direction she saw Sanchez and Han sitting cross legged. Moving closer to them did not rouse them as they were sitting peacefully, in a deeply relaxed dual meditation with their eyes closed, focusing their breath into their skulls to strengthen and bring the intense calming of their minds.

Evangeline stood at the furthest point of the bow where the railings joined, looking down at the two men. Because the sun was now higher in the sky, the sunlight flooded onto the decking to move Han and Sanchez out of their meditative state. Opening their eyes, smiling boldly at Evangeline, Sanchez spoke out:

"Mateno, Pablo! When I came up here at 4.30 this morning, Han was sleeping on the decking under the canvas, and when the sun rose he woke up. I have talked with Han about the universal power, so let's now all go down to the galley and have some breakfast."

Evangeline inquired:

"What does Mateno mean?"

"The word MATENO is from the international language of Esperanto formed from the collation of many languages around the world, which is why all cultures and people on the planet who could speak in Esperanto would accept each other without conflict of religious beliefs, fortifying their own characters with freedom and devotion."

Raising his arms up into the sky, Han began to present his worshipping to the sun:

"Breath is the power of the universe. Meditation and breathing will bring Peace to the World. Always use your last breath to let your soul rise to eternity."

Appearing from under the canvas that Han had used to sleep under, the baby lamb poked his head out and began trotting along the decking next to Han, bleating and joyfully tapping its feet on the timber. Leaving the lamb skipping about on the decking, the three seniors strolled down to the galley. The time was only 6.10am, Aturo was preparing foods, and the deckhands were all sitting in the seats, chatting, telling jokes and laughing; waiting for their breakfast – bone broth with pearl barley, chick peas and onions.

Pablo sat down with Han and Sanchez. Twenty minutes later, the breakfast was ready for serving. Because Davy was still working at the helm of the ship, Aturo took on the job of serving breakfast and spoke out into the crowded space:

"Just come in here, to the kitchen and take one of these bowls, line up here and I will pour the broth into your bowl, and top it with goat's yoghurt, kale and fried garlic."

The five deckhands were so hungry, they leaped up from their seats and charged into the kitchen; accidentally, one of the men barged into the bench, thrusting a knife into his stomach, penetrating the wall of his large intestine:

"Wooaarghh."

Collapsing on the floor, he pulled down some saucepans with him, a heavy iron pan banged onto his skull, causing his sudden death. The noise of the steel saucepans bouncing around on the flooring bought Ortuga, Amir and Flintlock into the kitchen. Captain Ortuga appeared upset by the death of another one of his deckhands:

"Oh no, we now have only four men left to help sail the Liberty Bell. Flintlock, shall we recruit some more men when we arrive at Puerto Caballas?"

"Captain, the township I have known to recruit the best deckhands is the Colombian port of Cartegena. It is packed with Caribbean seafarers and highly experienced sailors from defence forces and military zones around the planet."

All the crew grabbed their foods and sat in the main room of the galley. Aturo dragged the dead body of the deckhand out through the exit doorway leading to the rear of the ship, below the steps from the cabin quarters of Captain Ortuga. The power of the ship's wake was easy going because the sails were not raised onto the masts, also the Sledge Ray creature had departed from its minded trade of swiftly carrying the Liberty Bell way above the waves. Trekking in the same direction as the Liberty, the magical sea creature swam to the port that the ship was travelling to, Puerto Caballas, on the western coast of South America. The Sea Goat reached the port 24 hours before the Liberty Bell; stomping up into the hillside searching for a cavern habitat to reside in.

Being so low and close to the water where the huge wooden rudder was positioned, Aturo slid the dead body of the deckhand out through the shuttered windows, trying to launch it beyond the rudder; the body banged onto the rudder and shattered its spinal column. The flesh and bone of the dead deckhand gorged out into the water, which attracted a group of hungry school sharks to scoff the human burley that was scattered into the ocean. At 9.00am, Aturo returned to his kitchen galley along the corridor inside the ship's hold. The crew had finished their breakfast, and had left to get on with their work.

The Liberty men were up on the top deck, scrubbing the decking and setting up the sails, ready to sail off in the precise direction indicated by the lodestone to arrive at the port of Puerto Caballas in 20 hours' time. Once the preparation jobs were completed. Captain Ortuga stood on the bridge with, Sanchez and Flintlock, casting their commands to the four remaining deckhands.

Dressed in his Scottish kilt, Flintlock was playing his drum to motivate the men. Davy was back up in his high position in the crow's nest. He removed the chained Turnkey out of his pocket and placed it around his neck so it wouldn't jab into his groin again. Han was sitting on the bow while Pablo, Amir and Aturo were all in the kitchen cleaning up the dried blood on the bench tops from the accident.

The ship was sailing rapidly over the South Pacific ocean; with its capability and proficiency established by the skills of the fundamental labouring of the deckmen. Ortuga spoke out gently, way up into the sky:

"You won't be able to get anywhere in this world if you wait for things to come to you, you must make your beliefs and visions take place. This year of 1732, I am 28 years old – Thanks to you, you are welcome to my celebration party tonight at 7.00pm."

Looking eager, Pablo rose up from the galley, marched off to the bridge to try and be pleasantly sociable with Sanchez and Flintlock, for they both wanted to hear the insights about the routines of how to open their meridian lines to transport life energy through the body and to facilitate the structure of the foundation and expansion of their personal empires. In great detail, Pablo explained the dynamics of energy and that all forms of life and activities, both anatomical and physiological in structure, are supported by and simultaneously deplete the energy within the body.

Pablo spoke to them about two super power, ancient routines, derived from the Chinese physical and breathing disciplines of Tai Chi and Qigong. Han told Pablo that the routines can be done sitting cross-legged, lying down on the back or standing, to empower the body and cleanse the mind with balance and harmony.

Pablo and Sanchez followed the first exercise that Pablo instructed, The Pole Dantian. Standing with their postures straight but not stiffly upright, with their legs a shoulder width apart and slightly bent at the knee joint.

Pablo told them to be aware of their breathing in through the nose and expansion of the abdomen, imaging the power of the universe entering the body and flowing down into the Qi Hai, the sea of energy. Pablo also said that this particular routine can be practised as long as one feels comfortable and empowered, and then stop and relax. The next meditative practice was another breathing routine, called Bellows Breath; its aim is to raise a person's vital energy and increase alertness by inhaling and exhaling rapidly through the nostrils while keeping the mouth closed. After practising the meditation routines for 20 minutes, instead of surging his loud penetrating voice, Richard Flintlock spoke out very passionately:

"Pablo, you are a genius, thanks for helping me. Because I feel so pleasant, calm and balanced, I now feel more compassion to others…

"If we are attacked in the forthcoming journeys by any enemy vessels, I will try to save our lives by talking with the assailants about the reason why they are attacking, what are they searching for and what they want."

Sanchez supported the statement of his colleague:

"Yes, Pablo, you and the Chinese monk, are genius gurus – thanks for your open-hearted, expressive commentary, delivering information to myself and Flintlock, to help make us both supermen."

Rising into the atmosphere on the portside of the ship, there appeared a massive clicking rhythmic noise, sounding like an animal crossbred with an elephant, a parrot and a dog whining, all trying to communicate with the fellow companions of their pack. Davy leaned over the railing to glimpse what creature was producing the noise; his terrier dog friend also jumped up onto the rail and pointed his head down to view the side of the ship. Davy clasped his arm around the dog's neck to protect it from tumbling down into the water. The creature they saw was a giant of the deep: a Humpback, whale. Even though Davy had his arm around his dog, the animal slid off the railing and fell onto the whale's back. When the dog bounced onto the massive sea creature, the whale rolled over, sending the terrier dog into the water, then the whale flipped its fin up into the air which drove the dog also up into the air and back up onto the ship. In amazement, Davy stretched his arms out, and caught hold of his dog in mid air.

All the crew were now on the top deck; the four deckhands and six seniors stood around discussing what they would do when they arrived in South America and how they could find gold or treasures. Naturally, Ortuga's sniffer sheepdog had the ability to seek the trails of other animals and other treasure hunters, plus Ortuga was also in possession of a map of the whereabouts of the sunken treasure from the Spanish ship, Nuestra Senora de Atocha, that sunk in the year 1622. Translated as Our Lady of Atocha, the vessel was part of a famous fleet, which carried silver, copper, gold, jewels and gems stolen from other ships and South American communities. Captain Ortuga did not want to notify any crew members about the map until his celebration party that night when he would only tell his seniors. He was readying himself by recalling his memories about his early life, his journey to Valparaiso and how he got hold of the treasure map.

It was 2.00pm in the afternoon – five hours before the party would begin – Ortuga returned to his cabin to clean up the plans, sea charts and navigational tolls off the table, making sufficient space for the seniors who were invited to the party.

As the Liberty Bell cruised forward on its journey, it was passed by a 16 cannon loaded boat; the vessel was the Greek slave trader, Tecora, with over 300 African men imprisoned aboard. Deprived of their freedom, most of the slaves were naked, shackled together with different types of chains. The boat was sailing to the Caribbean island of Barbados, where it would sell the majority of the men as slaves to labour in the tobacco, cotton and sugar industries, and several would be sold as domestic slaves and personal servants. When the slave trader boat sailed close to the Liberty Bell, five men broke free from their chains and jumped off the vessel and swam through the waves towards the stern of the Liberty, towards the gateway and steps leading up to the main decking. Whilst swimming towards the Liberty, they were fired upon by the Tecora's officers, two of the slaves were killed; their bodies floated on the surface of the water and were carried away on the waves. The other three men, two strong Africans and one slender Dutchman, arrived at the stern. They grabbed hold of the huge wooden rudder, then lifted themselves up through a flap leading into the cannon galley and then walked out onto the stairway leading from the Captain's cabin to the top deck.

Hearing the racket of the gunshots and the men flapping their bodies onto the wooden rudder Captain Ortuga surveyed the activity out from the high stern window of his quarters. Noticing the three bedraggled males, he walked out to the stairway to greet them onto his ship, with a view that they might become deckhands to support his four remaining men.

Ortuga stepped downwards to meet with the escapees:

"Welcome aboard, fellow seamen, would you like to be recruits on my ship?"

Hardly believing their luck, the smiling men nodded their heads and shook hands with Captain Ortuga. Grouped together, they all stomped up the stairway to the greasy stern decking covered with fish scales and slime.

Once Ortuga realised that the men were slaves, he would pay them a basic salary, sufficient enough for their new responsibilities and share with them any gold or treasures discovered in the future. Carefully, they went along the decking, walked up to the top deck and met up with Tuli who said that he had been watching the whole incident from up in his crow's nest. The start of the escape strategy was triggered by the unchaining of many of the slaves, but only five people managed to carefully leap over the bow of the boat and swim to the Liberty Bell. Three other unchained slaves flocked down into the water from the stern of their vessel but toppled into the spinning brass propeller which hacked them into pieces, the blood flowing out of the severed flesh of human bodies attracted a hungry shoal of hammerhead sharks.

Swimming from their boat, the other two African men who had been killed by the officers, had been shot in their heads. Tuli was delighted that the other three men had escaped from the doom of slavery:

"What are your names?"

The handsome Dutchman from the town of Amsterdam replied, "My job was to patrol the deck on the Tecora and to whip and lash any offensive slaves that argue or fight with any officers. I became so very distressed by the ghastly, selfish nature of my fellow officers and the nasty actions of my position planned by the Captain that I took the opportunity to break away from their assembly and jump off the ship with the four slaves.

I unchained several groups of men that were chained on the main decking; the 24 individuals were all from the continent of Africa. Other slaves were captured from coastal settlements, raided by the crew. Only seven men jumped into the ocean, the others fought with the ships' officers and stormed down to the hold to release the other 300 slaves."

The two African males placed both hands in between their groins to cover their nakedness. The males breathed heavily and sighed to discharge their harmful feelings of leaving the ship and hundreds of companions who would be killed by the officers of Tecora. One of the high strength black guys removed his hands away from his crutch, flexed his biceps which expanded massively, clenched his fists in the air and spoke out:

"Captain Fantastic – I am Marley Waylon, and this is my buddy Samson Buju. We are both from the African county of Senegambi, and I will always be strong when we are together. I am a man who will fight for your honour; I'll be your hero. Captain, do you have some clothing we can put on? If so, we can then help your deckhands with maintaining your ship."

Ortuga asked Tuli to go down into the hold and search the deckhand's sleeping berth for some spare clothes used by the eight deckhands that had been killed; their clothing was gathered together in bundles under the hammocks. Tuli grabbed the worn clothes and carried them up to the Africans. When he arrived up on the deck, he dropped the clothes, and the men searched through to find garments to fit them. Samson Buju bent down and rummaged through the items, grasping a pair of leather boots, white trousers, a striped shirt and corduroy waistcoat; he confidently dressed in the outfit and stood proudly next to Captain Ortuga.

Marley Waylon picked up a pair of brown corduroy trousers, a cream coloured shirt and a woollen jacket with yellow braiding that had been an officer's uniform thrown away by one of the officer mates on Francis Drake's ship, the Golden Hinde. Searching through the pile of clothing, he also found a tricorn, a pirate hat crunched flat under the clothes. He pulled it out and used his hand to reform the felt material back to its original shape. Dressed in his selected attire, Marley proudly moved along to stand on the left-hand side, next to Captain Ortuga.

Chapter Seven
The Man Who Sold the World

The two African men, Samson Buju and Marley Waylon, evoked brilliance to work with the Liberty crew, sailing the ship onto South America with such great knowledge and skills. Captain Ortuga was so impressed with their passion of life that he expected them both to be part of his senior crew to manage the Liberty Bell. Marley felt some metal objects in the pocket of the admiral's jacket he was wearing; putting his hand in to the pocket he clinched his hand around the three items, two keys and a harmonica. He took the harmonica out of his pocket and placed it between his lips and played a joyful reggae tune. Dancing on the decking, his fellow comrade Samson joined him in a jig; they laughed and smiled happily at their new future of freedom. Ortuga invited both of them to his birth celebratory party and asked if they could play some reggae songs to entertain his senior crew.

In the Captain's luxurious cabin, the time quickly reached 7.00pm. Ortuga was sitting at the large wooden table with the two African men, waiting for his senior crew members to arrive. The table was bolted to the floor to stop it from sliding about when the ocean waters roughened. Davy had not been invited to the party, so he sneaked into the cabin before the Captain returned and hid inside the wardrobe.

A drumming sound on the cabin door came from the Bosun. Flintlock was leading four other seniors, Sanchez, Han, Amir and Pablo to Ortuga's celebratory night gathering. Aturo was still finishing the deluxe feast of roasted pork ready to bring it into the cabin at 7.30pm. Banging their knives and forks on the table, the two Africans, Marley and Samson, expressed their enormous appetites, for they hadn't eaten for three days, which explained why Juan Ortuga felt that their level of energy had become even lower since he first met with them. He got up and opened the door; calling down the corridor, he hollered out to the ship's Cook to bring the food down to his cabin.

Aturo arranged the delicious roast pork with crispy roast potatoes, parsnips and broccoli onto ceramic plates that had minor chips on them, produced from people jagging their knives into the plate when cutting meat. Aturo spooned out his favourite homemade apple sauce and placed the servings onto a brass trolley with a jug filled with flavoursome gravy made from coconut oil, soy sauce and flour.

Trundling down the corridor to the Captain's cabin, Aturo wheeled the trolley into the high ranking quarters and handed out a plate of the magnificent foods to each of the seniors. While handing a plate of food to Ortuga, he wished him a very happy birthday.

Sanchez was quite annoyed by the African males childishly tapping their forks on the timber table producing a plentiful sound of reggae rhythm, so he told them to eat with the deckhands in the galley, because Captain Ortuga wanted to recall his life story in peace and calm:

"You two slaving black boys! Can you stop making that Caribbean reggae racket, for it murks into my mind and I cannot hear clearly any conversations from the Captain or my mates."

Samson gave a silver-tongued view of the reverberating sound:

"Look, Quartermaster! Reggae is an ancient rhythm, its sounding sits harmonically with the flow of the soul energy of the world. So it must be your mind that is tainted by too strong a desire to feed orders out to everyone and rule the world."

The 48-year-old Sanchez responded politically:

"What? All you see is a dream within a dream. How do you think to know my character? I am only trying to help the world with my Captain, who is like the famous heroic outlaw, Robin Hood, except on the seven seas. Let's all get together in harmony, and accept each other."

Watching the two factions speaking with each other, Ortuga opened his mind to let knowledge flow into his head. When people get older, their immunity and physicality wears out. These beings lose their joy and happiness, forming disillusion and intolerance of other cultures and communities and don't want to help each other; they want to expand their empyreal egos through victory and carnage of rivals.

An insight swept across Ortuga's mind that his young, 13-year-old Cabin Boy, was always so full of joy and happiness even when negativity washed into his soul. The insight of this enlightening knowledge gave Ortuga a magnificent vision for benefiting the future; that the best way to help global communities would be to inspire positivity into each person's soul by accepting their cultural faiths and seeding altruistic kindness into themselves to create peace, goodwill and motivation to help each other.

Feeling like they were being enslaved again, both of the Africans jumped up from their seats, walked out of the cabin down to the food galley. Jigging along the corridor, Marley was playing the harmonica that he had found in the pile of clothing and Samson had pocketed two spoons from the Captain's table and was using them for a percussive unison with Marley's harmonica. Entering the food galley, the reggae seamen called out to the four hungry deckhands:

"Yo, Music Bros! Is this boat a transporting merchant ship or a pirate vessel seeking treasure?"

The deckhands were eating the same food as the Ortuga celebration meal, chatting with each other about the findings of Eldorado and how they could all search to find the gold. They also joked about the attacking galleon ship of the Spaniards. One of them posed a question of invitation to the African men:

"Captain Ortuga is searching all over the sea for gold and hidden treasures to give to the poor, so we might become pirates soon to plunder other ships. Can I buy you a drink or do you just want the money?"

Samson gave a well-mannered reply:

"When I have money, I have nothing to buy; when I don't have money, I want everything, so yes, can I please have a Piña Colada?"

The deckhand replied with courtesy:

"Money is not the root of all evil, intolerance and jealousy are. When we finally arrive at our destination, you boys can join us when we search for and discover the City of Gold."

Back in the Captain's quarters, Ortuga stood up on a metaphorical soap box to narrate inspirational tales to his group of seniors. He told them his captivating story of the walk from his Argentinean home town of La Rosario.

Posturely standing erect portrayed Ortuga's magnificent, solid athletic build, his rich olive skin and clear eyes of truth and altruism. While the seniors were munching away at their delicious roasted supper, Captain Ortuga told the story of the days of his youth, stating that he was last in the line of three sons and a daughter born to his parents, Anton and Hortensia Ortuga. His early childhood was not without problems, for he was afflicted with tuberculosis of the lungs when he was only eight years old. Judged incurable, he studied and reflected on all forms of animal and plant life, observing their ways of growth, strengthening and survival methods. Overcoming the malaise by the time he was 16, Ortuga had become a tall, strapping youth with a strong and positive determination to survive.

This resilience was to be a hallmark of his later life. With no formal or forced education, Captain Juan Ortuga was a non-religious, non-political man.

Having learnt basic life skills from his brothers and sister, combined with the community spirit and moral aptitude of his parents, Ortuga was always destined for greatness. Assisting the poor and needy to overcome life's problems, Ortuga forged a new life in the wider world outside of Argentina and his small village of La Rosario. As well as being an altruistic Man of the World, he was a pioneer in health and personal development viewed by all those that came in contact with him as an exemplary human being – a hero, a Robin Hood of the High Seas. Unlike his elder contemporaries, in his quests of finding funds to help disadvantaged communities, he never took the life of another man, priding himself and his crew on the fact that any riches taken were always confiscated by stealth and illusion.

Juan Ortuga started his working life shepherding Alpaca for the landowners that were located in Cuzco, Peru, in the rocky countryside and farmlands surrounding his village. To all those who knew him, Juan Ortuga was a man's man; some would say he was like an uncut diamond, a little rough on the outside but priceless on the inside. Even his peers saw him as a first rate role model and many followed his lead by supporting their local community. He was an honourable man of sharp intellect and humour, with a generosity of spirit and possessed a very positive attitude even in the most difficult of times. Listening with intention, three of the senior crew members, Flintlock, Amir, and Sanchez, finished their meals by scrapping and licking the mix of apple sauce and gravy off from their plates then piled them up in the middle of the table. Amir spoke to each of the gleeful patrons:

"Let's all drink to the Captain, and celebrate his birthday, but first can you please tell us about the ship you spoke of before that sunk, filled with treasure and its whereabouts? Captain, would you like a drink?"

Encouraged with inspiration, Ortuga smirked and replied:

"I am an active participant in life; the fullness of my glass is always half full, never half empty."

Sitting down with strength and certainty into his large, red-cushioned chair, Ortuga then told the story of the ancient mariner:

"Travelling along the roadways from La Rosario to the port of Valparaiso, I met an old man on the side of the road, he was one of three survivors from the most famous Spanish galleon – Nuestra Senora de Atcoca – which sunk in the year of 1622. Befriending and caring for the ancient mariner for two days, I listened to his many legends of the seven seas, including the tale of hidden treasures of gold, precious stones and antique manuscripts transported from the port of Cartegena. While close to his death,, the ancient mariner handed me a map of the treasure's location and with his last dying breath whispered:

"Change your life to Change the World."

Listening from inside the wardrobe, Davy was so thrilled by the story, as he watched through the crack between the doors. The Tibetan monk, Han, stated that the global commitment of mankind is to give and take; and that he has been changing his life to change the world for many years. He then asked the dinner party if they could view the firework display on the top deck set up by Davy and himself to celebrate Ortuga's birthday:

"Captain, I've also got a great magic surprise for your birthday, the Indian rope trick. This is for Tuli as well, for he has an Indian mother."

Ortuga agreed, emptying his cabin, he and the seniors left and walked up to the main deck to watch the magic trick and fireworks. After the group left the Captain's quarters, Tuli stepped out of the cabinet, laughed, and ran up the stern steps leading to the rear end to the top decking. Passing by the galley, the deckhands and the two Africans joined in with the group of seniors. Everyone stood under the main masthead, which had the crow's nest attached to the top. Han used his magic power to strike a flame onto the fireworks, the first ones that resulted were Rockets, which soared high up into the night sky and burst into expansive, illuminated spherical patterns of the primary colours of red, blue and yellow.

The crowd was absolutely amazed at the firework show and clapped loudly at the magnificent performance. The following display was that of Catherine Wheels, attached to the two masts, spinning around spraying sparks out from their wheels, falling onto the deck and sprinkling down onto some of the crew. The final showpiece was the Indian magic trick pooled together with Roman Candles. The routine had been dress rehearsed by Davy and Han that morning on the crow's nest platform. Han spoke out three magic words in two phrases:

"Indian Snuro Tirck – Magio Artfajrajo Eksplodoj."

Davy stood focused at the base of the main mast, standing next to a length of rope used to secure the ship to a port. After Han spoke out the words of magic the rope spiralled up into the darkness of the sky to the top of the mast, close to, but above the crow's nest.

The mooring line rope straightened and Han asked Davy to climb up, peering into the darkness Davy clasped his hands firmly around the rope and began pulling himself up into the night sky. The audience cheered and whistled to bring thrilling energy into the atmosphere. Reaching the crow's nest, Davy stretched out his arm to grab hold of the railing and sprung off the rope; the crowd clapped at his amazing performance. When he got onto the platform, he bent down and picked up four Roman Candles, fixing them symmetrically to the circular railings of the crow's nest to duplicate the points of a compass – North, South, East and West. Han murmured his magic words, *"Magio Artfajrajo Eksplodoj!"* Into the night air; the fireworks lit themselves up and within seconds they began to spray out their combustion, fireballs of multi-colour – doof, doof, doof, doof, doof, doof – into the sky, reflecting colours down onto the ocean waters.

The deep, heavy bass sounds of the Roman Candles probing into the darkness revealed a support rhythm that was used by the African men to bring reggae into the celebratory entertainment. Marley played the harmonica; Samson rhythmically clacked the spoons on the timber mast.

The reggae music was so stimulating that Han activated some more Rockets to join forces with the firework display encore.

Before the end of the firework display, Ortuga returned to his cabin to massage his painfully injured ankle, which was starting to ache badly. The injury was so painful that he sat down on his chair, closing his eyes for a brief power nap before any people returned to the quarters. Noticing that Ortuga had left the top deck, Han patted Pablo on his shoulder and asked him if he wanted to have a get together with the Captain, offering thanks to him for his birthday celebration and to heal his ankle:

"Yes, Han, that sounds really good. I would very much like to watch your healing power."

As Pablo and Han walked from the main decking into the corridor leading to the stern of the vessel, a stream of golden light flooded along the corridor. The light was flowing out from within the glass bottle that Flintlock had found in the ocean. The bottle was originally to be found at the base of the waterfall gateway to the Golden City, Eldorado, in June 1520.

After many years, the bottle washed along the Amazon River from the foot of the Andes mountain range down the Eastern coastline to the port of Valparaiso. The ship's Bosun, Flintlock, picked up the bottle in Valparaiso in 1732.

Although the light was flowing down from the main decking, no one there noticed it because they were all looking upwards to view the Roman Candle display, and all illuminations were perceived as lightings from the fireworks. Flintlock shoved the bottle under his jacket to conceal the illumination and raced down to the Captain's cabin to strengthen his companionship with Han, Pablo and Ortuga. Silently following behind Flintlock, Davy noticed the Bosun placing the bottle under his jacket as he walked around the food trolley into the cabin. Aturo had placed the food trolley to the right hand side of the cabin door of the Captain's quarters, so he could collect the dirty plates after he had watched the firework display.

Because Flintlock was in the Captain's quarters, Davy halted his intentional goal of being alone with Captain Ortuga to describe the crew killings carried out by Flintlock. Davy carefully kneeled down on the flooring and drew open the green velvet curtain below the top of the trolley, which concealed the wheels and drinking glasses. Shifting a large number of the glasses into stacks, he silently slid them to the left side of the trolley and then crawled onto the brass framework and closed the curtain to go into hiding. The moment he pulled the curtains together, Aturo came walking out of the kitchen down the corridor to wheel the trolley into the Captain's cabin to collect the plates and have them washed up before breakfast the next morning.

Aturo tapped on the cabin door, Pablo swung it open and Aturo wheeled the trolley into the cabin. After noticing that four plates still had some food on them, he left the trolley close to the porthole behind the dining table. The timing of Aturo was too early to remove the settings from the table which is why the Captain, Han and Pablo had returned to the quarters to finish their birthday treats.

As Han was pressing energy points on the ankle of Ortuga to relieve the torn cartilage, Aturo asked the Captain if he could sit down with them and wait until the meals had been eaten, then clear up the table. When Ortuga, Han and Pablo began eating, Aturo stood up smoking a large clay pipe filled with coca leaves. The pipe had the head of an ant-eater formed around the bowl that held the smouldering substance; he asked if anyone would like a celebratory drink or smoke his pipe. Waiting for the opportunity of privacy, behind Aturo, Flintlock pulled out the smuggled bottle from inside his jacket. Compared to earlier exposures, the golden glow was extraordinarily softer and the dissolved glow washed onto the table.

Because of the bursts of comparable illuminations from the fireworks, nobody questioned the exposure. Also, since Han and Pablo had viewed gentle glowings from moon light many times before, they did not appeal to Flintlock whether the light was flowing out from the bottle of liquid gold.

Looking across the table, crunching the crispy and highly-flavoured roast pork skin, Ortuga looked over at Flintlock and asked him what the bottle contained. Flintlock placed the bottle on the table and alleged his discovery:

"Captain, I found this ancient bottle at the port of Valparaiso before the Liberty Bell sailed off to Easter Island. I believe that it holds a combination of molecular phosphorescent creatures from the sand and some gold particles washed into the bottle while it had settled on the seabed.

The elements in the bottle created a watery gaseous mist, so when I open the bottle and pour the liquid into my cupped, hands the air will compound the vapour into solid gold. The treasure will only furnish my life and no one else's – I am not here to help anyone."

Upsettingly, Ortuga grit his teeth, shook his head and clenched his fists; opening the palm of his left hand, he swept it up from his chest towards the space in front of Flintlock to push him away from the table. Flintlock stepped backwards behind Aturo, who was serving the party drinks.

Motionless from underneath the trolley, Davy focused his eyes on the happening. Because Flintlock was hidden behind the broad, muscular body of Aturo, he tried to pull the cork out from the bottle to pour the liquid into his hands. To open the bottle, he firmly twisted the cork, then several minutes after, when he removed the plug an undetectable haze streamed out to create a physical constitution of an Aztec being.

Unbeknown to Flintlock, was that the bottle contained the spirit of the ancient Aztec King, Montezuma, who reigned numerous South American districts in the 1500s, and although he was extremely intolerant, he became a distinguished religious and political leader. The flowing spirit exiting the bottle intermingled with the smoke, laden air within the Captain's quarters to become partly invisible to human vision. Ortuga and Pablo were focusing their vision down on their plates. Not enjoying the roasted animal flesh, the psyche of the Tibetan magic monk, visualised the shadowed form of a chubby Aztec being standing behind Aturo. Han began to channel information into his mind that the bombastic energy belonged to the evil and crazy ruler of South America, Montezuma, who's spirit had been sealed into the glass flask by an Elohim race of advanced

Lightworkers from the Pleiadian star system. The Elohim race had worked with Montezuma whilst they had architecturally designed the Inca village of Machu Picchu located in the Andes Mountains in Peru as an energy gateway to their galaxy, which was designed to be linked by the Photon Beam.

The reason why the spirit of Montezuma was entombed in the glass prison was because he conflicted with the scouted beings, stole vast amounts of gold from the Pleiadian mines of Eldorado and attempted to stop them from building the citadel of Machu Picchu.

His imprisonment prevented his spirit returning to the universal energy and allowed construction of the township of Machu Picchu and The Elohim Throne to be fulfilled. The highly egotistical sovereign lord, Montezuma was the ninth ruler and political leader of the Aztec kingdom, Tenochtitlan, reigning from 1502 to 1520 AD.

Though Montezuma killed hundreds of humans during his reign, he also opened cultural gateways between indigenous communities and Europeans; his waddling, physical form was slaughtered during the early stages of the Spanish conquests within South America. After his death, the advanced Pleiadian beings chased his spirit and placed it in a bottle for another 200 years until it was discovered and freed by Richard Flintlock at Ortuga's birthday dinner.

Seeking a host body to co-habitate in, Montezuma moved stealthily towards Aturo. Because Aturo had been drinking tequila all night long, he did not sense the forceful entry of Montezuma's irritable spirit climbing into his body. Han and Davy were the only individuals around the table who saw the challenging event happening.

Although the constitution of Aturo was now jumbled, Montezuma was keeping his own hostility and destructive nature calm to halt any imagined elimination assaults or assassination that would kill the physicality of Aturo and Montezuma's spirit.

The barged spirit of Montezuma controlled Aturo's mental and physical actions. Drunkenly unbalanced and relaxed, Aturo casually leaned over the table and collected the plates from Han, Pablo and Captain Ortuga; placing them on the trolley, he wheeled the appliance out of the door passing back along the corridor to the galley kitchen. The weight of Davy under the trolley distorted the spinning motion of the wheels, making them skid along on the flooring. The two piles of glasses next to Davy, rattled and cracked, the glasses at the peak of the stacks broke and toppled onto the timber floorboards. Aturo wheeled the trolley into his kitchen close to the sink and food preparation workbench. Davy crept out from under the trolley, and swung his body under the bench to the far side. Standing up he talked confidently with Aturo:

"Thanks for your fabulous cooking tonight, the food was fantastic. Shall I wash up all the dishes, cutlery and cooking pans tonight?"

Aturo let his jumbled personality express a demanding tip to the cabin boy:

"Yes, Davy, your help will be very valuable to assist my drunkenness. But don't stay in the quarters with Flintlock and Pablo anymore, tonight you must sleep with the deckhands in one of the suspended hammocks in the berth of this ship."

To pursue the command, Davy moved over to the sink, lit the fire to heat the water, piling up the dirty plates next to the sink ready to wash them when the water had boiled. After a few minutes, he poured the boiling water into the sink. While he was washing up, he glimpsed out through a porthole opposite the sink. In the distance, he noticed a soft red light radiating from under the ocean. Wanting to know what was going on, he hurried his task of washing the plates and then charged upstairs to the top deck; still erected into the night sky he climbed up the Indian rope to the crow's nest. Davy looked out across the high seas onto the horizon, seeking the red glow.

The time was 11.00pm. The defaulted number of eighteen original crew members on the Liberty Bell had now reduced to ten. The four male deckhands together with the two African slaves, Marley and Samson, were walking to the sleeping berth to offer hammocks to the black fellows. Back in the Captain's quarters remained Han, Pablo and Ortuga talking about the power of the moon, for the night of Captain Ortuga's celebratory party was the night before a Piscean full moon. Ortuga asked Han that when they arrived at their new destination could he make a new figurehead for his ship, the object would be perceived as a birthday present for the Captain.

Aturo resumed his additive nature of drinking tequila to stabilise the tension created by the evil spirit entering his soul. The ship's Physician, Amir, and Aturo spoke together in the galley, agreeing upon the best foodstuffs to engage extra physical energy for the deckhands, because after the deaths of their numerous travel companions, there were hardly any recruits left in the crew that could toil the heavy laborious tasks that were needed to be executed tomorrow when the ship would arrive at its journey's end on the coast of Peru.

On arrival, the labourings would be radical, for the ship's canvases would have to be taken down, the anchor lowered, deckings would be scrubbed and polished to remove any damage to the timber caused from the firework displays. Then onwards, climbing amongst the hillsides to search for the City of Gold, and hopefully carrying heavy caches of treasure and gold bullion back to the ship.

Flopped over the steering wheel, Sanchez, was snoring intensely on the helm platform. Due to the colossal intake of tequila, the scurried spirit of Montezuma within the body of Aturo had also recessed into a deep sleep pattern. Therefore, feeling more clear headed, Aturo began to think about his work chores and menu for the coming day without the aggression and restraint from his new parasitic attachment.

Aturo began to contemplate how to empower the men by cooking batches of the coca leaves he had purchased at the market in Valparaiso; mixed with fried garlic and red chilies as it was well know that Peruvian locals chewed the leaves and drank coca tea to give themselves high euphoria, diminish depression and heighten their energy levels.

Chapter Eight
Queen of All My Dreams

Midnight arrived to welcome a setting of the partially eclipsed moon that had invaded the planet's energy by destroying crops, maddening livestock, influencing bacterial epidemics, pestilence, forceful conflict and warfare. With the acquired gift of speech, the separated creatures in the hull of the ship zoomed up to the main deck and conjuncted together – the dogs, five chickens, eight rats, the young baby lamb and a feisty rooster. Shadows of the animal flock herd splayed across the decking from the light of the eclipsed moon, blending with the red glow in the distance, bouncing off the waves through the portholes of the vessel. Sitting around the table with Captain Ortuga, Han, explained to Ortuga about lunar eclipses and their links to historical religious writings and texts within scrolls hidden in the Dead Sea waters of the Jordan River in Galilee; the scrolls were secretly buried in the caves by Jesus Almasih of Nazareth and his twelve apostle companions:

"Captain, please let me describe the power of the moon magic, and tell you about my visit to the Jewish community of Israel, where the earliest Tibetan monk met up with Jesus one thousand, six hundred years ago."

Ortuga was so thrilled by Han's passionate knowledge of spirituality and how the universal energy empowers human beings, he asked Han to tell him the facts about the glowing red light that was flowing into the cabin. Han began speaking gently:

"Share the faith of Jesus without fear, and your life will become harmonically balanced with love, devotion and surrender. Jesus Almasih used the ancient knowledge of the Taoist faith to compose his chronological writings, which were re-written by several human societies to establish the foundation of their religious groups such as Catholic, Mormon, Protestant and Quakers. As we observed on Easter Island, the universal energy flows into every natural life form to heal and evolve the spiritual constitution of super powered beings."

Whilst Han was describing the energy pathways of human evolution, an auric blue light glowed around Pablo. Lifting his left hand off the table, Han splayed his fingers apart and moved his hand towards Pablo to introduce to the Captain, the energy of Evangeline Moreau. :

"This being, Pablo, is a camouflaged Starseed with such incredible energy and insights of planetary alignments, the dawnings and happenings of future evolution that he must release his soul to help the world. As Jesus said 'Truth will set everyman free', Pablo live the truth."

Standing up in her heavy male disguise, Evangeline removed her bulky padded jacket that shaped her muscular, male appearance. Shaking her upper body and hands, the false beard fell off her face and her shirt dropped down onto the table to reveal her female form. Then she gaily danced around the room, singing a French melody sounding from her soul. Sitting back down at the table, she placed her hands around her head to doll up her hair, even though it was quite short like a man's haircut; without her beard, she looked beautifully attractive. Evangeline's eyes fluttered with adoration of her fellow male companions, for Han and Ortuga's, faith and energy vibrated so harmonically with hers. The astonished Captain was delighted at her beautiful presence, sliding to the edge of his chair, closer to Evangeline; he placed his tattooed arm around her to bestow warmth and honesty to her being and kissed her on both cheeks:

"Hey, Captain, when my being is in general public gatherings I have to be in my Pablo disguise because my father, who is the King of Spain, is searching the Pacific Ocean to capture me and take me back to his homeland to make me be part of the royal federation. But whenever I am with you, I will retain my female identity of Evangeline Moreau; I want the truth to be known."

Ortuga returned comments of devotion to Evangeline:

"My darling, your beautiful female being has appeared in my dreams ever since you stepped onto the Liberty Bell at Valparaiso, but I never knew that you were masquerading yourself as Pablo Medellin. You are the queen of all my dreams, your energy resonates with my soul. Right from the start of our new lives in Peru, I wanted to give you my heart. Now that I know you, I would like you to be in a partnership with my soul, for your spiritual insights will help us work together.

"Due to your heavily disguised male identity, I never recognised your womanhood. You must not expose yourself to my crew because their desire will cause conflict between each other to win your adoration and beauty. Please keep your beauty hidden until the crew's consciousness is advanced then I will introduce you to them all. "

Leaving the table, Evangeline sat down to relax on the cushioned lounge in the corner of the cabin. Responding to the Captain's truthful and devotional remarks, the strength of her blue auric light glowed brighter. As Captain Ortuga's eyebrows raised, Han told him about vibrational glowings. He said that Evangeline had a Starseed energy linked in with the Photon Beam from the Pleiadian Galaxy, and if the Captain wanted to find the secrets of the universe, he should think in terms of energy, frequency and vibration:

"Everything is energy. The Big Bang was the birth of the universe when its energy exploded outwards at the speed of light. It then subsequently condensed into solar planetary matter. Our physical mass is composed of energy vibrating at different frequencies resulting in diverse manifestational aspects of physical appearances."

When the primary Taoist monk met up with Jesus of Nazereth, Jesus explained to him about the universal power of the moon. Three days before the full moon, its ebbing power drains energy from human beings; the night of the full moon is the start of returning energy back upon the planet and three days after the full moon energy re-strengthens all life forms. Based upon the seven day timing of the moon, Jesus composed his biblical scrolls that developed into the religious belief that God created the world in seven days and that God has the power of wind, water, gravity and physics.

Still clutching the length of rope raised into the night sky from the Indian rope trick, Davy noticed the red light drifting smoothly from a vessel on the horizon along the hull of the Liberty ship illuminating from underneath the keel. Glancing downwards, he saw the wings of the Sledge Ray extending out on the portside of the ship, with the soft red light radiating from the creature. Several days ago, when he first saw the sea creature, Han had told him that the red light indicated a warning signal of danger; the intensity of the illumination specified the magnitude of danger.

Gazing back over the ocean he recognised a ship in the distance, it was the pirate sloop ship, Santa Ana, that had crashed into the figurehead of the Liberty Bell on its journey to Easter Island. The other danger intensely identified by the red light of the Sledge Ray was the evil spirit of Montezuma. Who was also known as the Butcher of Peru. Estimates for the number of opponents who were killed, tortured or imprisoned under the rule of this brutal leader varied from 100 thousand to half a million beings; he also structured a killer squad throughout the eastern coastal regions of South America to hunt the Spanish military. After his evil planetary energy had possessed the body of Aturo, the demonic phantom character quickly devastated his host's opinions, outlooks and insights, within the short period of twenty-four hours, completely over-powering his totality and his mental attitude.

The pirate vessel sailed closer and closer. Davy swung off from the rope and jumped onto the crow's nest platform, he bent down to pick up the Jolly Roger pirate flag that he had collected from the sloop boat when its mast smashed into the Liberty Bell figurehead.

Unrolling the flag, he tied it to the mast rigging and raised it up to the summit of the flagpole above the platform. When he turned around to look at the pirate sloop boat, a thought entered his mind:

He Who Dares, Wins.

This was the universal statement channelled from the Photon Beam, supporting Davy's strength of mind to act confidently when carrying out tasks that would help himself, his friends and the global consciousness. Reaching inside his pocket, Davy took hold of the golden Turnkey and removed the chain from it to unblock the visions. Clasping the shell, he visualised his mother and father trafficking refugees into the Cornish port of St Ives; Molly was helping Davy's parents. The group of eleven Chilean refugees comprised of two families with seven children, three teenage boys and four young girls. Most of the refugees that migrated from Chile in 1973 travelled to Canada, but the two families that were trafficked by his father, Joseph, and his Indian mother, walked together across the hillside from the sandy beach of St Ives to arrive at The Charter Inn guest house in Penzance.

Parvihn gave the refugees free accommodation until the parents found work in the English county of Cornwall. Briefly, another vision of his homeless school friend, Quinton, entered his mind. Quinton was sitting on a rock in his cave with his Retriever dog, watching lobsters crawling along the sand out of the cave towards the ocean.

The lobsters were exiting from behind the large rock where the hidden door led to the stairway up to The Charter Inn where the Chilean Refugees were entering the veiled gateway to conceal their entry to England. One of the lobsters was digging in the wet sand, revealing a golden Turnkey shell; Quinton's dog ran over and quickly side stepped the lobster and grasped the shell between his jaws which immediately transported the friendly animal onto the Liberty Bell next to Davy on the platform of the crow's nest. Then another vision rapidly flowed into Davy's mind; his friend, Tim, was being caned by the Headmaster of Penwright Grammar School. Bending over, looking out through the window in the Headmaster's office, Tim saw some class mates competitively playing rugby against the local comprehensive school, Rhodes Secondary.

Tim's mind was intently focused on the game, but he juddered by the shock when the Headmaster whacked his backside with the wooden cane six times. Standing up and wincing at the pain of the caning, Tim turned around to face the Headmaster:

"Sir, your caning has damaged the muscles of my upper thighs and as you can see, I cannot place too much weight on my legs to walk or run in sports training classes. I am the champion of Cornish cross country running, but now I will have to give up the activity. I am leaving this school to join Rhodes Secondary because of the argument I had about the Vietnam war with your history and French language teacher, Master Brinkley.

He told me that the British armed forces should have joined the Americans to fight the Vietnamese to declare victory and claim land for British civil ownership just like mass killings of

Australian aboriginal communities in 1788, and the mad, obsessive slaughter of the native Indians of American indigenous populations in 1775 by the Irish, French, British and Dutch military forces. My argument was that cultures should only claim possession of their own land and there is no truth or reason to start warfare with other cultures…

Do you agree with me, sir?"

"Tim, bend over again, for I cannot accept your atrocious comments about my teachers."

Tim leapt over the Headmaster's desk and charged out the door, along the corridor and down the weathered concrete steps leading to the playing fields where the rugby game was taking place. Speaking with the Sports Master from Rhodes Secondary School, Tim asked if he could be the Deputy Captain of the rugby team, for he knows how to win games. As the Sports Master said yes, Tim ran onto the pitch. Catching the ball, he ran down to the touchline; he bounced the ball on the pitch and kicked it over the goal posts to gain a win by three points. His team members hollered out in optimism at his victorious action.

Davy was so impressed by the opinions and deeds of his classmates that he felt perhaps he should return to Cornwall, gather them together and teleport them back to Peru in the 1700s to help the communities of the South Pacific against attacking and killings by pirate crews.

Removing his hand from the shell Turnkey, Davy looked down from the crow's nest onto the decking where he saw a group of pirates from the damaged sloop vessel Santa Ana climbing up the hull, swarming over the railings onto the main decking. The group of seven pirate men stood silently still on the bridge behind the helm. The red glow, warning signal from the Sledge Ray faded away, indicating to Davy that the anticipated danger of the pirate vessel was dulling and no longer present. Sliding down the rope, Davy marched along to the bridge to meet with the pirates, as the Santa Ana headed off into the distance, far away from the Liberty Bell. The time was close to 3.00am in the morning, he assumed that the crew members of the Liberty Bell were sound asleep in their quarters. There was nobody except Davy and the seven pirates on the top deck.

Assured that no one was watching his actions, Davy asked the pirate men if they would like to become part of the Liberty

Bell crew and to help island communities. From the shadows at the top of the stairs near the rear of the ship, leading from the Captain's cabin, Evangeline and Ortuga silently watched the gathering. After agreeing with Davy's proposal, he then led the pirates down to the berth and presented them each with a hammock to sleep in. Aturo, who was possessed by the spirit of Montezuma, brought them light snacks of wholemeal porridge topped with caramelised coca leaves and powdered valerian root.

After Davy and the seven men had left the top deck, Evangeline expressed her faith, as her blue aura flowed around her body and enveloped the Captain:

"Love of my life! Those friendly pirates acknowledged recruitment to become part of your seniors. Their understanding and acceptance of all cultures will bring a lot of joy to the world.

Juan, tomorrow morning, when we arrive at the ship's destination of Puerto Caballas, I will talk with you about how we can search for gold and treasures and also inform you about accessing the Photon Beam. In the Peruvian hillside, there is a Pleiadian citadel called Machu Picchu where the Elohim Throne is placed. By sitting on the throne, we can discover the hidden locations of gold, and visitations of happenings in the past and present."

In agreement, the Captain smiled happily. Ortuga adored her beauty, knowledge and compassion for all cultures and he thought she possessed so much love in her heart to help him to help the world:

"Let me be Your Teddy Bear, Lay Your Head on my Shoulder, for I Love You So."

Embracing Evangeline, he kissed her and felt words from the universe flowing into his mind…

'The Spirit of Woman – There's Something Beautiful in the Glow of her Smile and Female Being. A Notion from the Look in her Eyes brings Love, Light and Peace to the World. Listen to her Heart, and You can Build a Precious Love that lasts Forever. That little Piece of Heaven belongs to your Dreams and Mystical Knowledge to Expand and Multiply Global Love to Change the World guided by the Mesmerising Scent of the Super Female Form and Beauty.

"The Spirit of Man – Your Love is King, Crown your Power with Understanding, for your Strength and Wisdom makes Souls sing and dance. You're the Ruler of my Heart, your Love and Light shine to Help the World and bring Acceptance and Surrender to all Cultures. The Universal Soldier knows he will put an End to War without weapons; He is the One who gives his Body and Soul to bring Peace to all Nations."

Ambling back down to his cabin, Captain Ortuga opened his heart to let the spiritual diction congeal in his soul. Evangeline also walked down to her quarters, were Flintlock was snoring so loudly that he had woken all the animals and they were charging around the hold.

Entering her cabin, Evangeline noticed that Davy was no longer sleeping there because of Aturo's request that he should now sleep with the other deckhands, but there was the baby lamb and two chickens running in and out of the cabin. She decided to leave the door open to let them move out into the corridor.

Chapter Nine
Harvest for the World

When Davy had shown the pirate men their hammocks, he walked down the corridor to meet up with Aturo, asking him why he wanted him to sleep in the hammock berth:

"Sir, I understand that you want me to help the pirates become part of our crew telling them stories and explanations about Juan Ortuga and his heroic altruistic vision. By the way, what was that food you gave to them, would it help them sleep well?"

"Yes, young one. What you eat, effects your daily health and determines how long you will live. You have such a kind intellect that your personality and caring expressions will transfer to the pirates to become joyful men of the world on our ship."

"Okay, Aturo! Thanks to your nutritional beliefs, I am a little bit peckish now – what will you be cooking for breakfast?"

Waddling about like a drunken, long neck goose, Aturo blurted out his breakfast menu:

"Tuli! Captain Ortuga commanded me to make breakfast and serve it when the ship reaches the Peruvian port of Puerto Caballas, the food will be for all the Liberty Bell crew and the destitute people living at the port. The foods I have prepared are wholemeal rice porridge, goat's yoghurt and lava bread made from seaweed and oatmeal. Also, I have prepared a super bone broth made from a turtle that was smashed by one of the cannon balls; the ocean creature was swimming in front of the pirate ship – leading them to glory. The cannon ball plummeted down onto its shell, then the turtle died and floated over to the stern of our ship; I netted the dead creature and pulled it onto the decking."

The food flavourings and toppings that Aturo had fed to the pirate crew with the wholemeal porridge, had been administered by the angry strength of mind owned by Montezuma. The additives made the pirate men render their aggression; and they stealthily killed four originally recruited deckhands by strangulation, suffocation and stabbing. When the Liberty deckhands had been killed, the pirates left the corpses in their hammocks.

Sleeping amongst the four corpses were the two African slaves and seven pirates. Davy tried to fall into a doze slumber, but the noise of the animals roving around under the hammocks did not allow him to sleep very soundly. The two sleeping African men had also managed to drink excessive quantities of tequila and rum, with the alcoholic combination heavily mellowing their mental activity, producing deep sleep patterns of which the animals could not wake them from.

The Dutch slave driver, Wolfgang, had hidden in the same rescue boat that Bijan Bonapart had stowed away in. Nobody saw him hiding away from the two slaves that he had nastily governed when they were chained together on the Greek slave vessel; Wolfgang anticipated that they would want to kill him to offer themselves total expansive freedom. Although Wolfgang was sleeping under the canvas covering, he was woken up by Quinton's Retriever watchdog. The dog was up on the crow's nest podium, barking loudly at bats that fluttered around the skull and cross bones flag above his head. The furious barking sound made Wolfgang exit from the rescue boat and he strode down into the hold, seeing the cabin door of Flintlock's quarters open; he walked inside and rolled into Davy's empty bed. As all the animals had moved into the deckhand's hammock area, Wolfgang quickly fell asleep and began dreaming about his teenage life in Amsterdam when he rode a bike around the city; collecting rubbished leftovers of cannabis and hashish from local street cafés and parks. After which, he mixed the butts into brownies to relax his friends each weekend when they sat together listening to songs, playing instruments and laughing at every event and moments of speech.

Unaware of the killings of the deckhands, Davy awoke from his hammock in the darkness. Davy looked around at all the nautical sea recruits, sleeping soundly. He saw the eyes of numerous creatures that were gathering under the hammocks, sniffing and snorting the beefy blood stench that was emanating from the dead bodies of the stabbed deckhands; the other heady aroma attracting the animals was the vapour of roast pork tumbling down through the air onto the timber decking.

Several of the birds were perching on the hammock next to Davy. Even though the door on the sleeping berth was closed, a shaft of light channelled along the corridor from the kitchen galley penetrating through a small crack in the door. Gazing at the light, which began flickering, the door opened, and Aturo crept quietly towards Davy. The spirit of Montezuma forced Aturo to place his hand firmly over Davy's mouth to seize hold of him and drag him down to the galley where he threw him into the food larder room and locked the door.

After listening to the heavy footsteps of Aturo leave the galley, Davy, took hold of several empty hessian food sacks and used them to cover himself, making him sleep comfortably. He dreamed about the empirical days of Montezuma that he recalled from historical learnings in lessons with his school friends at Penwright Grammar. His dream clarified learnings about the construction of the monumental village of Machu Picchu, designed and constructed by the Starseed Pleiadian group of Lightworkers.

His dream showed him the stone stairway built on the Machu Picchu grassland, leading to the sacred Pleiadian object, the large stone seat titled as the Elohim Throne, carved from volcanic stone, and the golden shell Turnkeys hidden under the throne. Entering Davy's mind at the end of his dream, he observed and memorised a routed passageway leading from the port of Puerto Caballas, up into the hillside and the gateway, with two stone statues guarding the stairway up to the throne.

Realising that the following morning, the Liberty Bell would be docking at Puerto Caballas, he could walk up to the gateway with Evangeline and she could explain how to pass by the guards to enter visitation on the Elohim Throne.

The dust from the oatmeal buried in the hessian sackings woke Davy, sneezing and coughing for several minutes; he needed to drink water to soothe his throat from the compounding dust molecules. Sitting in the food larder he gazed around, seeking to find some water, but there were no liquids in the storage space; so he began calling to anyone nearby as he banged on the timber door to gain exit from the groceries penitentiary. Hearing his calling the baby lamb softly trotted out from the

112

hammock quarters along the corridor to the galley. Raising its right leg, the lamb pushed up the latch to open the door; Davy smiled abundantly and reached his arm out to stroke the lamb. He then walked over to the bench, picked up a large bowl of leftovers from Ortuga's party and placed the bowl on the floor next to the lamb; thanking the animal for his help.

The lamb joyfully darted its opened mouth into the bowl, gorging up the vegetables and apple sauce but it was unsure of the pork. When small pieces of the rare-cooked pig meat entered its mouth, it spat them out back onto the floor.

The rising sun indicated that the morning time was 8.30am; the ship was standing in the bay waters near to the sea brick wall of the Peruvian township of Puerto Caballas.

Davy raced up to the main decking, climbed up to the crow's nest and tied a band of canvas and a rope around the abdomen of Quinton's Retriever watchdog. Then he lowered the dog down to the decking to become friends with the baby lamb and Han, who spoke with all animals.

As the Liberty Bell was not secured by anchorage, the waves rolled the vessel around on the water, forwarding it closer to the beach front. Banging into rocks and skidding on sand banks, the abrasive movements awakened every crew member from their sleep, as well as all the animals in the ship's hold.

Although the sun had risen, the early morning outlook was cloudy, but as the sun became higher, hotter and expansive, the mist evaporated, clearing the viewings on the horizon and the indigenous township of the sun worshipping, Incan culture.

The Liberty crew actively motioned from the berth, up to the top deck to listen to Ortuga's foresight about the local community and its doings on the day of sun day. Ortuga realised that the remaining four original deckhands that he had recruited at Valparaiso were no longer in his ship's bounty squadron. In order to discover where they were, he posed a strapping enquiry to Davy:

"You must please determine where my four original deckhands are now, can you enquire with some of the people up here on the deck and search down in the hold for the deckhand men? Also, Davy, can you find out who was steering my ship to this port last night?"

Davy headed off through the group of pirates towards Aturo:

"Morning, Aturo, do you know which crew member was steering this vessel along the South Eastern passage from 3.00am this morning after the pirate ship sailed away from us? And by the way, boss, what are we all having for breakfast this morning? Because Captain Ortuga has told me that he wants to feed the locals up there on the street."

As the intense, alcoholic ingestion into Aturo's body had diluted his blood stream down, Aturo's energy tolerated the influential spirit entity of Montezuma gaining total control of Aturo's mind and his physical actions too:

"Look, boy! This day of sun, we will have a breakfast that brings us all together to follow my empirical building desire to take over the Inca natives and allow us to set up our own township on their land. Now, just go down to the galley and check out the foodstuffs that have been prepared, return back here immediately and tell me what we have – then we can mutually join as one with the locals to eat those foods!"

Knowing that the living being of Aturo Deshah was forcefully manipulated by Montezuma, the anxiety of Aturo himself was heightened. Davy walked away from the hostile energy of Montezuma, down into the hammock berth where he noticed four corpses of the deckhands. Not knowing that they had all been killed, he tried to wake them up. Moving closer to one of the deckhands that he had often talked to and assisted with his work, Davy gently tapped his chest to attempt to wake him. With no sound of waking, Davy shook his hand; blood spurted out from the stomach of the cadaver down onto the floor. Davy rapidly let go of the hand and projected his thinking out into the room to the other carcasses.

"Are any of you asleep and alive, have you all been physically destroyed by the alcoholic drinks, or are you unconscious from the valerian root powder that the ship's cook fed to you? Please wake up and speak with me so I can help you."

Looking down at the blood streaming around on the floor, Davy saw the group of eight rats licking up the pooled blood. As he moved towards them, they sprang away from their gathering, leapt onto the hammocks that were holding the deceased bodies of the deckhands and disappeared under the remains.

The rats' actions made Davy realise that the four crew members were all dead. He thought that because of the deckhands' incredibly deep unconsciousness caused by the foods that they had eaten the night before, the men would not have noticed the rats eating their way into their bodies to consume their flesh and organs, thus passing foul bacteria into their blood streams, thereby, bringing death to each man.

Walking out from the berth, Davy noticed a leak in the wooden hull, flowing salt water and sunlight into the ship's lower hold. Bending down to look closer at the split timber, he saw numerous barnacles that had weakened the hull by absorbing the strength of the timber, with the size of the gap being about 80mm wide. Darting through the hole, a large Conger Eel appeared and with its jagged mouth open, it began to snap at Davy. Davy leapt up from the hold floor decking and grasped a metal spade that had been used to dig up treasures, to thrust the Eel back out of the hole into the shallow waters. Falling out from his pocket, the Mollusc shell Turnkey slid through the gap into the waters. Quickly reaching through the hole, he clenched hold of the Turnkey before it sunk down to the sand, the Conger Eel quickly returned and curled around Davy's exposed forearm and tightened its body around his limb, causing Davy to release the golden shell. Sinking down, the teleporting object dropped back into the water, settling together with other Mollusc shells of the same shape on the sand bed surrounded by a cluster of tropical Angel Fish, Box Jellyfish and a Blue Ringed Octopus. As the lethal sea creatures possessed so much toxic danger that harmed humans and other creatures, Davy decided to leave the Turnkey on the sand bed for the time being, he then returned back to the main decking to join up with the crew. Arriving on the top deck Davy met up with Sanchez:

"Hi, Javir, can I use your telescope? I have just seen a breakage of the hull timber caused by barnacles; the damaged site is over there on the portside of the ship."

Both of them walked up to the railings and leant over, Davy pointed at the splintering timber and looked into the water using the telescope. Focusing down where the shell had sunk, he could see that the Conger Eel had been killed by the poison wrapped around it from the Box Jellyfish. His shell was hidden from view by the others shrouding it, even though the colour of the other shells were not golden they veiled the Turnkey.

The eager hermit crabs inside the other shells recognised the golden motivation; to gain strength from gold and they crawled over the golden shell masking its form.

Watching the movements within the waters, the Angel Fish swam to the Conger Eel and started nibbling its flavoursome flesh. Without Davy seeing its entry into his Turnkey, the Blue Ringed Octopus crawled under the hermit crabs into the golden shell.

After Davy passed the telescope back to Sanchez, Ortuga walked up to them, saluting them both, and bellowed out a message of intendance:

"Hey, you two! It is now time for having breakfast with the locals. Sanchez, can you secure the ship so it cannot drift back out into the ocean. Tuli, please come over here and tell me and Aturo the foods that are ready for eating."

Standing in the middle of the crew-gathering, Davy stood close to the Captain – hoping to tell him about the findings down in the ship's hold. From the being of Aturo, Montezuma was talking with the seven pirates about how they could join him to search for treasure and gold in Eldorado. As the pirates had eaten heaps of the additive foods readied by Montezuma, they were very hyper and thrilled about finding gold for themselves.

The first chronicle Davy explained to the Captain was the damage to the moulded wooden hull, that was letting ocean water flow into the hold after which he mentioned the list of foods that were on the bench top in the galley:

"Captain! Organic wholemeal porridge, goat's yoghurt, turtle bone broth and lava bread. These foods shall help overcome stress, low energy levels and insomnia, conveying faith of your vision of global altruism to the local indigenous community. This native community will allow you to be part of their society as you have the ability to grow acceptance of all personalities and healings."

Ortuga spoke with Han, asking him to go down into the hold and repair the hull, then to secure a gangplank from the Liberty Bell to the port, enabling access for the crew and the Incan locals. Samson and Marley assisted Han with lifting the heavy gangplank to the side of the vessel and once Han had fixed up the walkway, Pablo, Davy and himself walked across to offer gesture to the native community who were currently worshipping the sun. Escaping from the consumptive danger of humans eating animals, the dogs, chickens, rats and the baby lamb that rode on the vessel charged sprightly across the gangplank through the village and up into the bushlands, seeking homes for themselves.

The single animal that did not want to run away was the Retriever watchdog called Monty, that had befriended Davy, Ortuga, Pablo and Han. Returning from the watchtower streets, Pablo and Davy went down to the food galley, placed the breakfast on the trolley and wheeled it back over the plank to the natives.

The Aztec king – Montezuma, was sitting on the stern with Juan Ortuga, explaining to the Captain that he had entered the body of Aturo and also that he was very interested in knowing if Ortuga had any knowledge about Evangeline Moreau. He knew that in order to return to his empire he had to seek out this future spiritualist Starseed woman. Montezuma spoke about her:

"This woman was born in 1704 at a certain time when the earth and moon aligned during a seven day period, with the central planet of the Pleiadian System, called Alcione. This era of ingenuous enlightenment occurs only once every three hundred years and the earthbound humans born during this time are sheathed with the cosmic mantle and are termed as Starseeds."

These extraordinary humans possess an innate spiritual wisdom bestowed upon them from this rare planetary alignment, which the Elohim desire to channel back to their planet to further advance the spirituality of their race.

In order to gain the whereabouts of Evangeline, the Aztec King promised to reveal to Ortuga the hidden locations of hordes of Aztec gold that he himself stole from the Elohim City of Gold, Eldorado.

"Ortuga, whilst sailing over the oceans, have you ever met this woman? If you have, do tell me of her whereabouts, and I will exit from the body of your ship's Cook, Aturo, giving him freedom of expression and regenerating his own power."

Because of his deep love for Evangeline, Ortuga ignored Montezuma's bombastic questioning. As Ortuga climbed up the stairs, Montezuma clenched hold of his aching leg – Ortuga fell down flat onto the top decking. Crawling over to his deputy commanders, he issued instructions to the pirate crew to carry the rest of the food plus six flagons of natural mineral water up from the galley to the port, where everybody could sit together in devotion and listen to the spiritual teachings of Han, bringing inner peace to their souls.

Chapter Ten
Along the Watchtower

After trundling across the wooden gangplank secured to the bow, the total crew of the Liberty Bell stood together on the sandy beach known as Greenpatch Cove with the seniors and their Cabin Boy. Ortuga remained sitting on the stern of his ship, for his leg was aching so badly that he couldn't walk, which pressured the injured muscle, increasing his agony. Gazing over to the beach, he waved to Han, calling him back to the ship. Han walked back over the gangplank and strolled down to the stern to soothe the Captain's leg with his psychic energy healing. After Han had removed much of the pain in the Captain's leg, Ortuga spoke

"Han, you are a genius son of God. What can I do for you, how can I repay you? You have healed my leg so well that now I can regain my role as Captain of the Liberty Bell."

Han embraced Juan Ortuga with a powerful man hug: "Captain, I would like to have your support to let me meet up with the chief of the Inca tribe to talk with him about spiritual energy and ask him why his men kill young girls in their sacrificial rituals. I will also fix the wooden hull on your ship later today after eating foods with the Incas."

They then both walked forward to the bow of the ship and leaned over the railings, observing the Incan tribe with their chieftains.

The crew had moved from the sandy beach front onto a green patch at the foothills, where they were sitting with the Inca tribal men beginning to eat the foods prepared by Aturo. Whilst the foods were in the galley, uncaringly, Montezuma had added blood and some intoxicating valerian root stock to the turtle broth to make the minds of both the Inca tribes and the Liberty's crew members open to his commands of taking over their Incan kingdom. When this vision entered Han's mind, he pushed his hand forward, releasing energy that knocked Montezuma down onto the grass. Jumping over the gunwale railings into the air of the blue skies filled with white clouds, Han soared down onto the grassland spot to halt the native men from eating the toxic foods. By chance, he arrived before they had started to consume the hot turtle broth; Han took hold of the large container and poured the liquid into the mouth of Aturo, causing Montezuma to fall into a deep sleep.

Meanwhile, inside the submerged golden Turnkey, the Blue-Ringed Octopus was teleported back in time to a memory point from Davy's mind. Davy was so impressed by the historical happenings he learnt at Penwright Grammar School, that the Mollusc shell was transported back to the history class that happened several days after Davy had been teleported to Valparasio.

In the classroom of twenty-seven children, were his close friends, Molly, Tim and Quinton. The livid female history teacher, Miss Fanny Gardener, was educating the group of young teenagers about the year of 1918 when Britain granted women suffragettes the power to vote politically to acquire a conservative, liberal or democratic government. Hidden under her writing table, Fanny Gardener kept her large Alsatian pet dog that timidly reserved quietness in order not to cause any fear in the classroom. Molly, who was sitting next to Davy's empty school desk began to notice the golden Mollusc shell manifesting its form on top of the desk. Smelling the oceanic odour, the black-tanned Alsatian crept out from under the table and padded towards Davy's vacant desk. Gnashing her teeth, Fanny Gardener lectured her thoughts:

"Boys and girls, we all possess the same physical and spiritual energy but with different characteristic forces. Male is Yang and Female is Yin. Even animals contain identical life forces, but they are slaughtered to strengthen us with vitamins and minerals by eating their flesh."

Standing up, Molly eagerly expressed her knowledge of health and wellbeing:

"Miss Gardener, I will be your creature teacher. Being a vegan myself, I know what it is like to be feeling fantastic all the time, and I question why people can love one pet animal and kill all others?"

Back in the Peruvian port, the native community began to worship the sun, which made their spirits rise to immerse its extreme power into their bodies. Rousing from his eliminated energy, Montezuma commanded the seven pirates to begin attacking the Incas, but by means of the influence of the sun, the Incas punched the pirate men and floored their physicality down onto the ground. Han sat down with the Incan chief, looking at the pirate men lying unconsciously on the grass; he expressed a comment to beg forgiveness for their aggression:

"Overcome your hatred through love and kindness, extend love to your enemy."

The multicultural gathering of the senior Liberty seafarers and South American natives watched Captain Ortuga walking across the gangplank to join them; he wanted to apologise for the mischievous actions of the pirates. On joining the group, the Inca chief shook hands and asked him to sit with him; explaining the workings of the Incan community and the foresights of the retreat village in the sacred valley hillside, called Machu Picchu:

"This land is a place where you will reconnect with nature. I can overturn space and time to help you settle here with your crew members."

The aged warrior chieftain, Pachacuti, was filled with the spirit from one of the Pleiadian Lightworkers that architecturally designed the citadel structures of the ancient estate. His energy harmonised with Han's magical power:

"Chinaman – I invite your magic into my village."

He cordially received the Liberty crew, but the bad incident actioned by Montezuma and the seven pirate men changed the accepting frame of his mind, to become harsh towards Aturo. Pachacuti believed that to destroy the spirit of Montezuma, Aturo could be held in a bushland fire up on the hillside when the days of summer arrived in four months' time.

He told Ortuga that he recognised the spirit of the Aztec King – Montezuma inside the rolling body of the Jamaican cook. Explaining that the evil spirit had been captured by himself and that it can be subdued by sounds, like, ringing bells, vocal chanting and prayers. While the chieftain was talking, bells began to ring from a stone roundhouse, high on the hillside:

"There you go, Captain, welcome to Peru – The Land of Hidden Treasures. There is gold in these hills. My tribal congregation rings bells up there inside the watchtower to bring their friends and family together here on every day of sun worship."

After listening to Pachacuti's liberal words, Han ambled away from Ortuga and the Inca Chief and walked up to the defending castle watchtower, which was an ancient building that had the functions of a military hospital and also an arsenal. Entering its roundhouse, he walked into the courtyard to rally with a group of four men pulling ropes to ring the bells. Shifting behind the group, he walked up a tight spiral staircase to the viewing corridor along the open rooftop of the watchtower.

Han pulled out his flute and played a piping melody whilst looking over at the many goings-on of the gatherings down on the Greenpatch Cove; Han also saw the rustling movement of animals, a herd of eight Llamas plodding down from the hillside.

The animals stopped at the spot where the unconscious pirates were lying and began to eat the bread in their hands. Swooping down from the beach palm trees, a flock of brightly feathered Parrots landed onto the grass and joined the Llamas snapping at the hands of the pirates to release the lavish bread wraps filled with pork. Pork was rarely eaten in Puerto Caballas, as the meat delicacy of Peruvian natives was rodent Guinea Pigs; the small creatures are skinned and roasted in the extreme heated ashes of bonfire footings, providing a staple food for many native communities.

Walking into the gathering, a tall, slender woman carried a large sack of the cooked rodents over her shoulder and a basket full of coconuts. Opening the carriers, she served the foods to each person sitting within the get-together. Scoffing them for breakfast, joyful smiles appeared on the faces of every tribal member, but the highly flavoursome roasted creatures were refused by most the Liberty crew except for the two Africans, Marley and Samson.

Holding a steel drum, Marley stood up:

"Hi, baby! Your body is so gorgeously eye-catching. It's the most wonderful time of the year, can you dance for me?"

Placing the left over foods onto a rock on the beach, the attractive woman replied:

"Yippie Yi Oh Ti Yay. Yes, I can dance for you. I dance when the men are worshipping the sun, for I am a South American musical goddess living up there in Machu Picchu. The alignment of the planets is creating positive energy and sounds that will favourably change the lives of those who know how to take advantage of it."

Padding away from the pirates and Llamas, five ravenous Toucan birds flew down to the beach to nosh up some of the roasted Guinea Pigs. After eating the small creatures, the birds then flew onto the shoulders of muscular men within the congregation; attracted by the sounding of the flute, one of the Toucans soared up to the watchtower and landed on the left shoulder of Han. Because of the hunger aggressions of the Llamas, the pirates regained their consciousness mounted the animals and began riding the Llamas up into the hillside.

Playing the steel drum, Marley encouraged the whole congregation to stand up and dance with each other. In rhythmic harmony, the other senior Liberty officers played their instruments, Trumpet, Violin and Pan Flute. Dreadlocked, Marley gazed longingly at the Peruvian goddess, as she swirled around him whilst he played the steel drum. Because he wanted to dance a body bumping motion with the pretty woman, he passed the drum onto his mate Samson. She embraced him, as they bopped a gender tango dance together.

From the roundhouse castle watchtower, Han spied upon the groups dancing on the grass and the sandy beach; the tribal males danced in an assembly, setting up a human sacrificial symposium offering the precious energy of a young girl to the Aztec God of Sun and War, Solnazi.

In order to discover protective routines, Davy and Pablo walked up into the watchtower to talk with Han about his magic power and how they could use their own energies to stop the slaughtering of both humans and animals.

Reverting back to the 1976 happenings in the Cornish history classroom of Penwright Grammar so impressed by the golden shell, she tried to barge the Alsatian dog away from the Turnkey by thumping her hand on its ribcage. Turning its head around from the desk, the dog snarled at her and angrily snapped its teeth into the air.

Creeping out from inside the Mollusc shell, the deadly Blue-Ringed Octopus flattened onto the desk. The classmates all focused on the unusual sea creature while the dog pointed its nose towards the octopus and sniffed at it. As it began swirling its eight limbs towards the dog's nose, the hound quickly jumped away from the danger.

Experiencing the probable disaster, Miss Fanny Gardener used green chalk to write the words EVOLUTION of the OCTOPUS onto the blackboard, she then walked away from the blackboard and stopped at Davy's vacant writing desk. Pushing past the Alsatian, she reached her right hand out to grasp the shell. But before touching the Turnkey, the octopus sprung up from the desk and wrapped its tentacles around the teacher's wrist.

Using its limb suckers to open the pores of her skin, it injected its venom into her forearm. Sensing the poison entering into her bloodstream, flowing around her body into her brain, Miss Gardener slurred:

"This deadliest sea creature has three hearts; their oceanic homes are in the oceans of Australia and the Indo-Pacific. Not all bites transfer the venom, but this octopus has done so. No one should touch the creature. Can someone please call the hospital immediately to send an ambulance to pick me up?"

Sitting in the back of the class, one of the boys, Bruce Clarendon from the Australian coastal resort town of Huskisson Bay – grabbed hold of the teacher's left arm, and led her to the blackboard. To reduce the infiltration of venom into the woman, he used an ink pen to jab into the body of the Blue-Ringed Octopus. Falling off from her wrist, the creature dropped onto the floor, where the Alsatian ran up and gorged it into its mouth. The octopus then wrapped its tentacles around the dog's snout to bite and kill the attacker, the dog howled. Bruce picked up the phone to call the school Secretary, asking her to phone the district hospital, telling her that a poison had been transferred into his teacher's arm, causing severe symptoms of nausea, numbness, breathing difficulties and paralysis, subsequently, leading to cerebral anoxia and death.

As everyone was looking at the blackboard at the front of the classroom, Molly grasped hold of the golden shell. Putting the Turnkey into the pocket of her navy blazer, she entered the teleportation plan of transporting her into the past from the English county of Cornwall to Peru, visualising her destination to the sea port of Puerto Caballas. Before moving on, she waved farewell to her friends, whirling around she floated into the energy channel moving her out of the class room window high into the sky; sitting on a fluffy white cloud she travelled on her journey, sailing swiftly 200 years back into the past. Arriving 20 minutes after departure, the cloud lowered close down to the gathering at Greenpatch Cove; it split apart, letting Molly channel down to the ground. Molly landed upon a stone altar, flanked by two men ready to sacrifice her energy to the God, Nazielsol. The method used by the men to sacrifice the girl would be firstly, knocking her unconscious with a rock then passing the blade through her heart.

Rapidly gaining awareness of the sacrificial procedure, Molly quickly sat upright, to try and stop the Inca tribal man from banging the rock on her head. Moving about under her leg, a bull ant created an annoying itching on her flesh and stung her with its toxic venom. Han and Davy noticed her sitting on the altar with an anxious impression of petrification showing on her face.

Blowing powerfully into his pan flute, Han used the wind instrument to shoot bullets of air at the two Incans, to stop the sacrifice. At the same time, Evangeline used her Starseed energy to compound the rescuing of Molly; spellbinding the Llamas to gnaw the ankles of the tribesmen standing at the sacrificial altar. When the air bullets skated across their foreheads, Han sent down his magic power to raise Molly up from the altar. Her body floated upwards, gliding across the sandy beach front, then she soared up the hillside to the watchtower. The flock of Toucan birds from the beach front rose in the air and surrounded her as she flew towards the watchtower. Molly was so excited that she spread her arms out to fly like a winged bird. By means of the power channelling from Han, she flew high above the watchtower over to the citadel of Machu Picchu, and descended back down to the open walkway at the summit of the watchtower. To cradle her landing, Davy leaned over the stone turret catching her with his outstretched hands as she dropped into his arms. He then pulled her back over the limestone bricks and laid her down onto the cushioned timber walkway set along the open corridor behind him at the top of the watchtower:

"Hi, Molly, it is so good to see you. I am here to help you regain your presence, then I will tell you how you teleported yourself from Cornwall."

Sensing that Molly needed to regain strength to heal the venomous bite from the bull ant, Evangeline laid down next to her on the timber walkway. Although Evangeline was dressed up in her male disguise of Pablo, she cuddled together with Molly and whispered into her ear:

"Are you the girlfriend of Davy? He has been so supportive to the Captain of that ship down there on the beach front that I am seeking to invite him and his friends to become part of our troop to discover the City of Gold, of which the treasures and gold will be donated to communities around the world.

Molly, did you travel here with a Turnkey that is formed like a Mollusc shell? If you did, then we could use the same permit shell to collect Davy's other friends from your English town in Cornwall."

Not realising that, as she had flown over the beach front, the golden shell Turnkey had fallen out of her blazer and descended down into the water close to the Liberty Bell. The water current swirled the Turnkey down under the hull of the vessel, returning it to the shallow waters where Davy had dropped it through the split timber.

Over in the cove, a commotion had started, the two muscular, Incan males that were expected to carry out the sacrificing practice began yelling as they were suddenly attacked by the Llamas.

The herd of threatening animals sunk their teeth into their ankles and bulging calf muscles. Before collapsing, both of the tribal males climbed onto the Altar and threw rocks at the llamas, attempting to send them away. After running out of rocks to destroy the herd, the Incan men noticed that one of the Llamas remained at the altar; the animal had lost the seeded mind pattern of biting the men's ankles. Climbing off the altar, the men loaded straw onto its back to depress its strength, and shoved the blade into its buttock. The Llama then limped across the Greenpatch Cove to obtain healing kindness from the congregational gathering.

By this time, the majority of the rural Inca community had returned back to their village in the hillside. Souls lingering on the ground of worship were the Liberty fellowship consisting of seven pirates, five senior officers and Captain Ortuga. Sitting on the grass under a shaded palm tree was the Inca Chief, Pachacuti, together with the two African slaves and the Chief's wife, the capricorn Goddess dancer that joyfully danced with Marley.

Trampling down from the ancient stone watchtower together, Han, Davy, Evangeline and Molly sung a melodic Chinese tune of motivation. Composed by Han, the harmonic song of praise was sung to gain inspiration, to heal and balance one's mind. Once the wording seeded into the mind, compassion and caring would be offered to help all living human beings and animals.

Davy and Molly giggled about the fantastic time they had experienced with the teleportation of the Turnkey. Han and Pablo held each other's hands. As they arrived at the palm tree on the ground of worship the Inca chief perceived that loving of the same gender of male or female defined the transcendence of love to all beings. Standing up, the chieftain fellow gave a man hug to Han, asking him if he could give a speech to his community when they worshipped the sun:

"My citizens will be worshiping the sun on the next sun day, can you let them all know about the beneficial power of Taoism and how we can transfer our existing beliefs and thoughts over to the open faith?"

In favour with Pachacuti, Han smiled beamingly and told him that the ancient wisdom of Taoism has remarkable methods of healing to restore global health and nurse the world. As a result, it would be so beneficial for his community to alter their present religion.

Han replied to the ruler of the Inca society:

"Okay, chief, I will meet up with you and your community on the next day of sun to preach a Taoist sermon of the aspects of meditation, energy and spirit. The best time to gather would be just after sunrise, is that time acceptable?"

After agreeing with Han, Pachacuti walked off to the altar and ordered the sacrificial workforce team to guide him and the four bell ringers back to the village and the beautiful wife of Chief Pachacuti, Sofia Polkatango, remained on the beach with Marley. Ortuga then asked Han to get back to the ship with Davy to fix the splintered timber on the hull. Furthermore, he asked Han if he could remove the broken figurehead that was smashed into by the pirate sloop vessel and to carve another decorative figurehead for the bow of the Liberty vessel during the following days before the day of sun. The Liberty Bell was going to dock in the Greenpatch Cove for several weeks before Ortuga and his men were to set out to discover the location of Eldorado, the Spanish City of Gold. All folks moved off to the Liberty Bell, marching along the beach across the gangplank down into the galley to have lunch. Marley lifted Sofia onto his back and carried her into the ship. Watching the charming action of Marley, Davy crouched down and nodded for Molly to mount his back giving her a piggyback ride over the grass, onto the sand, up the gangplank and down into the galley which is where Aturo was preparing foods. Because of the extreme heat of the sun, the evil spirit of Montezuma had been suppressed, allowing Aturo's character to openly present itself.

The foods Aturo was serving to the crew members consisted of minced beef, husked sweet corn, brown rice, tomatoes, topped with a chilli sauce, coriander leaves and goat's yoghurt. Plus a drink of lime juice and the refreshing coconut juice from green coconuts, mixed together and placed in the shell of the turtle which the ship's Physician, Amir Noorian, considered as a catalyst to cleanse the intolerance out of pirate men.

Finishing their lunch, Davy walked Molly down to the hull zone where the timber planking on the outer hull had been attacked by barnacles; hence weakening the timber causing decay and splintering. The shell Turnkey that Molly used to transfer her from Cornwall to the past had swirled around in the ocean current, returning back to the sand bed below the hull; close to the cavernous dwelling of the Conger Eel.

Since Davy had last seen the cavity of the splintered oak timber, the hole had enlarged, accessing water from king tides into the ship's hold and also when heavy waves flowed along the ocean towards the beach the water trickled through the opening.

Trying to find the Turnkey, Davy knelt down and looked through the hole into the shallow water where he had dropped it before the Octopus teleported inside the shell to the history class of Penwright Grammar School.

Clasping his hands onto each side of the splintered cavity, he moved his head further out through the opening. Turning his head to the left and right, he saw that many barnacles were still attached to the hardwood plankings fastened to the hull frame. The observation informed him that if the crustaceans were not removed, then the hole would enlarge colossally and create havoc for the ship on its ocean going journeys. Moving back into the hold, he looked over at Molly; sitting on a timber hull frame, she was watching a group of crabs climbing up the frame to the food galley. Davy sat next to her, explaining to her about the miraculous functions of the shell Turnkey:

"The reason you were teleported here is because you must have gripped hold of the Mollusc shell quite strongly and the powerful memories contained in the Turnkey defined your journey to visit the past or the future. If you had gently touched the shell, then you would have only visualised some of its memories. So Molly, in order to command transportation to a location where you would like to travel to, like going home to Cornwall, you need to clearly project definite information of the return address such as:

"Please teleport me to my home in England – in the year of 1973.

"The address location for visitation is the grammar school called Penwright at 42 Mangrove Road, Penzance, Cornwall. Thank you very much."

Davy went on to explain to her that to commence teleportation, the memory energy of the shell Turnkey takes five to 20 minutes to begin the teleporting process. If the Turnkey memory does not correspond with, or relate to the energy or mentality of the person or group of people looking to travel back or forward in time, then it will not teleport to the location.

Davy also told Molly he was very devoted to Juan Ortuga because of the Captain's altruistic vision. Which is why he was teleported to Valparaiso and was recruited along with Evangeline Moreau to work with her harmonising energy;

bringing her close to him, to reveal the truth of her life and visions of the future.

The memory response of the Turnkey is quite sensitive, which is why the octopus was transported back to Cornwall. As Evangeline explained to Davy, the optimum way of halting the sensitivity is to attach a chain to the shell, which lowers the screen to blind its memory sensitivity. Davy glanced beyond Molly to the rear bilge of the ship; he noticed a movement of shadows at the stern. Because the ship was moored on an angle with its bow near the beach front and its rear angled down into the shallow waters, any water that entered the hull flowed downwards to the stern of the ship, creating a pool of deep salt water. Living within the pool were tiger prawns, lobsters and tropical fish.

Davy asked Molly to go with him to see the pool of water so they could get an understanding of how it could be removed. Close by to the pool, he again saw the heavy fluttering movements of a dark shadow shaped like the tail of a shark.

Settling down by the edge of the water on the timber frame, they both looked into the depth, and saw the shadow prancing around at the bottom of the bilge. Suddenly, a large green tail flipped out above the water, then curled down below the surface; the form rose again to the surface revealing a mermaid. As she leapt out and sat next to the shocked children, Molly kindly put her arm around the female aquatic creature:

"Hello, fish girl, how long have you been in this depth of water? Do you want my friend, Davy here to help me carry you back to the ocean?"

Listening quietly, the legendary mermaid understood the questionings but could not reply in English, so she replied in the global language of Esperanto: "Bonvenon al mia mondo, mi lavis tra la damaĝitaj malfermo en la lignon kareno de la forto de reĝo tajdo, sed mi ne povas trapasi ĝin ĉar miaj koksoj kreskis pli larĝa. Ĉu vi povas porti min al la pruo de la ŝipo kaj malaltigi min en la oceano?"

Turning around to face Molly, Davy translated her Esperanto reply:

"Welcome to my world! I was washed in through the damaged opening in the timber hull by the force of a king tide, but I cannot pass through it because my hips have become wider.

Can you carry me up to the bow of the ship and lower me down into the ocean?"

Suddenly, the noise of someone stepping along the base of the wooden hull was heard by all three of them. Glancing around, Davy saw Han, strolling along the hull, getting closer to the bilge. The mermaid quickly slid off the timber frame seat, back down into the water hiding from view by laying in the darkness at the bottom of the depth. Standing above Davy and Molly, Han was looking down into the water trying to find out what creature had made the fluttering shadows on the timber wall inside the hull. Below the surface of the water, the tiger prawns and tropical fish scurried around – the form of the mermaid's body creating a solid background, which amplified the dynamic colours of the fish.

Then a group of crabs skated all over the mermaid, nipping at her skin and making her spring up out of the water again. Rising out of the bilge water, Han noticed that her body was very beautiful, and he raised his eyebrows whilst thinking of creative ideas to carve the new figurehead for the bow of the ship. The magnificent image of the female sculpture that entered his mind was a figurine joining body parts of three females: the upper body of Evangeline Moreau, the tail of the mermaid and the head of the Peruvian Goddess – Sofia Polkatango.

Davy told Han that the mermaid wanted to be taken up to the main deck and lowered into the ocean so she could swim back to her marine grotto dwelling. Smiling, Han agreed with her request. He then leant over and gently pulled the mermaid onto the timber flooring that was covered with algae, making her body slide gently onto the timber hull. The three gleaming characters, Han, Davy and Molly put their hands under her body and lifted her off the flooring. They then carried her up to the galley, placing her onto a platform trolley to wheel her up to the bow of the ship. At 2.00pm, reaching the galley, the culinary room was still packed with crew members finishing their lunch. Preparing additional foodstuffs to feed the pirates throughout the afternoon, Aturo stir fried the group of crabs that had clambered up from the hull. After cooking the crabs, he placed them in the turtle bone broth with sweet corn, beetroot, green olives and green kale, naming the wholesome sea food meal as a Rock Pool Chowder. As the sea mermaid had not eaten for 48 hours, she nodded to Davy, inducing his acceptance of letting her sit down to eat a portion of the Rock Pool Chowder.

As the heat intensity of the sun had diminished, the spirit of Montezuma had minimal power over Aturo allowing the cook to put together the chowder from organic super foods.

Charmed by her beauty, all the men in the galley stared at the nudity of her upper body locked into the green strapping scaled tail. While she was slurping the food into her throat, Han pencilled a drawing of her tail for him to reproduce into the carving of the figurehead replacement. Aturo spoke to Han:

"Mr Monk, mermaids are the Goddesses of the seven seas. I adore their beings myself, but I will not become their partner, for I cannot swim more than just one mile."

Within minutes, she had finished gorging Aturo's sea food chowder. Then wheeling the platform trolley next to her, Davy asked one of the pirates to lift the mermaid onto the up folding, trolley platform. After curling her tail around her body, Davy and Molly pushed the trolley out of the galley along the walkway up to the main decking. Reaching the bow of the ship, Han was sitting cross legged on the ship figurehead where he mentioned to Davy and Molly that they must be cautious when dropping her into the shallow water for the hard fall would shatter her bones, or break her tail:

"Davy, I will teach you how to convert your energy into magic to lower her down with ease into the ocean. The forceful power of magic can also be used in your life to shield yourself, friends, family and global communities from harm."

Davy was amazed at his comment:

"Han, thanks for your delightful aid! Can we show Molly the teachings of magic as well? She might travel back to England to cure our history teacher, Miss Fanny Gardener."

Thrilled, Molly burst out with an excited response:

"Chinaman, I will take on the knowledge of magic to lower the mermaid into the ocean, and to also help the refugee communities in Cornwall – thank you, sir."

Han informed Davy and Molly, to implant magical power into themselves, they should stand with both hands raised up in the air and sing a mantra that calls the energy of the universe to load up into their bodies through their left hand. Once their bodies are full of energy, they must clasp both their hands together and continue the mantra which converts the energy into the power of magic. After the energy inside their bodies is converted to white magic power, they will have more good luck, good health and prosperity. The magic creates an energetic shield that protects the body from negative vibrations and it can be flowed out of the right hand for psychic healings and also to stop quarrelling fracas and aggressive conflicts.

Han said that the essential elements to creating magic were the terms of the mantra, with the central wordings being:

"BLESS MY MOUTH THAT I MAY SAY THE TRUTH. GOD IS LOVE, LOVE IS ME, LOVE IS THE UNIVERSE."

Raising their hands in the air, repeating the wordings for one hour gave the souls of Davy, Molly and the mermaid a magical power. In the autumn twilight, Molly uttered the mantra followed by a gifted spell to raise the mermaid above the decking, float her over the railings and lower her down into the waters. Swimming away from the ship to the horizon, the mermaid waved to them and dived down into the sea to lodge in her marine cavern.

The darkness of the night streamed into Greenpatch Cove. Davy walked Molly down to the quarters that he had shared with Evangeline and Flintlock. He introduced Molly to her new companions, for she was sharing their quarters and going to sleep in Davy's vacant bed. Davy then walked back down to the hull and as he glanced through the damaged timber down into the water he saw the golden shell Turnkey. After lifting it out of the water, he attached the chain to the shell and he then placed it around his neck inside his shirt, with the shell glowing softly inside his clothing. Walking off to the galley, strolling into the kitchen he sneaked behind Aturo, opened the door of the food larder and laid down under the sackings to fall asleep. Because the sun light had disappeared, the temperature in the ship had lowered down to 16 degrees Celsius, allowing the spirit of Aturo to govern himself; overwhelming the aggressive spirit of Montezuma in dictating actions to his physicality and his mind.

Chapter Eleven
Stairway to Heaven

Whilst sleeping without any fear or anxiety in the cabin with Pablo and Flintlock, Molly heard a mellow sound of music streaming down from the grassland at the foot of the hillside; the music woke her up just before midnight. Gazing out through the porthole up into the hills, she noticed several small bonfires with people drumming and dancing around them.

The melodic sound of music was being played by a band of four indigenous men together with the two African slaves, Marley and Samson. The Africans were playing a steel drum, tambourine and harmonica; the Incan band played a recorder, a bass cello and a medieval string instrument called a rebec lute which produced a similar sound to that of a guitar. The fourth instrument was a set of bagpipes made from the skin of a goat; the profound sound of the bagpipes delivered a dream to Flintlock about his youthful days in the Scottish capital city of Edinburgh during the annual occasion called The Royal Edinburgh Military Tattoo. At an event in August 1708, at the age of 15, he played a drum along with his father who played a set of Scottish bagpipes, his mother was there dancing – leading the military forces around the Edinburgh castle. The images of people stomping along to the marching sound of music that entered his dream reflected the Greenpatch gatherings.

Waking up in a state of harmonious bliss, Flintlock melodically tapped Molly on the shoulder, asking her if she would like to join up with the tribal gathering. She said:

"Yes, sir, as with all life forms, humans, animals and even plants, my life is highly motivated by the sound of positive music; an inspirational rhythm seeps into the mind, flows in the bounds of the working glands to produce super power, healing and immunity."

Flintlock grabbed hold of his own military snare drum and walked out of the cabin with Molly and proceeded up to the top deck and strolled over the gangplank to the edge of the grass. The sound of the tribal gathering grew stridently louder, penetrating the minds of Flintlock and Molly, persuading them to connect with the gathering to worship the female energy of the moon. As drumming is used to communicate as well as entertain, Flintlock started to play his snare drum to convey his commanding role of Bosun as they walked towards the Inca congregation.

So inspired by the Incan music, Molly raised her hands up to the moon, generating her magical power to fly along to the foothills. As she rose into the night sky, a colony of fruit bats united with her, fluttering all along together for 300 metres, then swooping down to land onto the grass next to the Peruvian woman, Sofia Polkatango.

She was dancing so wonderfully that the fruit bats circled around her body in a motion just like the moon orbiting the planet Earth. The bats of the Chiroptera mammalian species drew her energy into their souls; they then soared back up into the sky towards the moon that was sitting above the Pleiadian citadel of Machu Picchu. Molly landed up on the hillside, close to one of the bonfires, roughly 5 metres away from the bottom of the hills. Laying down on the grass bedding by the fire, she relaxed into a calming presence watching the bats sailing up into the night sky as their flight wove through the beams of moonlight.

Expressing his seniority, Flintlock drummed with a tempo of 100 beats per minute so loudly that his sounding triumphed over the tribal band so much so that they all stopped playing their instruments and started marching down towards the ocean front. Molly quickly turned around to view the awesome happening, and because she was laying at an angle on the sloping hillside, her sudden movement and her hunched weight made her roll down to the base of the hill. Rolling and rolling, she ended up in a shallow swamp filled with lotus flowers. The pure floral vegetation of rebirth and divinity had been planted by Sofia and her chieftain husband, in the spring season three years ago to beautify the religious site used by their community to worship the sun.

Major cultures that associated with the symbolism of the Lotus flower are Hinduism, Buddhism and Egyptology. The young seedlings of the Lotus flowers were given to the Incan chief from a fleet of Chinese pirates commanded by Cheng Yi. His wife, Cheng Hai, related so well with Sofia that she profiled the characters of Sofia's family and relatives using ancient Chinese Astrology, revealing planetary energy that defined the highest skills and talents of each individual. Additionally, defining shockingly accurate information that outlined what those people cannot do in their lives. Combined with the western astrological symbology, Sofia's character was found out to be the Chinese zodiac sign of a Capricorn Water Snake, which is why she carried so much love for the world and adulation to seek friendships with other men in her life as well as maintaining her relationship with her husband.

The intoxicating perfume of the Lotus flowers and the charcoal from the glowing bonfires sailed into the sky, spiralling down to the beach to enter the Liberty Bell through the top deck; falling down into the ship's hold to permeate into the cabins. The fabulous scent of the Lotus flowers woke Evangeline, who hurriedly dressed into her male outfit and raced up to the main deck to view the energy of the equinox moon.

The equinox dictates that the sun shall return the following day; therefore, Han would be greeted by Pachacuti and the bell ringers to voice his sermon from the watchtower tomorrow on sun day.

Even though the loud music and the potent aromas were flowing down to the beach front, Davy was still sound asleep under six densely-woven hessian sacks. Because the hessian material covered his head, Davy was unable to hear any outside noises, as he was wanting to sleep well to increase his strength so he could help Han fix the damaged hull the next morning.

In his bed, Aturo had also covered himself with thick woollen blankets after the sun had set as the tepid coldness of the night air had dropped down to eight degrees, but the moonlight did not let him go off to sleep. Also as a sleeping aid, he had made himself a large mug of warm milk with turmeric and cinnamon. He did not know that when his body temperature increased, the spirit of Montezuma would rouse to take over his mind and actions. The expansion of Montezuma's aggression geared up Aturo to get out of his bed, and return to the kitchen where he saw the dim golden glow of the Turnkey from around Davy's neck flowing under the door of the larder. Montezuma had been captured in the bottle because he was thieving the gold manufactured by the Elohim Lightworkers. During the several hundred years that he was captured in the bottle, he gained great knowledge and understanding of the gifts presented by the Turnkey.

Aturo silently unlocked the door to the storage food larder and noticed the glow around Davy's neck. He gently pulled the sacking off to discover the golden shell; the spirit of Montezuma knew that the Mollusc shell was a type of key that connected into a throne made of volcanic stone that was carved by the Pleiadians. The throne itself could be accessed through a hidden gateway above the rocky countryside township of Machu Picchu. The knowledge that he gained from the Pleiadian Lightworkers who had captured his spirit after his death made him realise that as his spirit existed inside a physical body, he could be transported back in time to his empire to relive his life as the famous Aztec King. After midnight, around 1.30am, the tribal community had all returned to their village to sleep. The solo characters left on the grassland were Molly and Flintlock. As they both gazed across towards the Liberty Bell, they noticed Pablo standing alone on the ship's bow. Flintlock rose from his position on the grass and began to walk back to the ship, as he felt that he needed to get some sleep in order to direct his crew members to carry out the huge number of jobs needed when daylight arrived, as he knew that strong commanding would be very essential to instruct the crew to disentangle all structural problems and mechanical errors on the vessel. So Flintlock returned back up to the main deck and as he walked past Pablo, he saluted him and strolled down into the hold to his sleeping quarters.

Montezuma forced Aturo to carefully take the golden shell from around Davy's neck. He then silently woke him up and put his hand over his mouth and dragged him out onto the kitchen bench, gagged him with a drying cloth and placed him inside one of the hessian sacks. Hurling the sack over his shoulder, he stealthily climbed down the ship's stern to a small rowing boat and began rowing to the shoreline to begin his passage to the

Elohim Throne. As he arrived on the beach, Aturo clasped hold of the sack with Davy inside, then he strolled beyond the cove to the foothills. Passing by Molly, Aturo deceitfully said that he was going up to the Inca citadel of Machu Picchu to find some more crew members to help carry out the everyday jobs on the Liberty Bell. Though in reality, the reason he was walking into the upper mountains was to find the aid of more men living in the granite stronghold that would help him to travel to the lost city of Eldorado and steal the gold.

While standing on the bow of the ship, in the cool morning air, Evangeline kept an eye on Aturo as she listened to his treacherous words of selfishness. Even though the cold air had suppressed the influencing energy of Montezuma to about half its potency, Aturo still appeared on edge.

In the stillness of the early morning, Evangeline worshipped the moon, because she knew that the Elohim Throne needed to be accessed through a hidden gateway above the Aztec township of Machu Picchu and the gateway could only be opened by the energy of the moon.

The gateway freely opens for seven days of each month governed by the power of the moonlight, three days prior to the full moon and three days after. By accessing the power of the throne on the full moon, a trip can be forecast to visit a maximum of six historical or future time phases, and at about 8.00pm, when the moon reaches a certain position in the night sky, the angle of moonlight deflects to unlock the door which can then be easily slid open; revealing the shimmering moonlight on the pathway and steps leading to the throne. Within the hidden stairway to heaven there are three stone figurines, two sentinel guardsmen and the throne master. When the light bathes the statues, they magically return to flesh to protect the entrance until the moon moves on roughly six to seven hours later, which turns them back to stone and locks the sliding door. The 'human beings' that conveyed the instructions on how to access the gateway were a reconnaissance party of three beings from the Pleiades whose roll it was to enter human bodies to establish a community at the chosen geographical longitude and prepare the local civilisation, thus structuring the time and place for the future arrival of the Elohim. After which, they were placed in the throne room as stone figurines to watch over and shield the secret channel, and block access of any evil beings that may create turmoil to other people, with intent to harm other races or transmit obtrusive or malevolent energy to the Pleiades.

The Elohim beings selected the geographic location of Machu Picchu for its strong masculine energy because the area attracts the softer female energy to create harmony, balance, devotion, respect and pure, unconditional love for each human being. After collecting yin – female wisdom – the Elohim reconnaissance team left the Planet Earth in the late 1600s. However, the Elohim Throne and the three stone figurine guardsmen remained in place for their return.

In order to gain access into the prophetic channel, a Turnkey is required. Only eight sets of two golden Mollusc shell Turnkeys were created by the reconnaissance group of Pleiadians for accessing future visions, past events and desired physical visitations. Only female Starseeds can access the gateway and sit on the throne at any time without the use of a shell Turnkey, as they are shrouded by the light of the moon which energises the force of the light to absorb the female knowledge, guidance and compassion. The wisdom that is immersed in the light then travels on the Photon Beam, onwards into the stratosphere and back to the planet where it is stored in a psychokinetic mind reservoir. Highly spiritual, humble and modest human beings can openly access the energy channel through the throne built by the Elohim, thus discovering where the most potent future Starseeds will be born.

If the person seated in the Elohim Throne wants to access the energy channel connecting to the Pleiadian Galaxy, a mantra needs to be recited which is shown in a relief carving on the wall of the pathway leading up to the throne and also the carving on the back of the throne.

At 3.00am, Aturo stomped up through the royal estate of Machu Picchu, where he mentally liaised with the spirit of Montezuma asking him to navigate the course to the Elohim Throne. On his arrival at the limestone gateway, the ship's Cook swung the sack off his shoulder and shook Tuli onto the ground. The autumn moon was in its first quarter of orbiting around the Planet Earth, setting at midnight, halting the moonlight power and closing the gateway. Stumbling alongside the concealed stairway Aturo discovered a hidden access into the area – ten metres above the throne. The opening gap between the rocks was so tight that Aturo couldn't pass his bulging body through it to gain entry to the legendary shrine temple and as the active spirit of Montezuma was still blocked, Aturo could not work out how to unlock the gateway.

Back on the Liberty Bell, Evangeline had psychicly observed Aturo's clumsy attempt to access the throne and she had felt the resentment and fury of Aturo as he was unable to enter the gateway. The daybreak time was now getting nearer for Han to perform his dawn meditation; Molly saw him walk up to the bow of the ship to converse with Pablo before he began his ritual.

Meeting up with Evangeline and Han on the ship's bow, Molly asked if he or she knew of any other method to gain access to the Elohim Throne. Evangeline replied:

"Good Golly, Miss Molly! Yes, there is another way of opening the gateway. You can use the power of the Turnkey by placing a command inside the shell, being the same method as asking the shell to teleport oneself."

With this knowledge, Molly leapt off the bow of the ship and flew eight kilometres across the panoramic valley leading up into the Andes Mountains. Soaring over the 15th century dry stone village of Machu Picchu, she saw Aturo talking with a group of three men about his desire to steal the gold from Eldorado and asking them if they would help him to find the City of Gold. Looking up at Molly's slurried presence in the misty mountains, two of the men thrust spears up into the sky at her, thinking that she was a prehistoric beast.

Flying swiftly beyond the iconic stone village, Molly hovered over the inner zone of the sacred temple where she saw Davy sitting on the throne. Carved in the shape of a pyramid temple, the throne was covered with relief carvings of holy symbols and mantric wordings to open the channel to the Pleiadian Photon beam.

Swooping down, she sat beside him, and began to tell Davy the method of commanding a request into the shell to unlock the gateway.

Thanking her optimistically, he laughed and began telling her about his desire to proceed on a visitation back to Cornwall. Molly was so excited by his plan that she asked if she could return with him to heal the school's history teacher, Miss Fanny

Gardener. Firstly, Davy informed Molly about his brief visitation back in time, where he discovered that the Aztecs had been endowed with an alchemical formula, explaining how to alchemise stone into gold. He committed the formula to the inside of the shell, remembering the procedure for the future when he would have the time to manufacture gold with his gracious super hero, Captain Ortuga. Getting up from the throne, Davy advised Molly how they would both travel back to Cornwall together:

"My Griffin Girl, I have learnt the knowledge of teleportation from the visions obtained from this golden Mollusc shell. A set of two Turnkeys are needed to travel because, when the traveller wants to visit a new destination, he places one of the Turnkeys into the throne and turns it clockwise for the future and anti-clockwise to visit the past. The other Turnkey must be taken on the journey to be used for one's return."

Davy then went on to inform Molly that whilst sitting on the Elohim Throne with the Turnkey inserted, visions would appear in the person's mind that related to the perceptive inspirations, compassion and humanitarian beliefs within the psyche of the individual.

Davy mentioned the visualisation that flashed into his mind of the occurrence of Francis Drake, stealing six sets of the shells from under the throne and taking them back to Penzance.

Memories are embedded into the Turnkey that is carried on the teleportation which is why a traveller can be taken to visitations within the memory of the golden shell and destination commands and requests can be verbalised by speaking into the shell. When returning from the destination, the Turnkey needs to be squeezed firmly and if it is just stroked or gently touched then the individual will visualise the most recent or aged memories contained in the shell. Davy only had the one Turnkey with him; the one that he had found that had fallen out of Francis Drake's bag, into the rock pool on the Cornwall beach at the front of the cave where Quinton lived. Davy now bent down to search under the throne trying to find the second shell. Privileged, without delay, he instantly found another Turnkey that matched his initial shell.

Looking onto the shimmering horizon, Evangeline and Han noticed the sun rising; in the distance, they could not see into the throne shrine because the gateway blocked their viewing. However, what they did see was Aturo standing at the gateway in between the two guardsmen. The mild heat of the morning sun roused the spirit of Montezuma, taking over the mind settings of Aturo.

Because of the closed gateway which was blocking Montezuma's access back to his Aztec empire, anger channelled into Aturo's mind as Montezuma made him pick up a rock and smash it onto the guard statues. The conflict act of annoyance broke a hand off one of the statues and a leg off the other. After the skirmish, Aturo stormed back down through the hills to the waterfront. Strolling over the gangplank, he entered the Liberty vessel and disappeared down into the galley.

Returning onto the throne, Davy clasped hold of Molly's hand and drew her onto his lap. Using the Turnkey that he had found under the throne, he carefully inserted it into a depressed fixture on the throne and turned it clockwise to expose visions of the future. Holding the other shell gave them both visions of the Penwright history classroom and the Blue-Ringed octopus wrapping its self around their teacher's wrist. As the power of the quarter moon was not flowing until midday, they could not teleport on the throne yet. Suddenly, a massive green light gushed inside the temple, Davy realised that the light was radiating from the Sledge Ray creature optimistically indicating that *it* would be able to safely transport them both back to Cornwall to the year of 1976.

Davy screeched excitedly to Molly on his lap:

"Whoo Whoo! My griffin girl, let's run back down to the beach and climb onto the Sledge Ray, as it will transport us back to the history class memory, that I have just envisioned."

Exiting the Elohim temple, Davy grabbed hold of both shells and ran up to the top of the shrine temple to slide through the rocks. Molly hovered up into the air above the temple and flew along with Davy down to the point on the beach front where the green light was glowing up from the ocean. The Sledge Ray was submerged in the water next to the Liberty Bell and when Davy arrived on the beach, he firmly held both Turnkeys and called out to the indigenous Sea Goat. The Sledge Ray rose up out of the water, Davy climbed upon its back and Molly lowered down from the sky to reside with Davy on their upcoming journey. Just as the Sledge Ray began to move forward into the ocean, the mermaid emerged out of the water; smiling, she handed a bottle of Phytoplankton super foods to Molly:

"Hello, young girl – Live your Life! This wonderful liquid is made from microscopic marine plants, which, when consumed, can produce the energy of longevity and it can also heal and strengthen all beings.

"Myself, whales, shrimps, sharks and jellyfish consume the aquatic herbs to help us to live forever."

Opening the bottle, Molly gulped two mouthfuls of the super food and passed the bottle to Davy, he then swallowed a mouthful too. Travelling with its light year energy, the Sledge Ray rode over the seven seas and seconds later, it landed on the Cornish beach front. Molly and Davy climbed down off its back and walked up the hillside to the Penwright Grammar.

Swiftly returning to Cornwall into the future of 1976, three years after Davy first left his hometown, he entered the history classroom with Molly. Walking into the classroom, Molly followed him down to the back of the room.

Lying with her head on her desk, Miss Fanny Gardener was in a subtle coma caused by the octopus venom and up behind her, on the blackboard was a cartoon drawing of the Blue-Ringed octopus dancing on its tentacles. Seeing the return of Davy and Molly, the classroom kids cheered and hollered out their welcoming expressions:

"Davy, welcome back to the best school in Cornwall, we have all missed your positive energy!"

The cheering stirred Miss Gardener from her coma. Molly quickly began to use her magical power to immediately heal her teacher, she got up, walked to the front of the class and passed the bottle of Phytoplankton to Miss Gardener. After slurping a teaspoon of the magic green liquid, within 30 seconds, Miss Gardener began to feel its healing power, detoxifying the venom out from her blood and allowing her energy to re-boost itself to motivate her knowledge of historical teachings:

"Molly Swanson, thank you. I owe you my life. Where did you buy this amazing medicine from, for I need some of it for my loveable pet Alsatian." Molly smiled back at her teacher.

Still 13 years of age, Davy sat at his desk and raved together in the 6th form classroom with his close friends Tim, Quinton and

Molly. Their history class went on for several hours, where they listened and viewed the historical world events spoken by Miss Gardener of malicious tyrants and their dark empirical voracity.

"1879 Anglo – Zulu conflict; 1939 Adolf Hitler; World War Two; 1975 the Pol Pot regime– forced labour and executions of the local populous; 1971 Idi Amin Dada – human rights abuses and extra judicial killings; 1964 Palestinean-Israel Conflict; 1974 Turkish invasion of Cypress."

At the end of the teachings, Davy felt tepid moisture dripping onto his ankle; bending under his desk, he saw the Alsatian dog with its sodden tongue aiming to lick at his calf muscles. With its jaw ajar, saliva was drooling out of the animal's mouth, trickling onto Davy's ankle:

"Excuse me, Miss Gardener, your pet Alsatian is under my desk, can you please call him to return to you? Then you could give him some of the Phytoplankton healing liquid."

Springing out from under the desk, the dog knocked into Davy, making his hand slide along the Turnkey flashing to a future visitation of the Syrian Conflict with ISIS which spawned from the Arab Spring of Jihadist Terrorism in 2011.

Davy saw a vision of himself, appearing about the age of 17, sitting with a chief jihadist, and the founder of the Islamic religion – Muhammad, innocently posing questions as to why the conflict had started and how it could be stopped. The chief said that the rebel conflict began after the Syrian government violently repressed a meek uprising; he would stop the armed war and killings with Syria if he was donated two billion pounds. The funding would help all the homeless people who were rebels, to build houses for them and make them happy and contented in their lives.

Davy saw himself writing down a section of the chemical formula that was given to him by the Aztecs. The formula described how to utilise universal energy to alchemise metals into gold. The chief was so delighted that he halted the rebellion warfare, surrendering on the following sun day of religion; issuing instructions to his Islamic military force to help himself and Muhammad transform their weapons, missiles and ammunition into gold, after which it was distributed throughout the land; bringing peace to Syria.

At 10.00am in the Greenpatch Cove, the day of sun was recognised by the Inca chieftain, Pachacuti, which inspired him to inform the bell ringers to play the watchtower bells and to invite Han over to the building to preach his sermon. Standing at the front of his community, Pachacuti gave an overview of the Taoist lecture:

"This sermon is not to be missed by any true believer or anyone with a passion for Chinese history and longevity; the bells are ringing to call everyone to the Greenpatch sermon."

Listening to the ringing bells notified Han that he should go to the watchtower to deliver his inspirational speech. He strolled through the Inca community which was worshipping the sun; passing on to the watchtower he met up with Pachacuti, who asked him to bring kindness to his community by explaining the methods of how they could remove irritation and aggression, save their energy and heal themselves. When Han made his way to the top of the watchtower, he realised that the distance between him and the community was quite great and that the congregation would not hear his voice clearly. Therefore, he declared a magical vow that empowered the strength of his voice; helping people all over the Greenpatch Cove to hear his words:

"Good Morning, you Shiny Happy People – I am going to tell you about how you can change your lives by opening the door to joy, acceptance and understanding, to live happily with all local beings, animals and global cultures. Gratitude is the most effective way to liberate your sense of happiness – thank you."

Hearing the introduction before the sermon, Ortuga called the seven pirates up from the hold to sit down with the Inca community. He commanded the pirates to apologise to the tribal natives for their aggressive behaviour when the Liberty Bell first docked in the portland of Puerto Caballas. The senior crew members then stood with their Captain on the ship's bow, listening to the secrets of ancient Taoism.

Beginning the sermon, Han described the pranic outline of three main parts of the human body that hold magical vibrations: the head, trunk and limbs. The trunk is curved like the moon; it houses all precious organs – heart, lungs, spleen, kidneys and bowels.

Air breathed and foods eaten, wander down into the trunk to upgrade the organs. Limbs are highly flexible and dexterous allowing us to move freely along creative and skilled pathways. The head is like the watchtower, it is carried by the trunk and limbs – thought seeds can be planted into the mind to grow into super thoughts to cultivate the land and the body, create beautiful artworks and serve others. When the mind converses with God, answers of truth and responding objectives relating to the energy of each individual bestow freedom, thus empowering and healing the being. After outlining the workings of the three parts of the body, Han expounded seven condensed thought seeds to summarise the flowing power of the miraculous energy to create human Super Heroes. The thought seeds Han informed from the watchtower were:

- When you are content to be yourself and you don't compare or compete, everyone will respect you.
- To be at peace – live in the present, now.
- Don't worry – be happy. The best fighter is never angry.
- How people treat you is *their* karma. When you judge another, you don't define them, you define yourself.
- Our own brain, our own heart is our temple; the philosophy is kindness.
- Enjoy the slow life – everyday.
- Learn to extend your love, even to your enemy.

The Incan congregation stood up, raised their hands into the sky to give thanks to Han for his sermon:

"Thank you, Han – thank you, my lord."

The passionate atmosphere of the blue sky above Greenpatch held an abundant number of white arcus wall clouds drifting from the ocean onto the beach over the hills to the top of the mountains.

At 12 noon, the autumn quarter moon raised up, spreading moonlight over the Incan society. Using his magic power, Han called down a cloud; it surrounded him in the watchtower. Lifting his body up into the white mass, he rode upon the cloud which took him back to the Liberty Bell. Stopping above the ship, Han stepped out from the cloud onto the crow's nest platform. The cloud moved on back to the hillside, exposing

Han, his appearance was clearly seen by the members on the bow, Captain Ortuga, Pablo, Flintlock, Sanchez and Amir.

They began clapping to thank him for the triumphant sermon that fruitfully sewed altruism into the minds of everyone.

Unaware of the sermon, Samson and Marley patrolled around the ship's hold and top deck with a whip searching for the Dutch slave driver, Wolfgang. The two African slaves were possessed with rage to take the life from the Dutch slave driver. Discovering Wolfgang, hiding in the timber rescue boat, Samson pulled him out from under the canvas cover and whipped him. Marley grabbed one of the oars, swung it at Wolfgang's head and knocked him over the boat; plummeting down onto a rock he broke his neck, slid into the water and drowned. Minutes after his death, facing down into the shallow water his body was attacked by fiddler crabs and spiny lobsters. Sensing the predator energy of Wolfgang, the mob of marine crustaceans bit into his flesh, stripping it off his bones to share with their aquatic companions, anemones, shrimps and barnacles; leaving little but the skeleton of Wolfgang laying on the rock.

Gushing into the water, Wolfgang's blood invited many other sea creatures to his body; racing from the ocean depth, a large Killer whale tried to take his body down to the seabed, to store the food for its family, but the skeleton magically crawled through the damaged timber hole into the ship's hull.

Washing across the hillside and up into the mountain regions, the moonlight energy opened the gateway to the Elohim stairway, vitalising the three stone figurines into living beings to watch over and shield the secret channel, and block access from any evil beings that desired to impact detrimental actions to other people or transmit obtrusive or malevolent energy to the Pleiades. Reverting from statues to human forms, the two gate sentinels suffered pain from the smashed amputation of their limbs by Aturo, one hand and one leg. Understanding that the moonlight would open the gateway to the Elohim Throne; the invisible king, Montezuma stepped out of the Cook's body and raced up to Machu Picchu. Barging past the two guardsmen, his spirit moved on to the stairway to the throne. Punching the throne master down to the ground, he then sat on the throne and was teleported back 200 years to his Empyreal Aztec kingdom.

Back on the Liberty Bell, Captain Ortuga and the crew members gathered together to nourish themselves with fun and laughter, drinking spiced ale and eating foods; having an afternoon meal of crabs, jacket potatoes and spinach. Aturo was very relieved to be rid of the Montezuma aggression, making him now feel great joy to all his companions.

Sitting down in the galley with the men, the main issue in Captain Ortuga's mind was what had happened to the Cabin Boy, Tuli. Even though Evangeline knew that Davy and Molly had transported themselves back to their Cornish hometown of Penzance, she kept silent. Retaining stability and balance of the ship's crew, Evangeline remained in her burly male disguise in order not to reveal her femininity to the males. For exposing her beauty and female compassion could launch competitiveness between the men to fight for her relationship. Knowing that she had told Juan Ortuga that she would guide him to the Elohim Throne that night, she left the gathering and went down to her cabin to have an afternoon nap.

Twilight shadows rose upon the ship and across the land, sending the Inca community back to their mud-brick homes. The moment in time was reaching 8.00pm, when Evangeline walked along to Ortuga's cabin to forward her Starseed knowledge of Machu Picchu and the Pleiadian Galaxy to him. Knocking on his cabin door, Ortuga opened it and asked her to remove her beard displaying her beauty to him.

Sitting together holding hands, Evangeline described the story of her Starseeded knowledge relating to the Elohim Throne, and how to transport oneself to the past, to the future and into the Photon Beam; to travel to the Pleiadian Galaxy to rally with advanced beings, gaining spiritual information that would help the world.

Born on the 18th of October, 1704, Evangeline was one of the primary human beings to naturally envisage peace, harmony and expansive understanding streaming from the Pleiadian Galaxy, quickening energy to spiritually evolve the Planet Earth to move away from primal aggression through war, massacre and terrorism. Each time, when the Photon Belt envelops the Planet Earth, spiritual beings would be born such as Jesus of Nazareth, Muhammad Abdullah and Siddhartha Gautama.

These extraordinary human individuals possess an innate, inner wisdom bestowed upon them from the universal intelligence which the Elohim desire to channel back to their planet to seed their society, further advancing their race with greater transcendence, compassion, understanding, and prophecy.

At 10.30pm, Evangeline told Ortuga that the moon that night was a Piscean full moon, in which case, it would be super to sit on the throne when the moon was at its most powerful and enter the Photon Beam to travel to the open cluster of Pleiadian stars. She then mentioned to Ortuga, that perhaps they should leave the ship soon and venture up to the mountains as the time needed to walk the eight kilometres, up to the Shrine took at least two to three hours.

"I think I may have advised you about the Elohim Throne before, on the night of your birthday. Even if a person sits on the throne and does not intend to travel to the past or the future – those beings consent admission of the Pleiadian spirituality to be channelled into their energy field, allowing their lives to be altered – to become children of God."

Leaving the ship, walking hand in hand across the gangplank down to the beach front, they mounted up onto Llamas to ride up towards the stone citadel of Machu Picchu. On reaching the temple gateway, Evangeline nodded kindly to the guardsmen, whose broken limbs had been re-grown by the moon's energy. Resonating with the future vision of altruism to help the world, the two Pleiadian guards welcomed her and Ortuga to the stairway.

Evangeline then led Captain Ortuga up the stairway to heaven. As they walked along the pathway towards the steps, she showed Ortuga the relief carvings, explaining their meanings and interpretation of how to enter the gateway in her absence. She also told him how to pass the two guards and seek direction and advice about the most dangerous places of visitation from the throne master whose roll it is to usher the seated traveller to their intended destination.

Passing up the stairs, they arrived at the ancient stone monument – the Elohim Throne. She explained to Juan about the monument, declaring that each Turnkey retained the memories of places visited, and, therefore, when the shell is just touched, images of the visitations are induced into the person's mind for likely exploration. A teleporter can take up to four colleagues along with them on the journey by placing their hands on the Turnkey. The second Turnkey should be taken along with them which when gripped and pressed returns their physicality to the energy foundation. If the person seated in the Elohim Throne wants to access the energy channel leading to the Pleiades, a mantra needs to be recited which is shown in the relief carvings on the wall of the pathway leading up to the throne and also into the back of the throne. Ortuga then sat on the throne and asked Evangeline to chant the mantra to take him to the Photon Beam:

"Thanks for helping me with this transportation, would you like to come with me so that we can both meet with the Pleiadian community?

Moving slowly behind the throne master Evangeline spoke to Ortuga saying that the first opening journey of anyone using the throne to take them along the Photon Beam to the Pleaides, where their spirit is embedded with knowledge, is brief and must be made alone. And that the journeys after the initial foundation of knowledge is when he could frequently meet up with the advanced beings to talk about numerous issues such as personal aggression, cultural hostilities and warfare. Ortuga smiled lovingly at her as she began to softly sing the mantra harmonically; layered with beauty, love and compassion, opening the galactic pathway to interconnect the Pleiadian system with the earth:

"T'Jen Yar Day
Beautiful Day, Beautiful Life
You need to Love Yourself, to Love The World
Show Me the Way to Love
Yar Day Ta M'kas…"

Darkness entered into the temple, surrounding Ortuga, then a glowing beam of sapphire light swirled around the monumental throne. The power of the light lifted the throne up towards the edge of the mountain side, sliding it onto a rock ledge.

Staring way out into the distant night sky, Ortuga saw a brilliant white star with the sapphire blue light circling around its luminary sphere. Sitting on the throne, Ortuga was drawn out into the darkness at the speed of light and as he headed towards the star; the throne transformed from solid rock into shimmering light. Zooming through the night sky, gravity made him enter into the Photon Beam with streaming beams of white and blue plasma flowing rapidly passed him along the pathway. Rolling around corners and curves inside the vortex tunnel, he passed by hundreds of miniature, polka-dot-patterned stars that implanted advanced knowledge of compassion and love into his mind.

Exiting from within the inspirational, sapphire streaming passageway, he sailed back into darkness. Again, focusing out in the distance, he re-envisaged the brilliance of the starlight that he saw initially from the mountain ledge above Machu Picchu. The size of the star seemed very modest, but in a matter of moments its size began to expand together with a rhythmic drumbeat of blasting flashes of white light; pulling him closer and closer to the globe.

A massive, explosive flash of colossal energy mimicked the action of a human breath, being the final exploit of the Pleiadian invitation to their universal address. As he entered the Pleiadian constellation, he observed brilliantly coloured cosmic islands inhabited with crimson, purple and blue light forms. As Ortuga exited from the Photon Beam, the Light-Throne form diminished, and returned back to monumental stone, then a statement of fantastic stimulation lectured by Han, entered into his mind:

"Your last breath takes you to eternity."

Channelling from the central planet, broad wisdom and compassion flowed into Ortuga's brain, progressing his mind to that of an advanced Elohim Lightworker with seeded knowledge from the star. After the cosmic happening, once again the throne set in motion, spinning around to transport him back to Machu Picchu.

During the return journey, stirring thoughts of loving impressions, implanted by Evangeline entered his mind.

Evangeline's inner spiritual wisdom acted like a pure channel of intuitive knowing, giving her the ability to open her mind to allow peace and loving energy to flow from and to the Pleiades.

Wisdom and female compassion is channelled out of the Starseed beings on the nights of a rare planetary alignment such as Aquarian Dawnings, opening galactic pathways to interconnect star systems. Thirty minutes after departing from the Pleiadian Galaxy, the throne landed back onto its position in the temple at the top of the stairway. Evangeline had stayed there, talking with the throne usher about the future vision of Juan Ortuga. They both welcomed Ortuga back to the Planet Earth, sensing and harmonising so well with his new light energy; Evangeline embraced her arms around Ortuga, cuddled him and kissed his lips. The transcending passion founded their relationship, holding hands they walked down the stairway. The time was nearly 4.30am in the morning, as the moon power had begun to wane, diminishing the Pleiadian reconnaissance team of the two guardsmen and the throne usher back to stone figurines.

The two Llamas were sleeping on the grassland at the front of the gateway. Thinking that they should reward the animals with food, the loving couple woke the creatures, removed the straw from their backs and allowed them to feed. They then climbed upon them ready to ride back down to Greenpatch Cove. Suddenly, Juan realised that he should sit back on the throne to seek the lost City of Gold, Eldorado. The gold would give much needed help to the Inca community, and would also help him assist other needy communities.

Chapter Twelve
After the Goldrush

Before returning to the Elohim Throne, Evangeline told Ortuga about the moonlight dream she had had whilst he was away in the Pleaides:

"The Age of Aquarius – The dream was about the future when the solar energy of the Planet Earth is linked into the energy of the Photon Beam. This particular planetary alignment occurs only once every two thousand one hundred and fifty years. The energy seeks to bring forth a new Saviour for the age of mankind – which I believe is you. Can I be the Slave to Your Love?"

Holding a Turnkey, Ortuga sat down on the throne. As the historical story of Eldorado was in his mind, the shell channelled a series of thoughts and visions to him regarding the city's foundation, construction and the location; he also visualised the indigenous Aztec people creating tonnes of gold with the alchemical formula of transforming stones and rock into the precious metal.

Waiting at the temple gateway, the two Llamas heard Evangeline's declaration. Humming to each other, they trumped into the entrance and trotted up the stairway. The humming of the Llamas at the gateway echoed out into the hillside, moving the ship's dogs and the baby lamb across the gangplank, up into the mountains. Reaching the temple crest they brayed loudly, calling out to Ortuga and Evangeline to climb up onto their backs.

Thunderous hooves and pounding hearts, took them down the hillside. Racing along, the animals met up with the Llamas at the foot of the hillside; excitedly, the three dogs, the terrier, retriever and sheepdog, blathered with the Llamas about why they were carrying the ship's Captain. The Llamic reply informed the dogs that Ortuga was going to become the new saviour of the world, progressing from his identity of a legendary super hero to a global spiritual leader. Arriving on the beach front, Ortuga entered the ship and threw some food down to all their animal friends.

As the morning progressed Han noticed two strong men walking out from the dense woodland on the northern part of the cove. Two lumberjacks carried the trunk of an oak tree, dropping it down onto the sand close to the Liberty Bell. Han asked the pirate men to haul the tree trunk up onto the ship decking so then he could start his creative line of work to carve the mermaid figurehead and replace the existing female sculpture smashed into by the pirate sloop vessel. Two of the pirates climbed down the anchor rope, unchained the anchor and re-tied the rope around the tree trunk. Hauling the tree trunk upwards, the five other pirates span around the capstan that was winding the rope to raise the tree; as it arrived close to the railings, the other two pirates joined together with their mates, adding strength to hoist the tree over the railings onto the bow. Han shook hands with each pirate, giving thanks for their assistance; then they stomped down to the food galley for a snack.

In the distance, Han noticed the wife of the Inca chieftain, Sofia, talking with the lumberjacks.

Whistling over the bow he drew her attention, calling her across the gangplank. Striding below the ship' hull, she met up with Evangeline dressed up as Pablo Medellin. Evangeline walked up to the decking with her and they both stood with Han to talk about his idea that he had imagined for carving:

"Hello, ladies! The three dimensional shape of the new figurine I have in my mind is a blend of three beautiful women; You two, and the mermaid who was living in the bilge water down in the ship's hull."

As most of the crew were on the top decking preparing the vessel ready to sail away, Han led the two women down to his cabin. He asked them to remove their clothing so he could see the physical shapes which he could then replicate onto the wooden oak trunk. So by reproducing their naked beauty onto the ship's figurehead, this would flow inspiration to the male seafarers, encouraging them to pleasurably sail the vessel around the seven seas.

Inside the quiet cabin, the two beautiful ladies undressed. Evangeline removed her male disguise, the beard, muscular paddings and the uniform revealing her torso. Even though Han sought to only replicating the head of Sofia, watching Evangeline, she too proceeded to remove her clothes, grass skirt and cotton blouse. Standing gracefully in front of Han, the women smiled, giving a blissful posture to their bodies. Han returned smiles to both of them, for he was attracted to the Peruvian Goddess, Sofia. Placing the images into his creative mind, combined with the tail of the mermaid, he thanked them both for their serene confidence to become nude:

"Gosh, the beaming form of your bodies will create a strong magnetic centre of attention to all ships passing by the Liberty Bell. Because of your exuberant beauty, I don't think any military vessels will attack our ship. Thank you."

Kneeling down onto the floor, Han worshipped the female beings, for their energy radiated calm desire around his cabin. Admiring the energy, he placed his hands onto their feet, cradled their ankles, closed his eyes and let his appreciative energy of adoration flow into their bodies. His spiritual, compassionate link to the idealistic doings of how animals bonded with other dogs stamped into his mind, the mode dogs used greeting to each other was the action of sniffing at all erogenous and highly odorous regions on their bodies. Following the insight authority, he relished the smell of Evangeline's feet, then stood up and placed his nose into each of the two girl's armpits to breathe the intense body odour into his nostrils. A wide smile appeared on Han's face, moving around in his head was a contented sensation stemming from the fondness their beauty and smellings. Pursuing the final canine expression of dogs, he poked his tongue out of his mouth and licked the skin on their forearms. Because smells bring memories from the past into the mind, he knew that when humans grew to higher levels of spirituality, they joyfully bonded with smelling all earth life forms of plants, liquids, pets, nature dwellings and odours flowing out from bodies of other humans and themselves.

After the channelling and aromatic deeds, he thanked the women and left the cabin, strolled up to the main deck to use a hatchet axe to create the basic, solid form of the figurehead. Noticing that a pirate was sitting behind the broad tree trunk, Han asked him to remove the existing, damaged figurehead that was still attached to the bow. Clumping the axe heavily into the oak trunk and cutting large chunks of wood away, Han produced the basic shape of the solid foundation block of the merged three female forms.

Then to complete the final carving of the physical forms of each body, he used a cutlass and his magic. By using the grouping of the mermaid tail, Evangeline's body and Sofia's head, the finished female sculptured figurehead looked magnificent. Having removed the damaged figurehead, the pirate men mounted the new carved figure onto the ship's bow.

Together with the Peruvian Goddess, Sofia, Evangeline returned to the top deck in her male disguise outfit to view the finished sculpture. Leaning over the railings, they looked down at the wooden form and smiled at the replication of their physicality. As they did not know that Pablo was a women disguised as a man, the pirates thought that Pablo was attracted by the naked body of the figurehead which made him smile compellingly at the sculpture:

"Hey, Pablo. Where is the woman that Han has carved her body image into the sculpture, do you know her?"

Han then left the front of the ship and went down into the bilge hold to find the areas that needed sealing with tar; he began fixing the damaged timbers. To remove the moulded timber on the outside of the hull, he crept through the damaged hole to work on the outside of the ship.

After Han left the top deck, Flintlock commanded the pirates to go down into the shallow waters of the dry dock to scrap off all the barnacles stuck to the hull. Understanding that the next day Ortuga wanted to sail off into the ocean, Flintlock told the pirates that their work must be finished by the afternoon. Before heading down to the shallow waters near the shingle beach front, the men marched down into the hold to shift the ballast weight to heel the ship over to the right-hand side. With this sudden action, Han tumbled over and was pushed back through the hole by a rock that banged against the hull, where the angle of the ballast's heeling locked him into the bilge area below the top decking.

Exposing the barnacles to the intense heat of the sun, dried the marine crustaceans, making it easier for the men to scrap them off the hull. Several hours later after scouring the timber, the men returned down into the hold to move the ballast, weighing the vessel over to the opposite left-hand side. Now that the damaged section of the ship's hull was re-appearing, Han began to remove the damaged timber planks but because the weight of the ship had crunched down onto a rock, the hole had become much larger. Han's advanced carpentry skills let him remove the damaged timber, replacing the planks and strengthening the hull to increase the ship's speed on its next journey.

Whilst working, he saw the mermaid, Marina, swirling around under the water, together with a school of highly-coloured tropical angel fish and two dolphins. She rose up from the water and spoke to him in a holy manner:

"Hola, Oriental Magician. The sculpture you have magically carved is fantastic, it has such charming beauty and attraction that I don't think any enemy ships would attack you."

The sun dried the side of the vessel so well, it encouraged the pirates to clean off the barnacle colonies and fouling sea moss from the timber sections that were submerged during the ship's ocean travels.

Because the afternoon was getting closer to twilight, Han quickly carried on working to finish the repair job. Swimming past the group of pirate men who were scraping off the organisms from the hull, the mermaid swam out to the depth of the ocean, down to a rock grotto in the reef that was stored with treasure that she had moved out from a sunken ship. One of the pirate men who was helping remove the barnacles slid down off the hull and dived into the ocean; grabbing hold of her tail he was taken down into the cavern. As the aquatic environment held no access to oxygen the dwelling was so deadly, it collapsed his lungs and stole his life. Then the body of the dead pirate slowly floated up to the top of the water.

Clasping hold of the body, the mermaid carried it back to Han who was sitting on the outside of the hull tarring the timber to seal the planks together. She left the pirate on a rock near the beach front and swam back to her dwelling.

Catching sight of the auric-coloured band of black light surrounding the body, Han realised that the spirit had not yet exited the body of the pirate. Han quickly used magic to send power into his open mouth to resuscitate the physical energy, and introduce sound and vibration into the black aura to subdue the past life problems and unreleased anger indicated by the colour of his aura. Suddenly the wide eyes of the pirate man glinted and standing up on the rock he put his hands together and bent down to worship Han, thanking him for giving life to his corpse.

Inside the ship, the other pirate men were lifting up the ballast, resetting the weight to its original position to balance the vessel on the water. Carried by the wind, the Liberty Bell slowly drifted about a kilometre from the cove, out from the dry dock to the ocean reef where the mermaid secretly hid the treasures in her cavern. To prevent the ship from drifting further out into the ocean, Captain Ortuga asked the two African men to hold the ship in its position by lowering the anchor down into the sea bed so it could be securely anchored until the following morning.

Around midnight while most of the crew slept, a flock of Brazilian vampire bats circled around the main mast gazing down at the ship's three dogs, who were sleeping on the bridge with the baby lamb.

Flickering shadows of the bats' flapping wings silhouetted from the moonlight bounced around below the mast and onto the bridge, waking up the dogs. The stroboscope form of flashing light upset the animals who were still lying on the roof, as they closed their eyes and tried to return to sleep. The vampire bats soared down from the night sky, sunk their teeth into the dogs, sucking blood out of their bodies to satisfy their appetite for oxygen and nutrients. The dogs leapt up and yelped at the bats, barking loudly to stop the attacks. The noise brought Sanchez out from his cabin, up to the top decking, for he wanted to make the bats fly away so that his crew could remain asleep so they would gain strength for the ocean journey tomorrow. Gazing upwards at the bats, he climbed up the main mast and sat on the yardarm, swinging his cutlass around into the flock, slashing into their bodies, forcing them to soar up into the mountains to settle back into their cave dwellings. Sanchez then placed his finger to his lips and whispered to the dogs to become calm and quiet:

"Shoosh, boys! Now go back to sleep, and in the morning, I will ask the ship's Physician to check your bodies for any dangerous bites from those hungry vampire bats. Goodnight – sleep tight."

The following morning, the sun rose from behind the citadel of Machu Picchu. Waking up at 7.00am, the dogs noticed that the lamb had a tiny cut on its upper leg, where a cluster of beetles were nesting in the animal's long-haired coat, eating the flesh at the edge of the cut. Gnashing its teeth, the security sheepdog blew the insects from the baby lamb and flicked them off the bridge roof. The four animals then ambled down to the main decking, waiting for the whole crew to arrive after they had their breakfasts.

At 8.30am, Captain Ortuga was the first person to make his way up to the top deck. He called the animals over to him and stroked their backs and he gave the lamb a little bowl of rice with milk. Minutes later, the rest of the ship's crew arrived to listen to his talk about the new journey which the ship was about to embark on. The present crew consisted of the two Africans, seven pirates and the six recruited senior officers.

Ortuga began his announcement of clarification, explaining his newly attained advanced Pleiadian knowledge of the awareness of kindness and how it is the most important power that can help all global communities:

"Bonan matenon! Welcome to my address today, we are going to sail to the lost City of Gold, Eldorado.

The sun is filling the sky and shining above you all. The reason why we are searching for gold is to manage the welfare of vulnerable people on islands around the Pacific."

For 25 minutes, the Captain's speech included several declarations of inspirational altruism, sewing seeds into the minds of his crew to comfort and enrich their lives so they would blissfully help him to help everyone needing caring and support. The first statement underlined the fact that pioneering adventures give freedom, happiness and joy to the travellers. The last statement indicated that the resolutions that serve your highest self are ruling motions that are aligned to each individual's unique purpose and guarantee rewards far greater than stolen riches and deceptive funds of provoked criminal fraud. Juan Ortuga then comforted his crew by telling them that he would donate riches from any discoveries of gold and treasures to each of them, reducing their levels of stress and anger:

"Adventures with nature take you high. Let's head out onto the ocean highway and then onto the Amazon River which leads to Eldorado. If we discover the gold then I will give some to each one of you."

Glancing around the group of men, Captain Ortuga noticed that his Cabin Boy was no longer in his crew.

Ortuga spurted out a wailing question:

"Has anyone seen Davy Tullman? I need his assistance to wash my clothes, to station him up in the crow's nest to view any dangers, to advise myself and to help all of you."

Raising the anchor, the capstan was swiftly turned around by the pirate men. The Liberty Bell was then drawn out by the wind through the heads onto the Pacific Ocean, sailing four hours south to the opening of the Islay Province estuary. The tidal estuary flowed into the river Amazon, leading to the massive lake – Lago Titicana. When the ship entered the river mouth, Sanchez began playing his guitar together with Samson, who played on the steel drum in harmony. The final leg of the journey took another three hours, sailing inland to the Lake District at the base of the Andes.

Finally around 4.00pm the Liberty Bell arrived at Lake Titicana. Spread around the lake were cereal crops of wheat and corn grown by the local villagers. Within the grain fields were several crop circles created by artistic extraterrestrials.

All the crew looked around at the circles, trying to work out what declarations or formulas the patterns indicated.

Before the sun set, Captain Ortuga headed the ship over to the sparkling waterfall that was shown to him when he sat on the Elohim Throne. The falling water streamed down from the Andes Mountains, forming a curtain that veiled the entrance to the City of Gold.

Settling nearby the waterfall, the Liberty Bell lowered its anchor to secure its docking position. The reason Ortuga moored his ship so close to the waterfall was that when the gold is found, the heavy loadings could be carried onto their vessel nearby without tearing cartilages, straining muscles or damaging the spines of his crew. The reason he did not want his crew injured was because they still had a lot of work to do, sailing the ship around the Pacific to distribute the gold to needy communities.

He knew that the best time to enter through the waterfall to find the gold would be in the morning, after sun rise at about 6.00am which would give his crew renewed strength and many hours of daylight to search for and load the gold onto the Liberty Bell.

Together with the two African men, Aturo began making an extraordinary supper for the crew members with the remaining foods that he had in the galley. The meal consisted of wheat dough and toppings – peri peri chicken, Spanish onions, tomatoes, green peppers, garlic, olives, basil plus goat's cheese. The foods were layered onto the dough to make a batch of delicious pizza flatbreads.

Earlier on route to the lake, Amir had advised Aturo to also make a health drink for the crew. So the Cook was busy blending milk and the inner bark taken off ancient Pau D'arco trees on the hillside of Greenpatch Cove as well as preparing the pizza flatbreads for the hungry men.

Amir was busy healing the cuts on the animals inflicted by the attacking vampire bats by applying a traditional, antibacterial liquid that he had distilled from the same tree bark when the ship was moored on the waterfront at Greenpatch Cove. Thanking him for healing the bites, the dogs licked his face. Inspired by the dog's action, the baby lamb rubbed her head along the side of Amir's face and licked his forehead. Before the main course of pizzas were brought up to the decking, the Africans were excitedly enjoying themselves with the knowledge that Ortuga would be giving free gold to them on the following day. Hence the mood of the crew was relaxed and carefree and the troop of men gathered on the top decking and began playing their instruments in an antipasto music mode.

Flintlock on his drum, Sanchez playing guitar, Amir – trumpet and Han with his pan flute, banging their feet on the timber decking, the pirate men clasped each other's hands and spun around Captain Ortuga in a rowdy circle:

"Hoy – Hoy – Hoy…"

Hearing the rhythmic sound of music, Aturo grabbed hold of his violin and walked up to the top deck to join in with the men, playing his violin in an artful finger picking South American style.

When the pizzas had finished cooking, Aturo told the Africans to serve the food and drink to everyone on the main decking. Just after he had left the galley, the food was brought up to the top deck; the pumping music of the drums then came to a volume standstill so the men could eat the sumptuous feast.

While he had preparing the pizzas, Aturo had scoffed raw foods and was not hungry; therefore, he wanted to play a beautiful violin love song to entertain the crew. The music that he played followed the rhythm played on a base trombone that was found by Amir under the bed in his cabin. Aturo inserted the tune of an ancient Spanish song called *La Isla Bonita*. Large, feathered birds flying in the sky tweeted along with the music.

The moonlight shone down onto the lake, fluttering around on top of the waves, spotlighting fish swimming in motion with the Latino rhythm. Dressed in her brawny male disguise, Evangeline strolled around the ship's railings; looking down into the lake waters at the fish, she noticed that the moonlight was penetrating deep down to the bottom of the lake, illuminating the naturally occurring Bolivian Moonstones around the ship. Trying to work out the reasoning why the moon was highlighting the moat region around the ship, she imagined that the power of the moon was attracted to the charismatic sound of the music surging into the night air.

The moonlight energy amplified into the silicate sea crystals, creating them into the iridescent Moonstones with the ability to heal personal energy. Grouping together in a choir, the dogs sat howling to the music as the pirates dived over the railings to swim with the fish that were, bobbing around the ship.

Trotting along from the hillside and following the stream of water that was flowing down to the waterfall, a small group of Llamas halted at the edge of the lakeside and gazed across at the ship. The native animals thought that the barking dogs were inviting them to dinner. The senior officers, Flintlock and Sanchez, had collected the left over foods and were throwing some to the animals and tossing the rest down to the fish.

The food attracted more creatures to the lakeside; Chinchillas, small rat type rodents. They bounded into the water, swam to the anchor rope, climbed up into the ship and raced down to hide in the hold.

Overhead, the large birds soared down to the ship's decking, perching on the yard arms and railings. Sanchez told his senior mates the impressive large birds were native, South American Condors. Whilst standing on the ship's bow, Flintlock gathered together with Ortuga as they noticed a group of three Galapagos sea turtles had joined the pirates in the lake water, searching for the pizza leftovers. When passing by any fish, the turtles opened their mouths and gobbled them down into their stomachs. Flintlock then turned his gaze to the base of the waterfall curtain, where a golden light glowed from within the water. He then told Ortuga that the light appeared to have the same radiance as the bottle of golden liquid light that he had collected from the waters at the port of Valparaiso:

"Captain, look Boss! That light is coming from behind the waterfall on that rock ledge over there. I think it is channelled from the moon."

As the pirates were swimming around the boat and Aturo was still playing solo love songs on his violin, Evangeline had gone down to her cabin to rest. Just as she was drifting into a deep sleep, the noise of the animals all talking with each other woke her up. She then unfastened the cabin porthole, stretched out through the opening and by using her Starseed energy, she lifted up a cluster of Moonstones. Reaching the surface of the water, she clasped a handful of the luminous gems, with the rest sinking silently back down into the lake.

One of the pirates swam under the bow; Captain Ortuga hollered down to him to enter behind the waterfall to try and find the source of the light essence:

"Hello there, buddy! Can you carefully tread upon those rocks and enter behind the waterfall, for if you find the source of the light, it might help us find the entry point to Eldorado?"

The pirate rose up from the water, pulled himself onto a rock ledge covered with slippery green algae; sliding through the water, he tumbled down into the depth of a stone valley that was concealed behind the water curtain. His sudden movement rolled the bottle through the waterfall onto the rock ledge.

Flintlock noticed that the light was in the same, ancient glass bottle that he had taken from the port at Valparaiso. Realising that the bottle contained the spirit of Montezuma, he walked away from the ship's bow down to the cabin where his mate Pablo was sleeping soundly, surrounded with moonstones and snoring softly like a woman.

Captain Ortuga remained on the ship's bow, facing the Eldorado waterfall, when one of the Galapagos turtles crawled upon the rocks and clawed at the bottle. Sliding the bottle on the algae, it toppled down, smashing onto the rocks below, next to one of the turtles. The glowing spirit of Montezuma flowed out into the darkness of the night sky; it stood proudly at the front of the waterfall, then it channelled itself into the turtle. The aggression of the Aztec King made the creature leap back into the water and swim towards the pirates, where it began crunching its mouth heavily into their upper bodies to remove their hearts and take their life force from them. Only one of the six men swimming survived the deathly incident; climbing up the anchor rope to the main deck, he crawled down to the hammock berth to recover from the frightening ordeal. The five bodies floating around in the water were quickly dragged down into the lake by a group of sharks. Noticing the sharks' ferocious appetite for any sea creatures and humans, in fear of their demise, the other two turtles swam away from the ship to the edge of the lake. Looking for a safe haven away from the sharks, they moved awkwardly onto the land, where the heavy creatures plodded along to a crop circle illuminated by the moonlight. After arriving at the circular labyrinth, the two turtles made their way along the spiralling path and rested in the centre point. Watching the movement of the creatures, Amir departed from the ship and ran bare footed into the crop circle.

Sensing the energy of spiralling currents, he cautiously made his way into the centre, and stood at the edge of the inner circle. Treading on the alien ploughed soil, he felt rubble shingles under his feet. Bending down, he saw chunks of raw citrine gemstones with energy spinning around inside their centres. Collecting handfuls of the yellow pigmented stones, Amir placed them into the pockets of his trousers and jacket; then he returned back to the ship. Passing through the entry to the crop circle, he felt knowledge flowing from the crystals into his psyche. Apparently, the knowledge had entered into the stones from the universal power that had initially set the patterns of the crop circles. The higher calling knowledge that flowed into Amir's psyche formed altruistic testimonials of how to be more caring to others.

Barely alive, one of the pirate bodies floated up from the water depth and drifted to the edge of the lake where he rested in the shallow water, with his hand over his heart. An octopus suddenly darted over to the pirate, clung itself around his waist, pulled his hand away from his heart and pushed in one of its tentacles to drain blood out of his body.

Knowing that he would soon pass away, he called out to one of the Llamas:

"Knowing there is divine energy in all life forms, do you want my life? If you do, then take it away from me now."

The Llama placed its head over the dying pirate's mouth, quickly suffocating him; the physical energy moved into the Llama, with the pirate's emerald green, auric soul flowing up into the night sky, returning to the universe.

Upset by the loss of the dead pirates, Captain Ortuga began sniffing and coughing. To veil his gentleness and sensitivity, he stomped noisily below the decking, down to his quarters. Inside the cabin, he pulled opened the drawer under the wooden table and clasped hold of a black velvet cloth wrapped around the shell Turnkey that he had brought back after his sitting on the Elohim Throne in the temple above Machu Picchu. Lying down on the blankets of his bed, he unwrapped the Turnkey and spoke into the opening of the shell:

"Can you please inform me why the spirit of Montezuma has reappeared? The female Starseed, Evangeline, told me that the Aztec King travelled back to the past, remaining in his royal kingdom to reclaim his commanding of the empire."

Visions explaining the occurrence quickly entered Ortuga's mind. The insights notified him that even though Montezuma did go back into the past, he did not make any changes to his life pattern.

After his death, the spirit of Montezuma had been captured by the Pleiadians, who locked it into the glass bottle. Picturing some of the repeated dates and timings, the bottle could originally be found floating around in the lake or at the base of waterfall gateway. But after 100 years, it was washed along the river Amazon to the port of Valparaiso by a strong current. However, the repeated occurrence did have a minor change by the stronger current hiding the bottle in the rock pool waters behind the Liberty Bell; therefore, no one took it out of the water.

On a gravitational full moon, the Aztec memory of the Montezuma spirit contained in the glass forced the bottle to spring out of the rock pool back into the sea current, returning along the Amazon River to the Eldorado waterfall, where it remained at the aquatic curtained entry to the City of Gold, until the conflict occurred with the Galapagos sea turtle.

Understanding the mystical explanation, Ortuga wrapped the velvet back around the Turnkey to veil the connections, and he fell asleep. In the still of the night, around 2.00am, a nightmare woke him. The story content of the terrifying dream was about Davy Tullman, and the Galapagos sea turtle which the spirit of Montezuma had stepped into.

Tuli was riding on the creature around the lake and entered through the waterfall gateway down into the valley to the Eldorado village. The Montezuma spirit powered the turtle to carry Tuli to the secret location of the hidden gold, all of which was then transported up a stone path by the villagers, who were loading it into a Spanish military ship on the lake side. Every one of the villagers boarded onto the ship and then sailed out of the lake to enter the river Amazon. Swimming at the front under the ship's bow, the turtle guided the ship along the river out into the ocean. As the ship passed through the mouth of the river the turtle shook Tuli off its back and then led the vessel toward a barrier reef of sharp jagged rocks. Ramming into the reef, the hull of the ship smashed open, revealing a massive hole in the timber planks.

Rapidly sinking into the ocean, the ship took every crew member to their death, with not one soul surviving; Tuli was also pulled down into the ocean from the massive swirling pressure of the ship's whirlpool – where he too lost his life in the depths of the ocean. Again, to bring the calming truth into his mind, Ortuga spoke into the Turnkey:

"Davy is a kind-hearted boy from the English county of Cornwall. Let me know where he is, for I want him to be with me to help deliver his kindness to those less fortunate around the world."

Images of Davy flooded into Ortuga's mind, which made him smile lovingly at the happenings. He could see that Davy was joyfully spending time with his family in the cave opening on the beach of Penzance; where he was gathered together with his beautiful Indian mother, Parvihn, his political father, Joseph, and his little sister, Jasmine. They were all standing in the cave where Francis Drake had hidden the golden shell Turnkeys and a sack of treasures. Parvihn was so happy that her son had returned to his hometown, she asked him where he had been travelling to:

"Davy, I have missed you, and your sister has missed your fun with her, playing imaginary games, hide and seek, jokes and board games. Did you travel to South America to help transport Chilean refugees back to Cornwall?"

Davy cuddled with his mum and sister, then shook hands with his father. Shaking his head, he was laughing so happily that he wondered whether he should spend the rest of his life with his family. His mother took hold of his hand and led him along the sand to the back of the cave, introducing him to a refugee family from Chile:

"This young boy here is my son. His favourite legendary hero is Robin Hood. He has been away for some time, I have just asked him if he had travelled to South America to help the refugees."

Davy shook hands with the Chileans. He then replied to his mother, but he didn't tell her that he was teleported 200 years back to the past:

"Yes, Mum, I have been in the continent of South America working as a Cabin Boy with a ship's Captain. I have discovered lots of treasures which I will give to you to help this family and the many other homeless people who live in Cornwall."

Davy moved behind the rock, searching for the bag of golden shells and the treasure, which were hidden on a rock ledge one metre above his head. He carefully placed his foot on a large rock and stretched upwards to look on the ledge, where he found a leather bag of Turnkeys camouflaged with green sea moss growing all over the outside of the bag. Slowly, he pulled the bag off the ledge and lowered it down to the sand. Sitting cross-legged next to the bag, he glimpsed into the water moat flowing around the rock. Surrounded by anemones and sea shells, he noticed the brass handle of the wooden treasure chest that was protruding out of the sand. Sliding his arms down into the water, he grabbed hold of the handle and yanked the chest up, out of the sand.

His mother had moved around the rock to see what he was up to, she looked at the chest with utter amazement.

Using his super magical power taught to him by Han, Davy unlocked the side clips, opening the lid revealing antique objects – gold, silver and jewels. Cradling an armful of the treasures, he walked back round to the Chilean family, sharing the treasures out with them to benefit citizenship within his home village of Cam Mellyn. He gave his sister, Jasmine, a lovely pearl necklace and his father a leather pouch full of pirate gold coins. Davy then opened the door leading up to the guest house, welcoming the refugees to his mother's world of peace and devotion. The people walked on past Davy and up the stone stairway. His father placed Jasmine on his back and also walked onto the stairway, leaving Davy alone with his mother. Embracing his mother, Davy whispered in her ear, telling her what he would do next:

"Mum, I have so much love for you and your vision to help the world. So I need to travel back to Peru to find lots of treasure that I can bring back together with my love for you."

Hearing Jasmine calling down the stairway, Parvihn kissed her son and stepped into the doorway to follow her husband. As Davy placed the treasure chest on the steps; Parvihn turned to him and said:

"Thank you Davy, my life is your life – you are a special divine being who inspires others to seek their highest truth. You have all my love."

Joseph then returned down the stairs to collect the treasure chest, and after Davy said goodbye to his father, he closed the door leading up to the guest house. He then sat for a while by himself in the darkness of the grotto, watching shooting rays of multi-coloured lights flowing into the cave opening.

Returning to the entrance, he clasped the leather bag of Turnkeys and ambled out to the beach front. Sitting on rocks outside the cave were his three amusing best mates, Quinton, Tim and the magical Molly Swanson, who were laughing at the light beams dancing around on the horizon like a universal disco nightclub. The scattered lights appearing in the northern night sky were streaming from the mania of the Aurora Borealis, that was beaming down on the four friends, who swirled around, waving their hands back and forth, disco dancing on the sand.

At the border of the ocean beach front, the Sledge Ray surfaced up from the water, the beams of light flowing from the Aurora Borealis were drawn into the body of the creature, energising its strength, giving it capability to carry the four teenagers back into the past. Sitting down with his mates, Davy told them about the creature's ability to transport them all back to meet up with Captain Ortuga. The marine Sledge Ray ducked down into the ocean below and darted out to the horizon; bouncing out from the water, it flew up to hide in the Cornish hillside of Portsmouth.

Davy and his mates danced into the cave home of Quinton and laid down on the soft sandy floor, falling asleep together in friendship with the acceptance and belief of each other's characters.

Ortuga was empowered by his satisfying vision of Davy and his mates, thinking that if Davy did return to South America with his three friends, the teenage group could become the new deckhands to prepare and maintain the ship before, and after its journeying around the globe.

On the lake close to the Bolivian border, the morning dawn appeared, inspiring the Liberty crew to enter the waterfall and begin searching for the gold in the city of Eldorado. Ortuga advised the surviving crew members, his six senior officers, the two Africans and the pirate deckhand who escaped from the killings of the turtles to mount onto the anchor rope. All the men stood by the side of the ship, on the portside and placed the gangplank across to the rock ledge at the foot of the waterfall. Ortuga then ran a command to his men:

"Proceed through the waterfall with caution and open minds, as we all search for the gold and allow the dogs to walk with you as they are able to sniff out the hidden treasures, especially the Golden Retriever dog that belongs to Tuli."

Following Ortuga, sliding down the rope, the crew were directed to the side of the waterfall where the air opening allowed the men to walk carefully through to the back of the waterfall curtain without getting soaked by the descending water. After stepping on the rock ledge, and gliding across the front of the curtain then entering the rear side where the ledge was dangerously narrow, the men halted. Only a group of three people could comfortably place themselves on the ledge at the one time; if more pressed into the group, someone would be surged off the ledge down into the valley. The first united group of three was Ortuga with his two African mates, Marley and

Samson. Behind the threesome, Sanchez was yelling orders over to the two black men, and then he squashed into the group. His expanded physical bulk made them both fall off the ledge, similar to lemmings falling off clifftops, tumbling down the rock slope to the cushioning grass land base of the valley.

Ortuga reasoned with Sanchez to remain on the ledge, to help the other six crew members move along by grasping their hand and lowering their weight down onto the safety pathway that led to the valley. Pleasantly agreeing with the Captain's command, Sanchez put his head through the siding of the waterfall and called out to the rest of the crew who were gathered on the rock ledge at the front of the waterfall. Diplomatically accepting his guilt, Sanchez cautioned the others:

"Our Captain is a Wise Man, he has the power to help us all. Please only pass through the waterfall when I request you to enter safely through this opening, and be very watchful on the narrow ledge."

When all the men had walked down the sloped pathway, the pack of three dogs followed them; chasing each other to join their masters. Eagerly bounding down the rock gradient, the animals reached the grassland to be happily stroked by the crew. Suddenly the canines began howling, so Pablo asked them why they were growling into the sky. The sheepdog pointed its clawed paw up the slope to the rear location of the waterfall; gazing upwards from the direction of the dog's paw, the whole crew noticed the Galapagos sea turtle that Montezuma had entered into. Staring down at the gathering, the creature was sitting under the streaming water travelling down from the hillside.

Han used his magical power to heal the African men, both of whom had broken knees and hips from the tumbling accident on the unyielding solid rocks. Whilst he was healing the men, the retriever dog ran off into the undergrowth of the jungle woodland, where he began to howl incessantly.

Understanding the soundings of all animals, Han interpreted the howling of the dog to Captain Ortuga and the crew:

"Hey, people. Using my sensitive canine skill of sniffing to find food and treasures, I have discovered the gold storage space under a large rock. That is why I am called a Golden Retriever."

No citizens or animals were living in the village at the bottom of the valley; all the mud brick dwellings, wooden huts and government chambers were abandoned. Therefore, there could be no conflicts or dangers when taking the gold away from the township. But the danger that no one noticed, was that the village based on the lakeside, was filled with enraged native Aztec pirates who once lived in Eldorado and whose role now, was to fiercely guard the City of Gold. Their energy corresponded with their king, Montezuma.

Strolling along inside the valley hideaway with his crew, Captain Ortuga walked along the main street into the jungle woodland. Along further, the Retriever dog was balanced on a large slab of granite covered with ferns raising its head up into the sky, howling to welcome the human assembly along with his two dog chums. Moving around the granite slab, the men lifted it off the ground, revealing a massive dungeon built deep into the solid clay ground. After sighting a bamboo ladder that was secured to the muddy earth brick wall, Ortuga began climbing down into the dusty darkness to search the cells. Opening the door of the largest chamber, he found the cell was crammed with gold. Getting down the bamboo ladder to be with Captain Ortuga, Han used his magic to flow the sunlight into the darkness which illuminated the entire dungeon. The other crew members climbed down, seized hold of the gold bullions and calmly marched back up the safe pathway that returned to the ship, where they walked across the gangplank and loaded the gold down into the hold. Becoming so arrogant with self-assured confidence, the men started to rush along the pathway. Removing the last remaining blocks of gold bullion from the floors within the prison chambers, exposed copperhead snakes coiled around skeletons of captive inmates that had been tortured and killed by the Aztecs. The crew were extremely careful to avoid the reptiles, as some of the snakes evolved the flaring reptile ability of the chameleon and the creatures could convert their skin colours into disguises appearing like the gold bullion blocks, and the bones of the skeletons.

Talking together, Ortuga and Han opened the door of the administrative centre that stored hundreds of files detailing offences of every custodian. Linking with his memory of the wealth prospectus of local villagers finding tons of gold in his

Argentinean hometown of La Rosario, Ortuga expressed his thought of the value of the Eldorado gold loaded onto his ship:

"Guess the value of how much the gold we have discovered in this dungeon is worth – I think the amount would be about 18 million dollars?"

Inside the headquarters was a Golden Throne of a similar structural design to the throne in the monumental Elohim temple above the town of Machu Picchu. The type of stone used to build the throne was white quartz, containing miniature traces of gold. A big quantity of the gold bullion stored in the dungeons had been extracted from the quartz rocks, separated from the ore using the alchemical formula declared by the Pleiadians. Wanting to take the Golden Throne away from the Eldorado valley, Han and Ortuga carried it out of the dungeon to the base of the path.

In order to stop the venomous snakes sinking their sharp teeth into their flesh, flowing venom into their bloodstreams; the Liberty men dropped the heavy ingots on top of the snakes, squeezing life out from the legless reptiles. Racing along together, everyone rushed up to the top of the pathway, where the waterfall had expanded, closing its side opening by stretching the width; forcing the men to walk through the vertical water curtain. Barefooted, tripping over the turtle, Flintlock violently booted the creature into the lake; the sea creature then swam forcefully back to the ledge trying to gnaw off his toes.

Ortuga reeled the anchor cable down into the valley, and tied the cable rope onto the throne. Han, Pablo and the two Africans then twirled the rope around the capstan, bringing the throne up towards the ship, bursting through the waterfall onto the rock ledge, where the Montezuma turtle hurdled itself up onto the seat of the throne. Watching the inhospitable actions of the turtle, Han lifted his hands up into the atmosphere. The energy power hoisted the throne up into the air; and as it angled forward, the turtle slid off the seat into the lake; Han then waved his hands past his head, instructing the power to float the seat over the railings down to the ship's stern. The throne was lowered onto the decking above the quarters of Captain Ortuga.

Swimming along to the bow of the Liberty Bell, the turtle dragged the vessel towards the Amazon river where the estuary opened out into the Pacific Ocean. Captain Ortuga recalled his nightmare of the ship ramming into the reef, sinking down into the deep ocean and drowning the entire crew. Reaching the pacific waters at the estuary heads, the turtle swam to the rear of the ship. Using its weight, the creature leapt onto the rudder to direct the vessel to the reef. Cradling a heavy cannon ball, Aturo stomped to the stern of the ship and dropped the solid, round projectile onto the turtle's back; crushing the creature's shell.

The evil spirit of Montezuma drifted high up into the air; and as there were no close physical forms for the ghost figure to step into, the spirit dissolved into the atmospheric space, where the Aztec being of King Montezuma vanished for all eternity.

Chapter Thirteen
Actions Speak Louder than Words

Amir had now arrived back on the Liberty Bell from his expedition to the crop circle. He began giving his crop circle stones to the crew to strengthen their muscles and heal any injuries. The knowledge that had flowed into his mind after leaving the mysterious crop circle informed him that the stones would support vibrant health and present visions of the future, as the stones unlocked hidden potentials of the mind, helping each individual to become aware of their astrological link to animal life forms and encouraging each human to be what they wanted to be, bringing them forward to kindly lend a hand to aid the world with joy and happiness. Amir then drew Captain Ortuga and his fellow officers' attention to tell them of the channelled facts that he had received from the mind of one of the turtles that he had encountered whilst he was in the centre of the crop circle.

"One of those Galapagos turtles told me that actions speak louder than words. Not even kings can avoid facing the consequences of their own misdeeds. Furthermore, the citrine quartz stones that I collected in the crop circle can be programmed by individuals to bring much needed rain to the environment."

Inspired by the factual intelligence inserted into the minds of the turtles by the crop circles, Han agreeably compounded the insights with his own Taoist wisdom.

"The power in those citrine crystals can be used to channel divine energy into the human, raising their soul so they can connect to higher beings. Holding a crystal in the left hand channels the energy *into* the body, and the right hand projects magic *out* to protect the being. The universal power of each and every one of us is defined by the colourful, multi-layered oval energy field that surrounds all living things."

174

Passing through the estuary heads, the Liberty Bell began to sail back up north to the Incan township of Greenpatch Cove. Dark clouds began to form in the east as the quartz stones stimulated torrential rain, pouring down onto the ship, furiously flowing around the top decking, making the crew descend down into the berth. The heavy rain swept around the ship, creating a water curtain similar to the waterfall located at the top of the Eldorado valley. Because of the bulky wall of rainwater, not one person on the ship had noticed that they were being followed by a sloop vessel manned by the lakeside villagers; chasing the Liberty Bell to plunder and reclaim the gold seized from the City of Eldorado.

Exiting from his cabin, Ortuga walked up the rear stairs to the bridge stern and sat upon the Golden Throne. Knowing that the throne had been formed by the Pleiadians who had created the Elohim Throne, Ortuga kept his Turnkey wrapped inside the black velvet fabric so as not to relay any visualisations into his mind.

Although an image *did* enter his brain, channelling from the yellow citrine crop circle stone that was inside his jacket. The image transmitted showed the sloop vessel sailing behind the Liberty with the lakeside pirate crew loading up their muskets and cannons, ready to fire upon the Liberty Bell as soon as their sloop had gained a closer proximity to attack. Sensing that his ship and crew could be destroyed, Ortuga quickly returned back down to the berth. Knocking on the cabin door of Han, Sanchez and Amir, he asked Han to walk up to the top deck with him:

"Han, can you use your magic power to reveal the lakeside villagers' sloop vessel that is chasing behind our ship?"

Standing on the bridge placing his hands together, Han pointed at the water curtain behind the stern, sliding the curtain apart to expose the sloop vessel that was filled with enemy attackers. Dressed in her male disguise, Evangeline was standing at the helm, steering the ship along the northern passageway to Puerto Caballas. Suddenly, a strong red light surged up from within the ocean depths, radiating around the Liberty Bell, indicating that the sloop vessel chasing behind them would attempt destructive acts to sink the ship and brutal killings of the crew. The alarming red light indicating danger, gushed out from within the body of the Sledge Ray creature, setting terror into

Evangeline. Away from the helm, Evangeline passed by the Golden Throne to the rear of the ship. Observantly, looking below the hull down at the rudder, she noticed the body of the Montezuma turtle was attached to the vertical section of wood. Rising up from the depth of the ocean, the head of the Sledge Ray opened its mouth to gulp down the crushed body of the turtle. It was unable to swallow the creature because of its awkwardly shaped protective shell jamming at the top part off the Sledge Ray's throat, causing coughing and gagging. Diving down into the ocean around the ship's bow, the Sledge Ray swallowed a mouthful of salty seawater, gargled to release the wedged creature and spat the turtle out from its mouth high up into the air. The limp body of the turtle clumped down onto the top deck, landing on the slimy timber panelling at the stern where hundreds of sea creatures had been caught and filleted for feeding the crews of Francis Drake.

Sensing the Pleiadian energy flowing from the throne motivated the Sledge Ray to lift the Liberty Bell up from the waves, swiftly transporting the ship to the intended destination of Puerto Caballas and dodging from the planned assault of the pirate villagers. Before the ship moored once again in the shallow waters of Greenpatch Cove, the marine Sledge Ray darted out to the horizon, ducked down into the ocean searching for sea moss to heal its throat that was coated with intense scratchings from the jagged, crushed shell of the Montezuma turtle.

When the turtle had plunked down onto the rear decking of the ship, the thunderous bass sound moved Aturo up from the kitchen galley to collect the sea creature's body. Understanding that the vital organs would still be very strong food, for they were protected by the shell; he roasted the protein meat for the crew, furnishing them with muscular growth and physical power to assist their strength with any future battles on the seven seas. The loud bass vibration of the turtle falling hundreds of metres down from the sky, then pioneered the start of a massive, onslaught of thunder and lightning.

On the ship's arrival at Greenpatch Cove, Pachacuti entered upon the stern of the Liberty Bell, and shook hands with Ortuga, Han and Pablo. Looking far behind into the distant rain, the sloop vessel was riding along on the waves to begin attacking the

Liberty crew. Pachacuti questioned Ortuga about the sloop vessel:

"Juan, what is that vessel behind us there, do you think it will assault you and my tribe? If so, where are your crew to defend the attacks?"

Answering back in an apologetic retort, pointing down into the ship's hold, Ortuga explained about the protective Aztec villagers sailing from the lake on the Bolivian border:

"Accept my regretful reply, for all my men are down under having food with the ship's Cook, Aturo.

I have collected gold bounty from Eldorado to donate one million dollars to eradicate poverty in your tribe. Also I will hand over two million dollars of the bullion treasure, to you to settle annoyances of any men aggressively irritated by governmental laws, who bring terror and tension to your homeland in an endeavour to build their own empires."

Even though Pachacuti officially headed the Inca council chambers, inscribing bureaucratic regulations and legal laws banning refugees and immigrants, he felt that the donations would enter ethnic kindness in the minds of all his indigenous communities.

Gaining closeness to the Liberty Bell, the sloop vessel began firing its cannons, powering onto the main decking, damaging the masts, yardarms and canvas sails. The thundering storm veiled the explosive noise of the blasting gunpowder from the artillery weapons.

Several of the lakeside pirate men threw grappling hooks across the ocean, clasping onto the gunwale. Thinking that the treacherous attack would become vastly dangerous, the Inca chief called his men to climb on board of the Liberty Bell to start fighting with the pirates after they swung across on the ropes.

Fifty of the Inca warriors marched across the gangplank, along the decking down to the stern with their weapons including daggers, whips and solid clumping mallets to bash the pirates off the side of the ship. Reaching the rear of the ship, a number of pirates swayed over the railings and stomped towards the bridge where Captain Ortuga was standing with Han and Pachacuti. Hiding from any killings, Evangeline ran to the ship's bow and veiled herself under a torn canvas sail that had been slashed off the foremast by a lightning strike.

Before the eight lakeside men got too close to the bridge platform, the Inca warriors swung the wooden mallets into their abdomens and thighs, pounding them over the side railings back down into the shallow water.

A huge number of lethal Box Jellyfish attacked the men, clinging their stinging tentacles around the men's legs and chests, piercing venom into their blood streams.

As the thunder and lightning faded away behind the horizon, the rain swept away down south, leaving a stillness in the air at Greenpatch Cove, making the attacks easier for another group of ten lakeside men to begin swinging across from their sloop vessel to board the Liberty Bell.

It was so timely for Captain Ortuga that Han left the food galley and returned to the bridge platform. The Captain then instructed him to quickly reset an energy force field around the ship to stop the cannon balls damaging the timber that had destroyed the ship's capability to sail out into the stormy ocean depths. The miraculous particle barrier also blocked the pirate men from entering the ship.

After the storm had moved on, the Liberty crew made their way up to the main decking detecting the threatening attacks of the unknown enemy sloop vessel. Aturo remained in his kitchen; he was the only person left in the ship's hold. Gaining an emotional desire to steal some of the gold in the bilge storage, he ambled quietly along the corridor. Pulling open the door revealed the gold bullion, and also a dangerous shadow hiding behind the gold. As Aturo tried to carry some bullion out of the bilge, the shadow of the skeleton of the Dutch slave driver, Wolfgang moved towards him. The eerie form shoved into Aturo's back making him collapse onto the timber flooring, with the bullion clumping under his chest, crushing his ribcage. Feeling off balance, Aturo waddled up to the top deck to gain healing of his vertigo and broken ribs from Han, with the Wolfgang skeleton following silently behind him.

Reaching the top deck the skeleton slid himself under the large canvas at the ship's bow where Evangeline was hiding away from the violence of the ship's attack. Sensing that the creepy skeleton had no energy resonating with that of her own loving energy, she let out a loud scream and quickly moved herself away from under the torn canvas sail. Passing through the dense crowding of the Liberty crew and the Inca warriors, she gripped strongly at her male identity of Pablo Medellin. Meeting up with Han, Evangeline asked him to create an arched rainbow air-bridge for the Incas to pass over to attack the lake pirates:

"Our lives depend on bringing the premeditated pirate killings to a standstill. Han, can you use your magic to create an atmospheric walkway from the Liberty Bell over to the pirate sloop so that the Inca warriors can then defend us?"

Swaying around with vertigo, Aturo felt crew members and objects on the ship spinning rapidly around him. His dizziness made his walking difficult, seeking support by leaning on the railings he spun around and toppled over into the water below. Luckily, the mermaid, Marina, was below the ship; she cuddled Aturo, helping him to regain his balance; she then sat on a solid rock with him on the edge of the waterfront watching the attack.

The Inca warriors trampled across the air-bridge; passing through the force field barrier, they arrived on the starboard edge of the sloop vessel. Using their mallets, they knocked the lakeside men unconscious and watched them fall down onto the decking. Grabbing up each one of the pirates, the warriors tumbled all of the bodies down the hull into the ocean waters, the forceful waves of the king tide drifted the comatosed bodies of the lakeside village men back down south to the estuary of the Amazon river. The clever actions of the Inca warriors were watched by everyone on the Liberty Bell and on their arrival back at the ship, Captain Ortuga gave each one of the Inca tribal men a block of gold. Smirking impressively, the 50 warriors returned to their hometown led by Pachacuti and his stunningly beautiful wife, Sofia.

With no crew members remaining on the lakeside sloop, the Wolfgang skeleton swam to the opposite portside of the vessel; he scrambled up the hull and ran down to the hold. Discovering a hiding place, he stepped inside the gun galley and sneaked under one of the cannons. Suddenly, with a huge jarring sound, a rush of water from the power of the king tide rolled the cannon down onto the skeleton, crushing its bones, making the skeletal soul float into the twilight atmosphere; Now the only remaining pirate, Bucko Felony, who survived the group attack and the Galapagos sea turtles stood on the helm of the Liberty where he dived over the stern across to the smaller vessel, claiming his intuitive leadership to be the new-fangled skipper of the sloop.

The next morning, the Liberty crew prepared their ship, ready to head off to the South Pacific to Easter Island, French Polynesian, the island of Tahiti and the British land mass of Pitcairn.

On waking, Han decided to apply colour onto the raw timber figurehead sculpture which he had mounted on the ship's bow. Whilst he was painting the stilted, merged female figures, Marina rose up from the water below him. She told Han that she possessed a treasure chest for Captain Ortuga to deliver to the world:

"For your love, I have treasure hidden in my ocean cavern. I will bring it up to you now, leaving it here below the bow of the Captain's ship."

Diving down into the ocean, Marina carried the treasure chest back up to the surface of the water and placed it next to Aturo on the rock. Aturo called out to Pablo to collect the treasure, giving it to Ortuga to enlarge his altruistic, gift donations.

"Hey, Pablo. Gosh you are looking really exhausted after all the repair work you have done since the sloop attack. Why don't you shave your beard off and massage your head with remedial focus, and can you get down here and help me take this treasure to Ortuga?"

Conclusively, after the repairing of the masts, the ripped sail canvases and the damaged main timber deckings; Captain Ortuga commanded his crew to sail off from Greenpatch Cove to the South Pacific.

The final surviving group of Liberty crew members now comprised only of eight seafaring people:

The tempered Jamaican ship's Cook – Aturo Deshah; the Scottish Boatswain Drummer – Richard Flintlock; the Charismatic Peruvian Guitarist – Javir Sanchez; the disguised female Starseed – of Evangeline Moreau – Pablo Medellin; the Persian ship Physician – Amir Noorian; the African slaves – Marley Waylon and Samson Buji, and the Magical Taoist flute player – Han Lipling.

Chapter Fourteen
He Who Dares, Wins

Outwards onto the South Pacific seas, the first destination of the Liberty Bell was Easter Island. Marina swam under the ship's bow, occasionally glancing up at the female sculpture of Sofia, Evangeline and herself. Concealed behind the sculpture, Ortuga moved to the right-hand side looking down to Marina. She spoke out to him about the treasure chest that she had gifted to the Liberty and also if she could use her navigational knowledge to faultlessly lead his ship safely on their seabound journeys:

"Captain, the earth is our Mother, so can you train your crew to treat her with respect. Evangeline told me that you might become the new global hero. I am sure, I and all the females would possess respect for you too."

As the treasure map, showing the final resting place of the sunken Nuestra Senora de Atocha vessel, that was given to Ortuga by the dying ancient mariner on his journey from his home town to the port of Valparaiso, had been destroyed by fire during the last pirate attack, Ortuga wanted Marina to help him discover the treasure on the island of Curacao. Recognising that the mermaid held so much wisdom and factual information of the whereabouts of every hidden shipwreck around the seven seas, Ortuga thought that she could guide him to the location of the hidden treasure of gold, precious stones and antique manuscripts in the sunken Spanish galleon.

As the morning progressed, Marina swam about a kilometre further ahead of the Liberty to scout for hidden reefs where she suddenly found herself surrounded by a pod of Humpback whales, travelling south to the Antarctic with their newborn calves. Seeing her as a threat to the pod, a huge male slammed its tail into her side and, Marina was catapulted high into the sky.

Plummeting into the ocean some kilometres east away from the ship, she floated on the surface of the ocean water to nurse back to health the injury caused by the thumping of the whale's tail into her buttocks.

Evangeline had sensed that something bad had happened to Marina and she went to Ortuga, to ask him to help rescue her. They both went to the helm bridge and Ortuga commanded Sanchez to steer the vessel north towards Colombia, then sail beyond to the northeast to get together with the mermaid soulmate. The Liberty's rescue journey took a number of hours and fortunately Marina was still floating around on the surface of the ocean when they finally sighted her. Reaching her position, the ship halted to raise her onto the stern podium close to the ocean; allowing her to slide without difficulty back into the water when she had regained her strength. Strolling along the main decking in her male outfit, Evangeline descended to the podium to watch over Marina; several minutes after her arrival, Han sauntered down the metal steps to gain energy companionship with the two female beings.

Sailing onwards, the first island that the Liberty Bell pulled into was an overseas British province. The Pitcairn land mass was the safest territory in a grouping of four volcanic islands. Way above, behind the sandy beach front was a range of blue mountains housing Aztec tribes, indigenous communities and a loyal British government that monitored the Aztec kingdom, restraining sacrificial killings of young citizens, thus keeping all ritual slaughtering under control. Viewing the ship docking into the deep waters of the temperate bay of Ulladulla, the mayor rode a horse down to the bay, welcoming the crew to determine their personalities. Teaming together along with the English man was a group of five indigenous natives.

When they reached the deep water bay, Juan Ortuga had set up the gangplank, where he conducted all of his crew onto the beach front. Gathering all together, Ortuga shook hands with the mayor and introduced his senior officers. Han bowed gracefully and began to explain his intuitive outlook on empowering the common ground of humanity. The foremost potent comments Han lectured were concise expressions of how to achieve longevity of human life:

"The core power of longevity is balance; validating seeded routines into the mind and physicality. Welcome to you all, balance will convey supremacy into your spirit on the day of death – returning to the sublime energy of the universe to eternally be with God."

The mystical intelligence of Han emphasised the inspiration of all the males, the indigenous Pitcairns, the Liberty crew and the leaders of both societies. Being a humble child of God, the ancient teachings he portrayed were of super love and forgiveness. Being an atomic element within the universal energy, after death, on the reincarnation of your energy into another human life form out of harm's way, you can live a life of déjà vu and salvage your kindness. Han went on to say that the opening remarks related to the mind, meaning Truth Will Set You Free and to Love One Another:

"Survival depends upon the acts of kindness and compassion, acceptance of all cultures and astrological characters of every human being."

Kindness and compassion are the principle temperaments that make our lives meaningful, sourcing everlasting happiness and joy, and inviting kindness into your hearts. Continuing his Taoist teachings, Han briefly conveyed wisdom of how to strengthen immunity by eating certain foods to prevent illnesses and death. Stating, that to obtain super health, avoid sugar, acid or mould and just eat fresh, pure, natural, medicinal foods like herbs, berries, nuts, vegetables, fruits, alkaline foods and whole meal cereal grains.

Celebrating Han's wisdom of health, the native islanders clapped hands. Smiling to himself, Captain Ortuga grasped hands with the British mayor; announcing the stored gold bullion that he had in the ship was to award to the poorest communities. Ortuga queried the ranking governor:

"Sir, what is your name, and where in England are you from – are you from Cornwall?"

Answering Ortuga, the Pitcairn mayor told him that his name was Robin Hood, born in Nottingham, but he did travel to the south of England where he escaped from his death penalty enforced by the sheriff of Nottingham. Reaching the British port town of Bristol, he sourced a ship to carry him to the Pacific islands of Pitcairn, where he was nominated to become the highest-ranking politician. Opinionated, Robin Hood replied with a heroic agreement:

"Yes, Captain, on my horse, I rode around the Cornish coastline visiting the five towns of Falmouth, Newquay, Portsmouth, Launceston and the renowned pirate village of Penzance."

Robin Hood is pleasant but hard hitting, all mouth and no trousers. In Britain, he stole masses of riches from the wealthy, giving the robbings to the poor which is what he secretly performs in Pitcairn giving treasures to the indigenous community. Han told Ortuga that the astrological character of Robin Hood was a Pisces Tiger, and that Ortuga was a Virgo Ox. The harmonising planetary zodiac energies of the two men defined that they could become close friends for they both have similar future insights, granting justice to global cultures and to help poor communities by donating funds to them.

Robin Hood and the group of five indigenous islanders then entered across the gangplank together with Ortuga. Joyfully exiting, each one carrying three blocks of gold bullion – financially estimated at the sum of three hundred thousand dollars. Treading down on the sand, the islanders ritually shook hands with Captain Ortuga, Robin Hood and Han then they strolled away from the water up towards their village situated on the edge, of the dramatically scenic range of the blue mountains. Witnessing the bestow donation of gold from Ortuga, masses of Aztec islanders headed rapidly to attack the native men; stomping towards the beach the Aztec muggers plunged their tough, wrinkly fists into the faces of the men. Returning aggression, the indigenous folk swung the solid bullion blocks deeply into the faces of the Aztecs foes. The huge number of attackers rapidly seized the gold bullion from the indigenous men, then ran into the mountains, hiding away from anyone who wanted to reclaim the donation.

Back in England, Davy and his three best friends woke up in Quinton's beachside cavern residence.

The time was 5.30am, 60 minutes before the dawn. Behind the large vertical rock with the water moat around its base, Davy slid open the rock door and began stepping up the stone stairway that was hacked inside the cliffs that led up to his father's clifftop guest house – The Charter Inn.

Due to the sea moss densely growing from the base of the jagged rocks that led up the stair passageway, the steps were quite slippery, staging hazards to anyone who did not walk carefully, holding the handrail with safety in their minds. Because of the dangers, Davy made use of the magic power he gained from Han.

Hovering up into the air, above the slippery rock stairs, Davy glided up the passageway drawing closer to the trap door hatch opening on the timber flooring in his parent's bedroom. Passing his head through the slight opening under the mat, he tried to gaze around the room, looking for his parents but the heavy mat filled with dust and dog dander distorted his vision. Davy then pushed the hinged trap door wide open and climbed higher out of the opening where he noticed a group of people in the room. Clarity of his vision identified the group of four people, two women and two men as the elders of the Chilean refugees. Silently, sitting cross-legged with their eyes closed, hands pressed together above their heads, the Chileans were practising yoga – tenderly chanting a yielding mantra to calm the mind. As Davy crawled out of the opening, the trap door banged down into the gap frame jamb, making a thunderous noise which pierced the meditated minds of the four refugee elders, jolting them from their dawn relaxation. With a surprised look on his serene face, the oldest man posed an enquiry to Davy:

"Hey, boy. Who are you, you are not a housebreaking cat burglar are you? You look so healthy and agile that you could climb in through the windows up on top of the building."

Confidently, Davy answered to the four citizens:

"Be careful. Look, I am Davy Tullman, the son of Joseph and Parvihn – welcome me back to The Charter Inn."

The Chilean lady told Davy that their five children were living in room number 10 next to the clifftop veranda with his young sister, Jasmine and his parents were living in the room at the top of the guest house. Davy asked her the number of the room that his parents were in. Replying, one of the ladies told him the room number:

"Your parents are living in room number 24. It has a stairway leading up to the rooftop, rendering an incredible view of the panoramic vista of the beach spreading around the Cornish bay of Penzance."

Thanking the Chilean lady, Davy left the room, passing out through the reception area and walking up the carpeted stairs to the highest level of the guest house. Reaching room number 24, he tapped gently on the door, the time was only 6.20 in the morning. Davy's mother, Parvihn, opened the door. Seeing her son alive, she smiled lovingly and cuddled him with her deep-rooted compassion. She mentioned to him about his father's part time employment as the Deputy Chief Customs Inspector, working three nights every week furnished a slight mental fatigue.

His father, Joseph, was still asleep in bed, so Davy whispered to his mother to come with him down to the dining room for breakfast. The other people that were in the dining room were the four Chilean refugees, so Davy and Parvihn sat down at the table with the migrants. Popping his head around the kitchen door, the Cook welcomed them to breakfast:

"Good morning to you all, it is a bit early for a cooked breakfast. Natural healing is what the world needs – instead, I will serve you a healthy mixture of fibrous foods."

The Cook placed large bowls of semolina, puffed brown rice, raspberries and honey on the table. Whilst eating, the Chileans celebrated by thanking Parvihn for her ministerial aid making them British citizens. After Davy had breakfast with his mother, he walked with her back upstairs to detect whether his father was awake. As they arrived at the room 24, the door was open – Joseph was not in there. Noticing that the door leading up to the flat rooftop was open, Davy and his mother carried on through the door meeting with their male admiral, Joseph. Firstly, shaking hands with his father, Davy then gave him a respectful, amorous man hug. Joseph pointed up into the hillside on the western bearing from the rooftop. Focusing on the direction, Davy saw the Sledge Ray leaping around in the misty hills:

"Dad, did you see that incredible creature over there? It is a Sea Goat. Those beasts do not exist in today's world; it must have travelled back from the 1700s."

After kissing his mother and father, Davy took the shell Turnkey out of his jacket, he touched the shell and saw the current happenings between Ortuga and Robin Hood on Pitcairn Island. Telling his parents that he would travel back to the past again, he asked his mother to cradle her arm around his shoulder to flow the vision into her mind, and his father placed his arms around both of them, revealing the heroic outlaw from Nottingham.

His young sister, Jasmine, also walked up onto the rooftop; hugging Davy, she too connected with the magic of the Turnkey and saw a vision from the past – the mermaid, Marina and the treasure chest, then she saw the mermaid slip off the stern of the Liberty Bell into the oceanic waters of Pitcairn Island.

Sensing the energy of the shell Turnkey, the Sledge Ray flew across from the Portsmouth hillside, landing on the rooftop of The Charter Inn. Before it landed, the Tullman family moved away into the door opening but lingered in the gap – looking at the Sea Goat creature. Davy kissed his young sister; walking out of the opening, he mounted onto the Sledge Ray's back and spoke into the golden shell:

"Take me down to the sandy beach front, for my best friends are down there, then we can all travel back to the past, to the moment in time of Captain Juan Ortuga and his encounter with Robin Hood."

Listening to the instructional wordings of Davy, the Sledge Ray turned its head around and snarled. Joseph ran out from the doorway and patted the creature's chest to embed comfort and tranquillity into its mind. Yowling, Joseph expressed his planetary understandings to Davy:

"The way of all creatures is dictated by the energy of the universe. Today is two days before the full moon lunar eclipse, the three days before the full moon extracts energy from all beings, both humans and animals – which is why the creature is a little disturbed."

Davy replied to his father's insight:

"Are you advising me not to travel on this creature? Dad, I have the gained boldness of adventure from Captain Ortuga and many pirate men. My power of daring strength will let me take on any beasts or human beings with kindness and acceptance."

Clutching hold of the hammerhead body part of the Sledge Ray, Davy steered the creature down to the beach, settling onto the rocks outside of Quinton's cave. The three friends, Tim, Molly and Quinton, strolled out of the cave and mounted onto the back of the Sea Goat creature. Davy asked them to grasp the shell Turnkey, letting them all transport together back in time to the island of Pitcairn.

Powering through the Northern Borealis lights in the early morning skies, the Sea Goat took the four friends back in time. Arriving on the Pitcairn beach next to some of the indigenous community who told them about the Aztecs stealing their gold bullion and running into the mountains of blue. Davy then asked Juan Ortuga and Robin Hood to climb on the Sledge Ray. Using its wings to flick away the Aztec thieves, it then drifted up into the mountain range. On sighting the stolen bullion, Robin Hood, Ortuga, Tim and Quinton slid off the creature, re-collected the gold and loaded it onto the back of the Sledge Ray. With its heavy load, it then flew down to the beach front, toppled the bullion off its back; returning the donation to the indigenous men. In telling Davy and his three Cornwall school friends about the British bandit Robin Hood, Captain Ortuga said that an outlawed hero sometimes has to fight with certain people and it is not always about just flowing kindness, for some cruel individuals might try to behead you; therefore, just make those that project evil to you, be aware that your courage and fearlessness may harm them. Have a super brave, valiant presence, with energy that suppresses their immorality. You don't have to kill people, just generate fear so any attackers are frightened by your heroic dominance and, therefore, won't kill you. – Those people that pass on darings will render their spirituality, building strength, boldness and confidence to help the global territories. He Who Dares, Wins.

Chapter Fifteen
The Temper Trap

Back on the Liberty Bell, Molly, Tim and Quinton alleged to Captain Ortuga that they could assist him with his world aid vision, so Ortuga informed them to set up sleeping divans in the cabin, sharing the room with Pablo and Davy. Flintlock was instructed to move out from the cabin and sleep in the hammock berth with the Africans.

The ship journeyed on to its next destiny – the French Polynesian Island of Tahiti. Whilst the vessel was sailing on the ocean, Han used his carpentry skills to secure the Golden Throne found in the Eldorado valley onto the helm bridge so the waves could not slide it over the stern. The throne was made from granite with layered veins of gold mineral embedded into the stone. Gripping the throne onto the timber platform channelled positive energy into Han, enlightening him about the beneficial effects of gold, bringing wealth, understanding, acceptance, spirituality and attunement to nature.

Strolling around the main decking, the three dogs, Sheepdog, Arlee; Black Labrador, Betsy; and the Golden Retriever, Monty, skipped behind Molly. Her magical ability demonstrated to her how to talk with the animals by way of using their sounds of woofing and whining.

When Molly pulled in past the helm bridge getting close to the end of the ship, she caught a glimpse of the charming mermaid resting on the timber decking. Lying down next to Marina, Molly enjoyed her being – the three canine dogs jumped off the bridge down onto the stern. The slippery covered layer of phlegm fish scales, flesh and guts made the Labrador puppy slide over the edge of the stern; it bounced off the rudder podium into the ocean waters. Surging out of the water, a large Bull shark gobbled the young dog into its stomach, then barged against the rudder, jolting the timber decking causing several of the planks to spring off from the framework and making one of the elevated planks push Marina over the stern. Sending out a loud scream, Molly instantly recalled the happening from a vision that she had seen whilst holding the shell Turnkey as she was soaring back in time on the Sledge Ray. On hearing Molly's call for help, Han ran to the railings just before the shark sunk its sharp pointed teeth into Marina's hard scaley tail, he rapidly stretched his hand over the railings down to the turbulent water below, grasping her arm firmly to pull her safely away from the hungry creature back up over the railings, onto the deck of the ship. Irritated, the dogs growled aggressively at the shark, sending it back into the ocean deep.

Comforting Marina, Han fastened a thick plank of wood to the decking which protected anything from sliding off the stern, Marina rested together with Molly and the two remaining dogs, smiling lovingly and thanking them for saving her life.

Returning to the helm to be with Ortuga, Han noticed Davy climbing up the main mast to the crow's nest. Walking up from the berth along the main decking, Tim and Quinton signalled Davy to stride to the helm to meet up with the two senior commanding officers, Flintlock and Sanchez.

Telling them he was born in the Scottish medieval capital town of Edinburgh, Flintlock asked the boys which county in England they were from. Tim confidently replied to Flintlock:

"Sir, we are from the same Cornish county where Davy is from, the pirate port town of Penzance. Can you let me become your assistant sir, for I am very good at instructions and commands?"

Sanchez heard Tim's appeal to become a superior crew member and feeling that Tim wanted to take over his role, he jabbed his elbow into Tim's belly, making him fall down on the decking. His body rolled away from the helm down to the stern, grouping with Molly, Marina and the two amusing dogs, Arlee and Monty. Upset by the unwarranted aggression, Quinton laughed at Sanchez's antagonism leaving the helm to gather with the stern group. Captain Ortuga seemed to be so upset by Sanchez's nasty behaviour, he thought that it might influence the four teenagers not to help him with the ship; he strolled down to the stern.

Quinton expressed his yearnings to Ortuga:

"Captain, can you deliver us all from evil? We want to join you on a joy ride, not with a criminal Commander."

Considerately, Ortuga replied to Quinton:

"Apologies for the malicious rulings of my quartermaster. Humanitarians all share and win."

At 12.00 noon, the weather was so hot with the temperature reaching 38 degrees. The stern group shuffled down into the ship's hold to the bilge lying in the water to recover from the intensity of the sun. From up in the crow's nest, Davy watched his friends, the dogs and the mermaid plodding down to the bilge; he followed them and paddled into the shallow water. As in a gathering of old friends, everyone put their arms around each other creating a joy division circle; even the dogs curled their bodies into the form.

In the distance, the southern destination of Tahiti was observed by the ship's crew, the seafaring members on the top deck were the senior officers with their Argentinean Captain, Juan Ortuga. The ship's Physician, Amir, told Ortuga that he estimated the distance to the island of Tahiti would be roughly one hundred and ten kilometres, taking about two hours to reach their new destination. On the journey to the French Polynesian island of Tahiti, the temperature had increased to a scorching 43 degrees, thus persuading the crew to stay down in the hold. The only people on the top decking were Ortuga and the two Africans.

The sea water was outstandingly turquoise in colour and much deeper than the Peruvian Greenpatch Cove and also the British island of Pitcairn. A haze of blue green algae bloom was surging under the surface of the water. Knowing that the ingestion of algae could be very deadly to human and animal life forms, Ortuga glanced favourably around the top decking, looking for any other crew members to advise them about the toxicity of the ocean bacteria. But not a soul was to be seen as the Africans had returned down to the hold, to play a dice board game with the senior officers.

Looking out onto the volcanic black sand beaches, Ortuga observed a tribal group of indigenous men with sunshade hats and parasols made from palm trees moving by a large waterfall, following the stream channel down towards the ship. When the men got to the Liberty Bell, they piled up the parasols, dived into the water to cool their bodies and swam to the ship's portside hull. Grouping together, the native men held onto the hull, treading water to remain in the cold sea. Below the water surface, their lower bodies chilled, but the parts above the surface, shoulders, arms and heads, were scorched by the sun.

Their Chief swam along the side of the ship to the stern, pulling himself up onto the podium; he mounted onto the stairway ascending to the main deck. Whilst he trod wearily up the stairs, a flock of blue winged jungle fowl birds swooped alongside the Chief. Communicating with the feathered creatures, the man began tooting in a calm natured way offering them kindness, protection, compassion and fondness for future feedings.

Arriving at the bridge helm, he shook hands with Ortuga and Han, who had heard the sounds of the Chief, talking with the birds. As the birds were perching on the railings, Han bowed to the man, giving him admiration for his kindness to birdlife and animals. Han then declared his perception of the feathered communication:

"Welcome to the vegan world of vegetarianism, I heard your conversation with those jungle fowl birds – you are a tooting calm man."

The Tahitian chief answered back to Han and Ortuga:

"I can sense your spiritual energies, are you both from the same monastery? Your descriptive vision of my being as a tooting calm man is intuitive. My name is actually Tutankhamun."

The chief told Han that his tribal community, that was holding onto the side of the vessel were ancestral Hunzas migrated from the territory of northern Pakistan seven years ago. The axis of the Muslim diets of the Hunza communities were cored with fresh, natural eating products such as fruit, vegetables, grains with no chemical additives placed in their foods. Drinking pure water, the Hunzas also try to breathe unpolluted air, up in their mountainous habitations such as all monastery groups. The Taoist knowledge of Han contracted with the consumptive conditions to gain health, youthful appearances and longevity resonated well with the chief.

Rhythmically tapping on the hull of the ship, the tribal Hunzas called the senior officers, the African men and the baby lamb up to the top deck. Ortuga asked them to bring bullion up from below and heave the gold bars over the railings onto the cushioning beach sand. Each of the crew members carried three bars each; standing at the railings, they hurled the bullion onto the sand observing the donation gleaming in the sunlight; the tribal men swam actively to the beach. After collecting the gold, they then walked quickly back into the mountains with their chief, Tutankhamun, strolling peacefully behind them, all surrounded by the choir flock of yellow warbler jungle birds.

A state of happiness filled the air as Molly sauntered up from the bilge. Together with the baby lamb, they trotted over the gangplank which had been secured by Han for Tutankhamun exiting from the ship.

Leaping across the gangplank, the two Liberty dogs joined together with Molly and the lamb to walk on the black sandy beach. The magical power of Molly gained her the communicative ability to chat with the three creatures. Barking and baaing, Molly enlivened the creatures, telling them that when they arrived at the ship's next destination of Easter Island, life partners of their own animalistic beings would be there for all of them. The baby lamb then scampered off ahead of the group, to the end of the beach where the lamb had caught sight of a ewe mother sheep, contentedly grazing on lush green grass at the base of the island' towering volcano.

The lamb finally reached the female ewe sheep and as the loving energy flowed from the mother and the baby lamb generated a heartfelt warmth and bond to both creatures, the lamb instantly decided to remain on the island and live with her new mother in the grassland at the edge of the volcano.

Noticing Davy and Quinton climbing up the main mast, back up to the crow's nest, Molly assumed that the ship was about to sail off to its last charitable destination in the South Pacific, Easter Island. She called the dogs and walked them over the gangplank down into the bilge.

Hoisting its anchor up from the deep, turquoise blue water, the Liberty Bell raised its main sails to catch the wind power;

sailing out of the cove down south, forwarding to its next future destiny – Easter Island.

The wind was so strong that it mightily heaved the ship across the ocean like a slingshot and in what seemed no time at all, the vessel docked into the same port as previously anchored when Evangeline, Han and Davy met up with the five spiritual stone heads, depicting core global religious insights of the universal power through the different languages of Arabic, Japanese, English, Hindu and Chinese.

The twilight darkened, rapidly filling the night sky, creating a star based staging for the Aries full moon, energising the stone figures under the earth. With the intense, thick heat of the daytime sun still lingering, Ortuga sat on the Golden Throne secured to the helm bridge, relaxing in the warm night air, reflecting on the day's activities. Closing his eyes, an image of the wonderfully lush vegetation of the grass land pathway leading to the Elohim Throne in Machu Picchu appeared in his mind. The Pleiadian usher, who advised travellers safe ways of transporting to destinations in the past or future, opened the gateway, showing the short-tempered guardsman. Wanting to receive answers about the Golden Throne, Ortuga spoke into his shell Turnkey:

"Usher man, I have travelled along the Photon Beam to your galaxy, the visitation engendered my soul with modest knowledge of advanced beings like yourself.

"Can you please advise me how to use the Eldorado Golden Throne to teleport beings to the past?"

A broad educating answer streamed into Ortuga's mind, explaining that the Golden Throne only transfers visions from the past or the future. The visions describe the global locations of gold minings, alchemical production laboratories and places of hidden gold and treasures. The mystically enhanced seated unit cannot teleport beings along the Photon Beam, but if the person sitting on the throne possesses a Turnkey, the throne can be used to travel the being's physicality back to the past or forward to the future. The next image that flowed into Ortuga's mind was the location of the lost treasure from the sunken Spanish galleon – Nuestra Senora de Atocha. A soft smile came upon his face as he rested back in the throne.

The full moon was spinning around under the clouds, flooding illumination into the dark night sky. Down in Davy's cabin, Evangeline was talking with Molly, Tim, Quinton and Davy, expressing her Starseed wisdom. Because there were no seafaring males in the cabin, she removed her male disguise outfit, revealing her beauty as she cautioned the four teenagers about the trouble why most men don't recruit females onto their vessels.

Midnight released the full moon higher into the night sky; a knock on the cabin door worried Evangeline, for she thought that it may be the burley Flintlock. She quickly dressed back into her male disguise, then opened the door to Han. Activated by the melodic energy of the full moon, Han then entertained the group by verbally interpreting the astrological animal portraits in each of the Cornish teenagers.

The planetary energies channelling into all beings, human and all living things at their time of birth determines their characters…

Tim – Aries Wood Rat

Molly – Gemini Metal Monkey

Quinton – Sagittarian Metal Pig

Davy – Piscean Earth Rooster

The astrological personalities of the four close friends together formed a joy division; Han declared that the sole energy of Davy would be super powered that night because the full moon was holding great astrological power. Invigorated by his new lunar energy, Davy headed off from the cabin to worship the moon at the ship's bow. Tim had followed behind Davy along the corridor and had diverted into the hammock berth where Flintlock was awake. Harmonising with his empirical energy, Tim swung into one of the hammocks next to Marley, thinking that when the morning comes, he could assist Flintlock to command the crew.

Whilst Davy was on the main deck, expressing thanks to the moon, he noticed one of the stone statue figures pulling itself up above the land surface from under the earth. The dynamically tempered male stone giant stomped over to the ship's bow, grasping hold of Davy, forcing him to believe in his religious faith. Identifying the belief of the giant as the Chinese faith, Davy spoke out to him:

"Don't hurt me. I believe in your religion, for my friend Han is from the Taoist monastery in Mount Cangyan in the Chinese province of Jingxing."

The stone giant dropped Davy back down onto the main decking, where he rolled along to the helm bridge and curled up against a pile of ropes. At 2.00am, he fell into a sleep pattern with the moon's energy flowing into his body, revealing to him that the homicidal military spirit of the Mongolian emperor, Genghis Khan, had travelled down from the continent of northern China, re-incarnating his energy and invading Easter Island to become the ruling king, baptising the island as his land. The Genghis Khan revelation was so strong, that it woke Davy and he returned down into his cabin, where Molly, Evangeline, Quinton and Han were all fast asleep.

Early at 8.00am in the morning, poor families from the surrounding area gathered on the beach front. Trying to enjoy themselves, the children chased each other, built sandcastles and played games; their parents sobbed as they spoke of their low incomes and the strict bureaucratic regulations to submit money to the ruling authority which gave little assistance to the poverty stricken communities. Together with the gathering was the Iranian stowaway, Bijan Bonapart, who knew that the Liberty Bell had returned to donate funding to the destitute island families, so he had guided them all to the waterfront to collect the donations before Genghis Khan woke up, trapping their human rights by ordering his soldiers to seize the donations away from them.

The bedraggled children chanted an ancient Christian song taught from the Syrian priest, Beth Gazo, who was a disciple of Jesus. Inspiringly, the children tapped drumming sounds on the ship's hull to wake the crew. Captain Ortuga observed the gathering from the helm bridge and when the crew rose to the top decking he called out to them to carry gold up and drop it over the railing into the shallow water. The poor people collected the gold bars, hid them in their jackets and trouser pockets, then walked back to their natural dwellings in the woodland hillside.

Covertly, Marley and Samson loaded gold into the rescue boat and after lowering the craft vessel down into the deep waters, they clambered over the railings and mounted onto the rescue boat. Having a strong desire for the gold to move them away from slavery, they silently rowed along the coastline into a secret cove covered with tropical palm trees and bushes.

Entering the boat into a cave, they decided to remain on the island possibly turning into musicians to entertain indigenous tribes and Genghis Khan with song tales of their colourful adventures. Their revelation of becoming musical stars was defined by Pablo, for after they had escaped from the slave vessel he told them that in life, there is nothing that can't be fixed by peace, music, love and a little understanding and community.

Samson and Marley had taken away a lot of the gold bullion stored down in the hold. They also took the board game played with Aturo in the galley, which Marley hurled to a group of children on the beach as they rowed the rescue boat along the coastline to their hidden destination.

The essential labouring crew had now decreased to just the six talented senior officers. In order to regain physical power of deckhands to prepare and sail the ship around the seven seas, Ortuga thought that he should visit the famous Colombian port of Cartagena on the Caribbean coastline to recruit more men. And as he had lost the map of the sunken treasure from the Spanish galleon, Atocha, he asked Marina to lead him to the location in the Caribbean Sea 500 kilometres north of Cartagena which he viewed whilst sitting on the Golden Throne.

The viewing showed him that the Spanish vessel was ravaged by a severe hurricane, ripping off its sails, scooped up by a howling wave and then slammed down into the reef, gouging out the bottom of the hull to let loose 20 tonnes of treasure onto the bottom of the seabed.

Spending loving moments with Evangeline in the cabin whilst the ship sailed to the north, Molly progressed her compassion with a historical tale about the attacks of foreign islands similar to the invasion of Easter Island by Genghis Khan. The legendary fable was the invasion of the early aboriginal Australian tribes by the British military headed by Captain James Cook. The erudite learning had been scholarly embedded into Molly's mind by the Penwright's history teacher, Miss Fanny Gardener.

Whilst on the top deck of the ship, assisting Flintlock, Tim also spoke of his historical learnings about Genghis Khan. Flintlock resonated so well with the explanation, for he possessed a similar character with the same desire to build an empire and instigate killings to survive. The title of Genghis Khan meaning Universal Ruler was given to him by other tribal leaders. He did possess a divine status, for his egotistical destiny was to rule the world by creating the largest empire on earth, uniting many nomadic tribes of northeast Asia, by merging the cultures together with peace and understanding. Historical teachings underline a famous quote made by Genghis Khan, explaining to his enemies why he was drawn to killings saying:

"I am the punishment of God. If you had not committed great sins, God would not have sent me as a punishment upon you."

To gain fastest route to the Caribbean Sea, the Liberty Bell passed through the Panama Canal – being only 77 kilometres long, with a little help from the Sledge Ray. After arriving in the Atlantic ocean, Marina connected so well with Evangeline and Molly, she asked them if they wanted to ride on her back to the Caribbean treasure location that Captain Ortuga was sailing towards. Carried up from the bilge water, Marina was laid down on the helm bridge next to the quartz throne; she now possessed a meek anxiety about sharks bolting around the ocean waters, searching for flesh and food.

Looking down at the mermaid, Ortuga justified the reasoning of killings. Aggressive killings to triumph empirical expansion are wicked. Attacks should only be made to defend against predators such as mosquitos, snakes, spiders, crocodiles and sharks. If human beings fight to kill, defending their actions can be restrained by banging them into unconsciousness. Anyone in the state of unconsciousness can be hypnotised with thought seeds to amend their minds, entering the acceptance of their rivals; all aggression and killings can be passed on by finding out what the attackers want and then hopefully giving their desires to them.

Ortuga asked Sanchez and Davy to carry Marina to the stern podium where they gently lifted her down into the cool green water. She floated for a while until Evangeline and Molly climbed on her back, then they graciously moved along on the surface of the ocean to the location of the sunken treasure, with the Liberty Bell following behind them. On reaching the location in the late afternoon, Marina shook the girls off and asked them to swim back to the Liberty Bell as she dived down into the ocean; whilst discovering the sunken wreck, she slid in through the decayed timber hull looking for the treasure. Searching throughout the holdings, Marina noticed that there were numerous sea creatures living in the vessel and also a small pod of white tipped reef sharks, but she could not see any treasure. Avoiding the danger, Marina swam rapidly up to the ocean surface. Rising above the water, she appeared next to a familiar Liberty vessel. The ship was a naval galleon of the Spanish armada, crammed with a crewed capacity of violent, military buccaneers and pirates. Not realising that the ship was in the Spanish division that attacked communities in the continent of South America, Marina climbed onto the stern platform and found a pile of old sails to curl up under, she then dozed off into a deep tranquil slumber.

Sitting on the throne secured to the bridge helm, speaking into the shell Turnkey, Ortuga realised the treasure's new hiding place. Before the Spanish galleon had sunk, the treasure was buried in the sand bed under rocks inside a marine cavern on the island of Curacao. Thinking that he did not have enough strong deckhands to hunt for the treasure and excavate it out of the buried sub marine rock quarry, Ortuga decided to sail the Liberty Bell down south to the port of Cartagena to recruit new deckhands, utilising them to dig up the treasure.

Davy, Tim and Quinton were all on deck, following commands issued by Flintlock and Sanchez. In secret hiding, Evangeline had rushed down into her cabin to re-dress into her male disguise outfit, returning shortly up to the top deck to sit with Han and Molly.

Because all the Liberty seafarers were facing forward searching for the portal entry of Cartagena, no one saw the Spanish armada vessel following far behind the Liberty Bell.

Arriving early in the morning dawn at 4.00am, the Liberty Bell anchored into the major port of Cartagena, docking next to a sloop vessel. Sanchez recognised the boat as the vessel sailed by the lakeside villagers from Eldorado. The solo pirate, Bucko Felony, who, after the bludgeoning of the Eldorado crew, had swam to the sloop and seized the craft, was now its new owner. Bucko too had travelled to Cartagena to recruit men for the crew of his new vessel.

At 7.00am, the Liberty crew and Cornwall companions woke up, finding their way to the cobblestone streets of the township looking for somewhere to have breakfast. Feeling extreme tiredness, Evangeline returned down to her cabin to fall into a sleep. The colonial town was bordered by well-built stone walls, offering protection and hidings from challenging assaults of enemies and violent foreign adversaries.

The hungry travellers noticed a massive brick-built customs warehouse close to the sea wall and a set of steps leading down to the port bay water. A five star food market arena was positioned under the agency headquarters with several restaurants opening to serve breakfast to the local community. The busy eatery that incited the seniors had a large hand painted sign above its front doorway saying 'Hello Fresh'. The breakfast menu outside of the bistro listed highly flavoursome foods – bacon, fried eggs, potato chips, mushrooms and grilled tomatoes.

Possessing ravenous appetites, Captain Ortuga, his senior crew members, Davy and his schoolmates all walked into the busy eatery that was tightly packed with many local people sitting at the tables scoffing bacon, fried eggs, buttered toast and drinking ground coffee grown in Colombia. While waiting for an empty table, the five seniors played their instruments at the front of the bistro as the seated customers laughed and smiled at the popular sounding music. The owners of the eatery asked the men to go over and play on the cobblestone streets, for the music was distracting the customers from ordering any extra foods. Just as they were about to move on, Sanchez noticed a group of people walking away from a large table in the bistro, that was big enough to seat six people. Refusing to leave the eatery, Sanchez eagerly stomped past the other tables that were crammed with clientele, over to the spare table. He then grabbed a chair and sat down with his arms stretched out to stop any of the locals from taking any of the seats. Ortuga and his four fellow senior officers then sat down and ordered breakfasts and coffee from a charming waitress. The Taoist vegetarian, Han, ordered mushrooms on toast with chips and tomatoes, and a glass of coconut water and Davy ordered, bacon and eggs sandwiches and chips, with coffee for his friends to take away.

Davy and his schoolmates then sat at the top of the port bay steps, eating their breakfasts. As they were jovially enjoying their food, looking out at the six ships moored in the bay, Tim noticed the familiar pirate sloop vessel from their previous travels. It was packed full with newly recruited men running around on the main deck, exercising and lifting ballast weights to strengthen their muscles. After the workouts, the sloop crewmen strolled up to the town streets and marched up the stairway, passing by the Cornish teenagers. Whiffing the strong smell of breakfast foods into his nose, the Pirate Captain, Bucko Felony, questioned where the breakfast had been purchased from Quinton replied with a mouthful of food:

"Good morning, Captain! We bought the breakfast from that eatery over there. Be careful though because the Customs Officers are standing at the front of the building. They are looking for vessels that smuggle goods into the town without paying taxes – are you smuggling anything?"

Without responding, Bucko Felony shuffled harshly past the teenagers sitting on the steps that escorted people from the waterfront up to the walled boulevards. One of the men barged Quinton off the step he was sitting on, making him tumble down towards the jagged rocks, falling towards a major injury or death.

Quick as a flash, Molly used her magical power to cushion Quinton in the air, safely floating him back up to the group. The Penwright school buddies then joined together and then ventured to a tavern hotel overlooking the bay. Davy led his comrades up to the hotel balcony and ordered some champagne drinks to commemorate the future world vision of Juan Ortuga. Davy then told them the story about Robin Hood and his attempted actions of stealing every day from the rich to give to the poor. Celebrating the efforts of their United Kingdom, Sherwood hero, the happy cheering invited the senior officers out from the busy breakfast restaurant into the tavern bar on the ground floor. Ordering another coffee, Ortuga stayed in the bistro talking with the waitress about her parents who owned the fresh eatery and her three children fathered by a Caribbean pirate from the island of Tortuga. Playing his flute, Han walked up into the back streets, finding a Buddhist temple; entering through the decorative archway, he sat down with the temple guru and an assembly of practitioners to join in with their meditation.

Whilst the other seniors were gulping alcoholic drinks at the bar, Davy could see a Spanish military galleon sailing into the port anchoring near the Liberty Bell. The first male from the military armada that walked up the port bay steps trailed by his arsenal crew was King Philippe of Spain, the father of Evangeline Moreau.

Overhearing the encouraging conversations between the Liberty seniors in the tavern about the Eldorado gold bullion, the Spanish uniformed men drew close to the entry doors, outside of the tavern. Sensing the aggressive energy developing under the balcony, Davy and his mates carefully looked down upon the armed military group. Hearing that the bullion was stored in the hold of the Liberty ship, the Spanish military men barged inside the tavern and used their cutlasses to fight with the four officers. After the Spaniards brutely jabbed their swords into their chests, Sanchez, Amir, Flintlock and Aturo all buckled down onto the floor with blood gushing around their bodies.

The noise of the commotion woke Evangeline from her sleep. So she quickly dressed in her Pablo outfit, and then hurried off the ship into the town. Watching her striding towards the steps, Davy noticed the Spanish King standing behind a horse outside of the tavern hotel. Walking near to the tavern, Pablo looked over to the right side of the town, glimpsing the bistro waitress kissing Ortuga. Whilst abroad in foreign ports, Evangeline would always dress in her wild male fashion, and when making her way to the bistro, she concealed herself by blending in with the group of drunken crew from the sloop vessel in the centre of the cobbled street boulevard.

In her male disguise outfit, Evangeline was easily mistaken for an outlawed buccaneer and her bad-tempered father, King Philippe, naturally did not recognise her. He jumped up from behind his horse and pulled his musket out of his jacket. As he pointed his firearm at the commotion and pulled the trigger, she was caught up in the cross-fire and wounded by a bullet entering her heart – being shot by her father, for he perceived her as a Colombian male pirate.

The newly recruited sloop crew members were all killed by the armada military men leaving only Bucko Felony alive. By chance, prior to the commotion, he had moved to hide secretly behind one of the lofty stone walls surrounding the boulevard. Devastated by the incident of Evangeline's probable death, Ortuga scampered away from the adoration of the bistro waitress and moved below the tavern balcony, where he called up to the Penwright school chums:

"Tim, I think that the Spanish military will soon steal all the gold bullion from my ship. Can you please remove the throne that is fixed on the platform of the helm bridge, taking it onto the sloop vessel – where it will be safe and sound?" The reason why Ortuga wanted to transfer the Golden Throne onto the sloop vessel was because he thought that rather than carrying all the heavy bullion onto their ship, the Spanish military would much rather prefer to steal his Liberty ship along with the throne fixed on the helm and return to Spain.

Ortuga then called out to Davy, "Davy, four of my wonderfully talented senior officers have been killed by the armada militia. Please use your magic, to carefully secure their spirits into bottles from the boulevard tavern. Then we can take their spirits with us when we leave this port township."

Molly went down to the Liberty Bell with Tim and Quinton. Wanting to meet up with Marina, she returned to the stern podium. Sitting on the stern on the Spanish galleon, Marina noticed Molly. She swam back to the Liberty, where Molly told her about the aggressive occurrences and killings of all the sloop crew and the Liberty senior officers.

Quinton helped Tim detach the throne from the bridge, and moved it up to the gangplank. Davy then arrived at the ship to collect all the personal belongings of Captain Ortuga, Evangeline and Han. After collecting the possessions, he used his magic to create an air bridge leading over to the sloop vessel. As he walked onto the magic bridge, he effortlessly moved the belongings through the air, with the ship's dogs following along behind him. Appreciating the magical power of their school mate, Tim and Quinton then lifted up the throne and confidently walked across the bridge to the waiting sloop.

Up on the cobble stone boulevard, Ortuga was in a state of shock, crouching down, embracing Evangeline. Slowly moving to her death, Ortuga expressed his deep love to her:

"Evangeline, you have all the love of my life. I will create hope to bring peace to the world. But I will not be able to empower my compassionate love to the needy men and women of the earth without your connection. If you are going to die, please let me have your Starseed energy. Rest in Peace."

Unfortunately, Evangeline's life ended abruptly at the age of 28, tragically killed by her father. Ortuga wept, kissing her cheeks to decant his love into her spirit, with his sobbing tears dripping on her face.

Feeling his loving sentiment, her spirit made her head rise up, her lips opened. Ortuga bent over her body and whilst kissing Evangeline, a reflective thought entered his mind. The thought was channelled from the long lost, mesmeric energy flowing out of the shell Turnkey.

To help rescue her life, he laid her dead body onto a wooden bench at the front of the stone wall; he then raced down the steps to the beach. Meeting up with Davy, Ortuga asked him the whereabouts of the Sledge Ray:

"Tuli, can you fetch the Sledge Ray creature to this sea port, so I can travel a voyage back to the past to modify the occurrence time when Evangeline walked out from the Liberty Bell dressed as Pablo. The revised happening will be for her to not be disguised; favourably recognising his daughter, her father would not kill her."

Grasping hold of his Turnkey, Davy appealed his humanitarian reaction into the shell, requesting the Sledge Ray to travel from the hillside on Pitcairn Island over to the South American port of Cartagena where the six vessels were docked and settle on the beach in front of the ships.

While waiting for the Sea Goat creature to appear in the water, Han had left the Buddhist meditation group to return to the Liberty Bell.

None of the Spanish military males were on the beach; they were all in the bistro eating breakfast. As Han walked down the stone stairway leading downward from the boulevard teeming with locals and animals, he met with Davy and Ortuga. The commander asked him if he could remove the carved wooden figurehead from the Liberty ship and place it on the bow of the sloop vessel. Han nodded as he moved onto the Liberty ship to work with Tim and Quinton, who had now returned from the sloop, to help with the removal of the female sculpture.

Davy explained to Ortuga about the Pleiadian expedition, that he had previously discussed with Evangeline in his cabin, were she had told him that if anyone wanted to change happenings in the past, the person would have to teleport to the Pleiadian Galaxy. Describing the only way to reach the galaxy, Davy clarified the practical methods that must be dealt with:

"Captain, the Sledge Ray can't take you back to the Pleiades for it cannot travel inside the Photon Beam but it can take you to Machu Picchu. You will have to travel back in time on the Elohim Throne, back to the time of several nights ago when the moon was full of Arian power."

Further advising the instructive routine of how to alter future occurrences by changing the past, Davy explained the routine:

"The only way to enter the Photon Beam is by sitting on the Throne and singing the mantra. After arriving at the Pleiadian Galaxy, one must settle down on the planet to meet up with the advanced beings, then by holding the Turnkey, bring the original happening into your mind, then visualise the required change. When the altered happening settles in your brain, then chant or sing the Elohim mantra to compound the latest event into the time.

Suddenly in the distance, the mighty Sledge Ray soared up from the horizon, powering along in the ocean to the South American port of Cartagena.

Reaching the fleet of six ships, it started to exude red illumination into the seawater, indicating the provoked dangers of the Spanish armada military. Manoeuvring around the ships to the beach front, the creature flopped down onto the sand with its wings spread out ready to transport the two passengers to their destination request.

To steer the Sledge Ray, Davy leapt onto its neck placing his hands on the hammer head, handle bars. Ortuga sat behind Davy, tightly holding his Turnkey as he began relaying his request into the shell. The destination that they were to be taken to was the grass land above the shrine temple which offered safe access to the Elohim Throne, because the two guardsmen were forever standing at the front of the gateway to protect entry from criminal beings. Within 15 minutes after departing south from the port of Cartagena in the Caribbean Sea, the Sledge Ray ascended up the grass hillside of Machu Picchu passing across the full moon through the stone citadel and past the gateway up to the shrine at the stairway summit. Davy spoke into his shell Turnkey, commanding the creature to gently land down onto the grass ledge above the temple. Accidentally, the Sledge Ray bounced off a rock, toppling Ortuga off its back; luckily, the grass cushioned his body, avoiding any accidental injuries.

Sliding in through the rocks, Ortuga entered the shrine and strolled down to the Elohim Throne where the throne usher shook hands with him. Then after taking a memorial implant of the mantra on the back of the throne; he sat down and sang the hymn. Setting into his mind, he recalled the wordings when he arrived at the Pleiades to change the evil killing of Evangeline by her father.

When Ortuga began singing the mantra hymn, a glowing beam of sapphire light swirled around the monumental throne, lifting it up into the luminescent night sky. Ortuga then noticed a brilliant white star planet with the sapphire blue light circling around the luminary sphere. Drawn out into the darkness by gravity, heading towards the star at the speed of light, the throne transformed from solid rock into shimmering silver light. Gravity made him enter into the Photon Beam with streaming beams of white and blue plasma flowing next to him, along the inside of the vortex tunnel.

Passing into the galaxy, the throne took him down to the star planet and settled on the celestial beach covered with white soil and amazing blue flower plants. Spiritual voices glided along the beach, asking who was sitting in the Elohim Throne. Ortuga replied compassionately:

"My present life is incredibly heartrending, for one of your Starseed ladies has been accidently killed by her father. – I want to change the past happening to bring her back to me."

Accepting his inspirational devotion and kindness to Evangeline, the Pleiadians walked along the beach with him and stood next to the throne. Looking around at the alliance of 11 advanced beings, Ortuga recognised them as Gods and Goddesses of Greek mythology. The confederation of male Gods were Zeus, Apollo, Cronos, Hermes and Prometheus together with six female Goddesses, Demeter, Aphrodite, Athena, Gaia, Artemis and Nemesis.

Sensing the ancient energy of the mythological alliance flowing into his body, Ortuga placed the vision of Evangeline's father shooting her into his psyche. When the vision established in his mind, he sang the Elohim mantra:

"T'Jen Yar Day – Beautiful Day, Beautiful Life.
You need to Love Yourself, to Love the World
Show Me the Way to Love
Yar Day Ta M'kas…"

After shifting the wicked killing in Cartagena out of the recorded events, Ortuga channelled another vision into his mind. He was with Evangeline in her cabin, she was dressed up in her male disguise and Ortuga suggested to her that in order not to be killed by her father, she should dress in her female clothing before she walked up to the cobble street boulevard.

Feeling the Argentinean man's affirmative energy, the advanced beings lifted the throne up from the white beach and returned it into the Photon Beam, taking Ortuga back to the Machu Picchu temple. On Ortuga's return, Davy was waiting on the Sledge Ray to transport his commander back to Cartagena. They flew to the hillside behind the walls close to the back streets where the Buddhist monastery was built. Dismounting off the Sledge Ray, they both walked down to the top of the stone stairway and observed the frequent events and the changed killing of Evangeline. The happenings showed Han placing the musical spirits of the four senior officers who were killed by the Spanish military into champagne bottles, sealing the cork with wax and inscribing the names onto a label and sticking the label to each of the bottles that contained the spirits.

Another occurrence illustrated the Spanish militia boarding the Liberty Bell, preparing the ship ready to sail away back to Spain, thieving every block of the Eldorado gold bullion stored down in the hold.

Viewing his schoolmates on the pirate sloop vessel, Davy walked away from Ortuga towards them, laughing and joking with his friends about changes of the past and the future.

Sitting alone at the top of the stone stairs leading up from the port water observing the final happening, Ortuga saw Evangeline appearing beautifully dressed in her female clothing, wading into the sea water, shimmering her energy into the ocean. Close behind Ortuga, the Spanish King, Philippe, leaned over his shoulder to view his daughter, walking up the stairs. Passing by, she blew a kiss onto Ortuga's face, then moved onward behind him, to be with her father:

"Bonjour, Daddy. I have missed your love, so has my mother. Can we sail back to Barbados to meet up with her and help the refugees?"

King Philippe hugged his daughter:

"Evangeline, Hola Carino – you have so much beauty, compassion and wisdom. I want you to take on your role of a Spanish royal princess, in a choir of angels to help my dominion."

Holding hands with her father, Evangeline walked down to the dock and entered with him onto the Spanish galleon. The vessel then sailed out of the port onto the Atlantic Ocean heading for the Caribbean Islands and then onward to Spain.

Strolling down to the pirate sloop vessel, Captain Ortuga smiled and shook hands with Davy and his schoolmates, for they had become the new crew members. The surviving senior officer, Han, carried the champagne bottles up onto the sloop vessel, to store them in the Captain's quarters, to secure the mystical, musical messages in the bottles, until someone asked them to be opened, allowing the spirits to flow into other beings.

A message then channelled into Ortuga's mind from the Pleiadian Galaxy: "Aye Aye, Captain. That town Cartagena was too big for both of us. Let's look into The Art of Noise to save the world."

Pirate
Glossary

Ballast
Heavy materials used to weigh down the ship, making the vessel stable enough to powerfully sail on the ocean.

Berth
The place in the ship's hold where the crew sleeps in hammocks.

Booty
Treasures and goods seized by violence, stolen or won by pirated armed forces in war conflicts and treasure discovery expeditions.

Bosun
The senior qualified member of the decking department, known formally as the ship boatswain or petty officer, is responsible for the components in the ship's hull.

Broadside
Attacks begin with a broadside, firing all canons from one side of the ship at the targeted vessel; shattering masts, slashing sails and riggings. The victims run below the deck to hide from the danger, after which the attacking vessel draws their ship alongside to climb aboard.

Buccaneers
Sometimes called Freebooters, the title was given to 17th century pirates and privateers, who attacked Spanish ships and settlements in the Caribbean provinces.

Capstan
A round, winding mechanism pushed around by the crew to raise and lower the anchor that is attached to the vessel by rope or chain.

Crow's Nest
A platform structured on the upper part of the main mast, servicing as a lookout point to spot approaching hazards, other ships and land; an additional close purpose of the platform is for the cabin boy or commanded crew members to look down on the main deck to observe the crew members.

Cutlass
A short, curved, slashing sword, perfect for fighting in nautical warfare at close quarters onboard a ship.

Figurehead
A carved, painted, wooden figure fixed to the frontage bow of the ship.

Gangplank
A long, narrow length of timber placed between the ship and the land, or between two vessels, so the crew can walk across.

Grappling Iron
An item linked to a rope, thrown onto enemy ships to hook onto its rigging or hull, used to climb aboard the vessel.

Helm
A wheel or tiller handle used to steer the ship to travel in the direction navigated by a senior crew member.

Jolly Roger
A pirate flag of black and white, decorated with fearful images such as skulls and devils, to scare marine opponents, and to attack and plunder their treasures.

Keel
The lowest part of the ship's hull.

Lodestone
Before the compass was invented, navigators used pieces of magnetic rock, lodestone for navigation. When the needle was rubbed on the rock, it would become magnetized and indicate the directional pathway to steer upon the ocean.

Musket
A long barrel rifle, held with both hands against the shoulder of the Musketeer to focus well on the object in order to soundly shoot the firearm.

Pirate
A man who commits acts of robbery on the oceans, a pirate seafarer attacks shipping or coastal settlements illegally.

Port
A town that has facilities for loading and unloading seagoing vessels.

Privateer
A nautical individual who is given government permission to seize merchant vessels and attack communities and coastal settlements that belong to an enemy country.

Rigging
The network of ropes that secures the masts and sails in place, on the top deck of the vessel.

Scurvy
A nautical disease caused by lack of vitamin C, defecting the skin and gums. Seafarers often suffer from scurvy because they do not eat enough fruit or vegetables.

Sledge-Ray
This flat-bodied nautical creature is a combination of a hammerhead shark and a manta ray. A light radiates from within its body and indicates effects that are around the ship or those in the distance moving towards the vessel – red glow indicates danger and green indicates freedom. When a Golden Shell

Turnkey is in custody, the wonder creature carries the human on its back across the ocean – back to the future or forward to the past.

Sloop
A small sailing-ship with only one mast, that holds the mainsail; the vessel can be rowed as well as sailed; also may have one or more small foresails.

Starboard
The right hand side of a ship when facing the Bow.

Stowaway
A person who hides on a ship.

Treasure
Gold, silver and jewels. Gold is of unparalleled value to pirate men. Buried treasure is a scarce commodity but when stolen treasure is recovered and placed in the ship's hold, the senior crew members, Quartermaster and Bosun, try to ensure that none of the treasure is taken away by the deckhands.

Spirit
Glossary

Altruism
Unselfish regard, concern and devotion for the welfare and wellbeing of other people, communities and cultures. Willingness to do things that bring advantages to others, even if the actions bring difficulty to yourself.

Astral Travel
Out of body experience when the existence of a soul or consciousness separates from the physicality of the being, exiting from the body to travel throughout the universe.

Aura
A subtle electromagnetic field that surrounds the body, produced by chakra energy, radiating from within the body. The shape and colour of the energy defines the strength and spiritual power of the person.

Citadel
This area is the defensive, core, fortified region of a town which may be a castle, a fortress or a hidden village holding a religious community such as Buddhist or Taoists.

Chakras
Seven energy centres within the human body, from the base of the spine to the crown of the head, which facilitate to empower organ functions, the immune system and emotions.

Channelling
When entering a state of trance, this fomentation opens communication gateways to all dimensions – the three dimensional realm of earth & the multidimensional spirit realm of ascended masters, spirit guides, and cosmic and planetary

energy. Often the energy tracking through the channel is healing and helpful.

Clairvoyance
The natural psychic ability, often expressed as conversations with God, to gain information about people, objects and events through extra sensory perception – clearly visualising the truth about the past, present and future occurrences.

Divinity
The state of sacred events derived from supernatural power of holy supreme beings and the channelled energy from the universe.

Elohim
The title of the infinite, all-powered, supreme energy of the universe that created the world and connected galaxies, allowing the opening flow of its energy to teleport human physicality to cosmic destinations.

Energy
Produces a higher being; the information gained and healing power are pure and direct, full of divine love, spiritual truth and integrity.

Evolution
A naturally slow process of genetic changes and mutation of the generations of plants and animals that drifted over millions of years, resulting in the development of new species of life forms – finally creating male and female human beings.

Extra Terrestrial
Alien life existences that do not originate from the earth, ranging from simple organisms to highly advanced beings within civilizations from distant galaxies.

Faith

Strong belief and trust; faith is the uplifting mental proof of acceptance of reality of things humans cannot see, receiving super confidence from the inspirational emotions of hope, love and peace.

Israel

The initial holy land of biblical teachings. The most sacred sites are in the old city of Jerusalem. The name Israel is united from religious Latin nouns of God – **Is** means to be: **Ra** is another god worshiped by Aztecs and Incan communities: **El** is the European noun meaning him.

Lightworkers

A lightworker is a volunteered spirit before birth, devoting their presence to raise the vibration of the planet by opening gateways to enter their spirit onto pathways leading to the knowledge and energy of advanced beings, to help the planet and its population heal from the effects of fear.

Life Force

Natural esoteric energy, the active principle forms part of any living plant life or animal with its energy flowing around living things to empower and heal.

Magic

The use of compounded energy flowing into rituals, symbols, and actions to defend oneself, friends and neighbours. Since the earliest cultures of mankind, magic created miracles and healings, continuing in the modern world to have spirituality, religion and medicinal roles.

Mantra

A repeated rhythmic series of syllables or word phrases, sung or prayed, enchanted solo or in unison by a crowd, used to attract flowing energy to gain supreme relaxation and empowerment of the mind.

Meditation

The practice where an individual trains the mind, focusing upon a sound, object, movement or breath to increase beneficial reduction of stress, promote calmness and enhance personal and spiritual growth.

Meridians

Energy flows through the pathways, accessing all organs and areas within the body mass. Ancient healings used the meridians to heal all illnesses.

Miracles

Power of universal energy produces miracles, such as walking on water, conversations with God, healings, visions, levitation, and the miraculous resurrection of Jesus of Nazareth.

Monastery

A building, structured for the residing kinship of monks or nuns, serving as a temple specifically reserved for meditation and prayer.

Monument

A commemorative, architectural structure built to honour people, cultures and the remembrance of historical events and times.

Photon Beam

A huge belt of inter-dimensional light that passes through the galaxy, streaming energy channels of etheric and spiritual nature that interacts with and affects the physical for transportation to other galaxies.

Pleiades

Of ancient mythology, the open constellation of hundreds of celestial stars was formed 100 million years ago – dominated by hot blue and tremendously luminous stars.

Prophecy
A prediction of what will happen in the future.

Reincarnation
Cyclical existence – after biological death, the mind and energy of living beings are returned into the universe and reborn into a different physical body.

Speaking in Tongues
A description of those people that can speak in different languages, for the manifestation makes one feel empowered by God to harmonise with many cultures.

Starseed
Beings that have experienced life elsewhere in the universe, in non-physical dimensions on other planets.

Taoism
A philosophical tradition of living life in esoteric harmony with nature's way. The theory is the source, pattern and substance of everything that exists.

Teleport
Transfer of spirit being or physicality from one location to another, without traversing across land space between the two locations.

Turnkey
When touched, the object transports people – individuals, groups and items to life's timings – back to the future or forward to the past.

Universal Energy
The collective good and bad super energies of the entire Big Bang cosmic space are omnipresent, omniscient and omnipotent; governing and strengthening all life forms, human emotions and planetary activity, and producing global and individual consciousness, and intellectual patterns.